# "Dad Doesn't Want to See Me," She Told Michael.

They were in his car. Rain mixed seas and sky into an indistinguishable blur at the nonexistent horizon.

"He doesn't even want to see Mom, or at least not all the time, but she can't stay out of that damn hospital."

She sat close to him, her head on his shoulder. His arm was around her and his cheek was against her hair.

"I wish there was something I could do, Sarah," he said miserably. "I really do."

She pulled away and sat up straight. "I've got to go home now, Michael."

"When will I see you again?" He started the car and backed out of the parking space. "Tomorrow? Can you get away tomorrow, for a while?"

Michael turned on the windshield wipers. She concentrated on his black hair, his profile, the strong neck, the shirt open at the throat. She took from her mind her knowledge of each of the parts of his body; and the hot cloud stirred in her belly.

"Tomorrow," she said blindly. "Yes, tomorrow is fine."

Whatever happens, she thought, this does not die; whatever happens, we have this; and it's warm and rolling and will keep us alive . . . .

# THE Favorite

## L.R.Wright

PUBLISHED BY POCKET BOOKS NEW YORK

POCKET BOOKS, a division of Simon & Schuster, Inc.
1230 Avenue of the Americas, New York, N.Y. 10020

Copyright © 1982 by L. R. Wright

Published by arrangement with Doubleday & Company Inc.
Library of Congress Catalog Card Number: 81-43308

ISBN: 0-671-45186-3

First Pocket Books printing September, 1983

10 9 8 7 6 5 4 3 2 1

POCKET and colophon are registered trademarks
of Simon & Schuster, Inc.

Printed in the U.S.A.

This book is dedicated to my mother,
Evelyn Jane Appleby

I also wish to acknowledge the indispensable contributions of my husband, John, to the creation of this book, originally titled *Hauntings;* and to express my gratitude to my daughters, Katey and Johnna, for their continuing love and support.

From Sarah's exercise book:

I am not resigned to the shutting away
    of loving hearts in the hard ground.
So it is, and so it will be, for so it has
    been, time out of mind:
Into the darkness they go, the wise and
    the lovely. Crowned
With lilies and with laurel they go;
    but I am not resigned.

                    —Edna St. Vincent Millay


The wind flapped loose, the wind was still
Shaken out dead from tree and hill;
I had walked on at the wind's will—
I sat now, for the wind was still.

Between my knees my forehead was—
My lips, drawn in, said not Alas!
My hair was over in the grass,
My naked ears heard the day pass.

My eyes, wide open, had the run
Of some ten weeds to fix upon;
Among those few, out of the sun,
The woodspurge flowered, three cups in one.

From perfect grief there need not be
Wisdom, or even memory:
One thing then learned remains to me,
The woodspurge has a cup of three.

                    —Dante Gabriel Rossetti

# THE Favorite

# PART I

# Chapter 1

SARAH HAD FALLEN ASLEEP ON TOP OF THE COVERS, FULLY dressed, expectant, and in the middle of the night she was awakened.

She looked up out of sleep and saw her mother sitting on the edge of her bed, Glynis standing beside her. Light from the streetlamp glowed upon their faces because Sarah had not closed the curtains, and she could see that Glynis was frightened.

"Sarah," said Margaret. "Your father is dead."

She sat bolt upright on her bed. "It's a mistake," she said. "Somebody's made a mistake."

She had watched him in his illness, and had thought she was waiting for it to kill him. It seemed now that she had not believed that at all; instead she had been waiting, innocent and stubborn, for a time to return which had now been extinguished.

"It's not a mistake," said her mother, face luminous. "He's dead."

Why did she tell Glynis first? thought Sarah, and knew that her mother had been afraid to come first to Sarah; and in that instant she was totally alone—except for her father, dead somewhere.

"Sarah," her mother said. "I'm sorry."

She sounds just like anybody else, thought Sarah. Her voice; it's ironed out and ordinary.

Sarah got up and walked from her room along the hall, past the open door to Glynis' room and past the door, also open, to her parents' room. Although she didn't look in, she saw that the bedside light was on and the covers were pushed back. She walked down the stairs, looking straight ahead, through the dark hall to the kitchen and out the back door, into the cold, damp night. Her mother and sister followed, scuffling their slippers. Sarah bent down beside the porch and looked underneath it. The tiny, waxy, bell-like flowers had not yet appeared. She only imagined them, glowing ghostily under there. But the leaves were beginning to grow again, soon there would be a profusion of them, wide green leaves; and then, later, the lilies of the valley would bloom, in the damp, in the perpetual shade under the porch. Her father had discovered them when they first moved into the house, seven years ago, when she was ten, and had hurried her outdoors to look under the steps. She had knelt down and looked and there they had bloomed, blowing hesitant perfumed smiles at the smiling faces peering in at them.

Sarah looked hard into the darkness under the porch, breathing the scent of another year's flowers.

She could not remember anything recent.

She got up in the rain-washed dark of the March night and went inside the house. Her mother and Glynis followed, patiently.

They got dressed and drove through the quiet Vancouver streets to the hospital, and three of them sitting in the front seat of the station wagon, the none of them said anything at all, it seemed to Sarah later, and she wondered if her mother and Glynis had thought, as she did, well, at least it's the last time I'll have to go to this damn hospital.

When they finally got there the buildings were bright with light. Once inside, Sarah was seized by an inarticulate rage. The hospital had cradled within its evil walls since the day her father had been taken there the certain knowledge that he would never leave the place alive. She watched as some white-coated people approached her mother and offered their sympathy. She watched Margaret accept it, and wished

4

they had offered some to her. I would grind it into their faces, thought Sarah, with the heel of my hand.

The hospital held a muffled stench, as though many substances had been scrubbed into it to try to hide the bad things that were there.

Nurses murmured to Margaret, and gestured, and Margaret put one arm protectively around thirteen-year-old Glynis.

The three of them followed the nurses down the hall, and when they reached the door to her father's room Sarah observed the nurses drawing away and she thought their attitudes of respect were artificial, and she hated them. She imagined them gossiping about inconsequential things. They couldn't have known much about nursing, or they would not have let her father die.

She could not remember, for the moment, what it was that had done this to him.

They stood alone in the hospital room. Sarah stood back, holding Glynis' arm, and watched Margaret walk to the bed and pull back the sheet and look down. Sarah was very warm, and her skin seemed to be rippling. Margaret got to her knees, her forehead resting on the edge of the bed. Sarah tightened her grip on her sister's arm. Then Margaret stood up, leaned over and kissed her husband's cheek. Sarah wanted to snatch at her, pull her away from the body, slap her. What kind of charade was this?

When they left the room, there were papers Margaret had to sign. Sarah, stiff with suspicion, wanted to know what they were and what unspeakable things would happen to her father now that Margaret had signed them. But she didn't say anything; she listened intently to the voices that screamed at her to do something, do something; listened, but did not do anything at all.

Before the funeral, they went to look at him lying in his casket. Sarah was made breathless by the succession of matter-of-fact but terrible things that were expected of her. This one was the most terrible, the most stupid, she thought, staring down at him.

He looked like a Madame Tussaud's image of himself. He lay, recognizable but unreal, a mannequin of himself, an impostor. Sarah saw that much care had been taken to make

5

him look like himself, accidentally fallen asleep on the way to an important occasion.

"He has not dressed himself," she said sharply to Margaret, who put a hand on her arm. "Why is he wearing his best suit? Why has he got that handkerchief in his pocket? My father never had a handkerchief sticking out of his pocket like that."

"Will the casket be open or closed?" asked a person from the funeral home.

"Closed," said Sarah furiously.

"Closed," murmured Margaret, as Glynis began to cry. Margaret led them outside.

People had to be told that he had died. Sarah guessed they had a right to know, some of them. But in the chapel they sat like rows of vultures, paying admission with their tears, and Sarah looked upon them with contempt. She half expected them to have divided themselves up into friends and relatives of the deceased and of the widow, and seated themselves on opposite sides of the church, but they hadn't gone that far, they were sitting all together.

As she walked in with her mother and Glynis, Sarah saw her grandfather stand up. His eyes were wet, shiny behind his glasses. He reached toward Sarah's mother, his daughter, but her grandmother tugged him gently back into his place.

Sarah knew all these people, or most of them. Yet she chose to dress them this day in wickedness. She wished she could slowly raise her arm high above her head and quickly bring it down, cracking thunderbolts and scattering lightning to set the place afire. Her hands were cold, and she shook slightly, with anger.

Before she sat down in a pew next to Glynis she noticed her other grandparents. She was surprised at first to see them; their presence seemed incongruous. People weren't supposed to die before their parents.

The minister hadn't known Sarah's father at all. Sarah knew he was just saying things other people had told him to say, plus more stuff he figured should do for any corpse. He appeared confident nonetheless that he, here and now, was all by himself shipping her father's docile soul to heaven. She wondered what would happen in that church if she suddenly got up and started yelling "fuck fuck fuck" at the top of her lungs. It was not a word that came easily to her, but it seemed absolutely the best one in the world to say, right now.

In the middle of the service Glynis reached over without turning her head and fumbled for Sarah's hand. At first Sarah thought she was offering comfort, and she splayed out stiffened fingers in rejection; but Glynis' hand clutched spasmodically, opened, clutched again, and Sarah, looking at her, saw tears falling down freckle-dusted cheeks, past the corner of Glynis' mouth. Sarah felt much more than four years older than Glynis at that moment, and much, much stronger. She took Glynis' hand in both of hers, gently, and let it quiver there between her cupped palms, and when it was quieter she stroked the back of it, concentrating on this one thing, Glynis' hand, feeding her anger, softly, with Glynis' pain.

Margaret sat on the other side of Glynis telling herself that it would soon be over. She was desperate to be in the room she had shared with Ted, alone with his belongings and the invisible texture of his presence. It was a room unsullied by death; death had not occurred there; and if she were to lie quietly on their bed with the clock ticking and Ted's clothes hanging in the closet she might be able for a few minutes to deny his death, to keep at bay the sudden and shocking aloneness which had already shown her its face. She would have to confront it, eventually, but not yet—not yet . . .

Margaret turned to look at her daughters, suddenly dispassionate. She knew that this was a terrible thing for them; still, they were at the beginnings of their lives. But there were so many old men around that Margaret had never expected Ted to die while he was still young. They had been married for twenty years, almost to the day, and she hadn't thought of her husband's life as having an expiry date.

She had been looking at Glynis' profile, and now she saw that Glynis was sitting ramrod straight, tears painting silvery tracks upon her face. Margaret felt a bloom of amazement—hers, then, was not the only private grief. Would each of their griefs be private? Would each of them suffer alone? Beyond Glynis, Sarah's head was bent, and Margaret saw that she was staring intently down at Glynis' hand, which she was softly, slowly stroking. Margaret wanted to touch

Glynis, but Sarah's absorption held her back; Margaret could almost feel the lean in Glynis' body away from her and toward her sister. As Margaret watched, Sarah raised her head, thick blond hair stirring as she moved, and looked at Margaret steadily with her father's dark blue eyes. Bitterness and anger flooded Margaret as she held Sarah's gaze; she was appalled by the strength of her anger, revolted by her bitterness. . . . She tried to smile at Sarah. Chasms and canyons, canyons and chasms, she thought; I have lived my life ineptly.

Things were very strange, throughout the days of Sarah's father's death and burial. The house seemed always to be filled with people, since Margaret had insisted that both sets of grandparents stay there, even though there was not enough room for them. Neither her own parents nor Ted's wanted to say no, because they knew she didn't yet want to be alone in the house with her children. Sarah was impatient with the visitors and wanted them to go to a hotel.

One of the strangest things about this time was that people brought food. Each time Sarah entered the house there was more of it. Casseroles crowded each other upon the kitchen table, cakes and plates of cookies thronged the counters. There was a baked ham and a huge roasted turkey.

"What's this for?" said Sarah.

"People do it when someone dies," said her mother. "They bring food."

"Why, for heaven's sake?"

"Because they can't think of anything else to do."

"We couldn't eat all this even if Dad were here to help," said Sarah. "What are you going to do with it?"

"We'll eat what we can, I'll freeze some of it, and the rest I'll throw out."

"Throw out? You're going to throw food away?"

"What do you suggest, Sarah? Just what do you suggest I do with it? Have a party?"

She almost did, as it turned out. After the funeral people converged on the house. Women bustled around in the kitchen putting some of the food on plates. Then they took it into the living room. They made coffee and tea, and served wine.

"Look at them," said Sarah, jabbing Glynis in the ribs; they were almost the same height. "Funerals make people hungry. Can you imagine? Maybe that's why they brought all that food in the first place, so they could come here and eat it after the funeral. What do you think, Glynis?"

Glynis shrugged. "I don't care what they do."

Across the room Margaret sat on the sofa and watched as her friend Moira in a jade-green dress approached. Moira studied Margaret's face, and put a cool hand on her forehead. "You're going to be okay, Maggie," she said.

"I wonder," said Margaret.

"How are the kids?" said Moira, looking around the room for them.

"I can't tell."

"Hang on, Maggie."

Margaret saw Harry Innes coming toward her, a glass in each hand, and saw his face relax as he spotted her.

"It's just what you need," said Moira. "Wine is just what she needs," she said to Harry, smiling.

"Scotch is what she needs," said Harry, "but the ladies in charge of this do haven't provided any of the hard stuff." He handed Margaret one glass and Moira the other. "Have three or four," he said to Margaret. "That ought to do it."

Margaret observed him cautiously, as though meeting him for the first time. Harry had a wide mouth and a sharp chin, and a habit of thrusting his head forward while pulling his body back. When he had started to put on weight it all went into a paunch, while his elbows and knees and chin continued to jut out as bonily as ever. His hair had begun to thin when he was young and now what was left of it was almost completely gray. He looked like he ought to have bad breath and smell of perspiration, but he didn't, he always smelled of Aqua-Velva, Margaret thought he must buy it by the case.

Despite his unprepossessing appearance, or perhaps because of it, he had never been a timid man. He flaunted a sarcastic drawl and a world-weary demeanor which he perhaps found useful in his job. He had wanted to be an actor, a long time ago. Margaret always found that hard to believe. He was much better off as a backstage authoritarian, she thought—and so was the theater.

"Funerals aren't exactly my line," he said now, strained, "but if there's anything I can do, holler."

"I'll call on you if I need you, Harry," said Margaret. "You can count on it."

Harry patted her arm and wandered off to talk to Ted's parents, whom he liked. He did not like very many people. He had liked Ted very much indeed.

Ted's parents were not looking good, he decided, and he veered away to collect two more glasses of wine. He'd spend another ten minutes here, not another goddamn second, and then he'd go home and get royally pissed, so pissed he'd pass out, thereby managing to get through this whole asshole of a day as quickly as possible.

"Maybe you'd better rescue your mother and father," said Moira to Margaret. She nodded toward the archway to the hall, where the Kennedys stood glancing uncomfortably over the shoulders of a man in a brown corduroy suit who was talking to them with enthusiasm. He was one of Ted's colleagues from the English department, an earnest young assistant professor with a gift for turning every conversation into a lecture.

"Oh, God," said Margaret wearily, and got to her feet. She made her way through a couple of groups of people, circled the man in brown, smiled at him and pulled her parents toward the dining room.

"It's very nice that all these people should want to pay their respects to Ted," said her mother, whose eyes were swollen, "but don't you think it's time they went home?"

"She can't very well throw them out," said Margaret's father, and Margaret hugged his arm.

She opened her mouth to suggest that her mother go upstairs and lie down when, "Excuse me," said a voice from the other side of the room, and it sounded very clearly above the clattering of the dishes and glasses and the rise and fall of conversation.

"Excuse me," said the voice again. "You're in my father's chair."

Margaret stopped and turned around. For an instant she thought it was Glynis' voice. Then she recognized it, and became unaccountably cold.

Sarah was standing patiently, looking down at a man from the history department. He wore a dark blue suit and a white carnation in his lapel. Talk ebbed away and the room became quiet. "It's his particular chair," Sarah explained.

Margaret stood as if frozen, watching Sarah move to the other side of the chair, between it and the fireplace. The face of the man in the chair, and his carnation, were starkly white, but everything else seemed normal.

"It's his chair," she heard Sarah say. "He gets quite annoyed if he wants to sit down and somebody's in that chair."

The blue-suited man fumbled his hands onto the arms of the leather chair, beginning to push himself up, and as he moved, so did Margaret.

She thrust herself through the people in her living room and reached Sarah.

"Everett," she said—thank God, I remembered his name—"stay where you are." She felt armed and alert and ready for battle, but with what, she could not have said. "Sarah," she said, taking her daughter's arm, "come with me. I need your help in the kitchen."

She led Sarah away, past Glynis, and for a second wondered if she should drag Glynis away, too, but decided she would be safe enough—from what? she thought frantically, as she pulled Sarah through the kitchen and down the hall and up the stairs to her room.

Margaret closed the door behind them. "Sarah," she said, "your father is dead. Do you understand that?" I will not get through this if I'm not careful, she thought, and swiftly calculated the number of years she could reasonably expect to live.

"Of course I understand that," said Sarah, agitated, distracted. "We saw him in that coffin, we saw him get himself buried; of course he's dead."

"That's not his chair any more," said Margaret. "He'll never sit in that chair again." Her legs began to shake. She sat abruptly on the chair next to Sarah's desk.

"Whose is it, then? I know he won't sit in it any more. That's a ridiculous thing to say. But whose chair is it, if it isn't his?"

"Do you want it?" said Margaret. "You could have it up here, in your room. By the window seat."

"What would I do with it? Sit in it? No, I don't want it. It stays right where it is." Her fingers fumbled for the locket which hung around her neck, and closed around it.

Margaret stared at her, trying to think. "Would you like

his ring? His university ring? Would you like his watch? His tiepin?"

"Mother, what's the matter with you! Why would I want any of that, it's an ugly thought, ugly!"

*"Take* something, damn it!" Margaret stood up. "I want you to *have* something of his!"

Sarah looked at her contemptuously. "To remind me of him? I don't need reminding of him. I don't want any of that junk. If I haven't got him, do you think I have anything at all?"

Margaret spread her hands helplessly. "Oh, Sarah, oh, God, somehow we have to help each other."

Sarah looked at her for a moment. She rubbed the side of her thumb across the front of the locket, feeling the soft-edged stone that was set into it.

"I think it's too late for that, Mother," she said.

# Chapter 2

TED GRIFFIN CAME TO VANCOUVER FROM KELOWNA, IN the Okanagan Valley, to go to school at the University of B.C. He got two degrees there, and then got a job teaching in Saskatchewan. When he returned to Vancouver in 1961 after a four-year absence he was very glad to be home.

He was a man tied by inclination to the West Coast, a man with no desire to live anywhere but Vancouver, although he would have gone to the far corners of the earth to see what they looked like. He arrived a month before the fall term began and felt so triumphantly possessive toward the campus that he spent most of his time there, just wandering around, hands in his pockets, exultant at the prospect of having his own office (he thought it would probably be a small one) in the English department, of teaching at U.B.C., the place where he had been taught.

He saw Margaret first on the stage.

One night soon after his return he wandered into the Freddie Wood Theater, then still housed in one of the old, dilapidated huts left over from the Second World War. He hardly noticed the name of the play that was being performed there by summer school students—it was *Dark of the Moon*—but thought only that he might run into his friend

Harry Innes at the theater. He didn't see Harry, but he saw Margaret, who was playing someone who fell in love with a male witch. Ted thought this a preposterous thesis, but he couldn't keep his eyes off Margaret.

After the play he considered strolling backstage and asking around for Harry, and he probably would have done this, except for Margaret: he didn't want to see her close up only to watch her eyes pass over him. So he walked quickly to his battered red Triumph, trying to shake off a growing impatience with himself. When he got to his apartment he went to bed, but he did not go immediately to sleep.

The next morning he decided she was probably empty-headed and self-absorbed; he had a feeling that most actors were like that. Then he wondered why it would matter. It's the superficialities I liked, he told himself, remembering; but he knew that he hoped for more.

He had nothing much to do, so he phoned Harry, who was at that time production manager at the Freddie Wood, and because he had never seen much point in dissembling—it just took up time—he told Harry he wanted to meet the girl who had played Barbara Allen.

"Hoo, hoo, hoo," said Harry. "What do you think I am, a dating service?"

"I can make my own dates. I just want to meet her."

"Call her up. I'll get you her number."

Ted leaned back in his chair and frowned at the wall, thinking. "Harry. Is there something you want to tell me?"

"Not a thing, pal, not a thing."

Ted sat up and shifted the phone to his other hand. "I think there is. Are you going out with her?"

Harry snorted. "No, I am not going out with her," he said.

"How can I meet her?"

"I told you. I'll get you her number."

"I don't want to do it that way," said Ted furiously.

"Well, what the hell do you want me to do?"

"What's the matter with you, anyway, Harry?"

"Going out with her. Jesus. Grow up, Ted."

Ted waited.

"You are single-minded, you know that?" said Harry. "You've been out in the boondocks for four years, you come back, you phone me up and all you've got to say is introduce me to this bimbo I saw on your stage last night."

Ted felt a flash of anger at the word "bimbo." He let it pass. "Jesus, Harry," he said after a minute. "I'm sorry. I really am." He heard Harry sigh.

"All right, all right," said Harry. "I'll try to get her to have lunch with me. Then you come too."

Margaret watched uneasily as Ted slid into the booth opposite her, next to Harry. His head was lowered.

"This man here," said Harry, slouched over a cup of coffee, "is Ted Griffin. Ted, this is Margaret Kennedy. Now can I go home?"

Jesus, thought Ted, furious.

He raised his head and stared grimly at Margaret across the table. He had the bluest eyes she had ever seen, and a chunk of dark hair had fallen across his forehead. His face was shaped like a triangle, with softened edges. She would tell her friend Moira later that she had been immediately smitten, but this was not quite true.

"I just told her about you," said Harry confidentially to Ted. "If I'd told her any sooner she probably wouldn't have stayed."

This is really a very juvenile situation, thought Margaret, studying them. Harry wore an expression of unconvincing boredom. The newcomer looked almost angry—but he was probably embarrassed. And so he should be.

"How old are you two?" she said.

"I'll never tell," said Harry, smirking.

"Twenty-eight," said the stranger. "How old are you?"

"You're acting like a couple of high school kids," said Margaret. "I'm twenty-one," she added lamely.

"I don't think so," said Ted calmly. "I've met most of the people I know through other people I know. Haven't you?" He shrugged, and finally smiled, a smile that hit her in the chest right where she breathed. "I saw you in the play last night."

"That play had a cast of thousands. Why me?" He looked exasperated. "I'm not being coy," she said. "I would just like to know why you've gone to all this trouble." She gestured to encompass Harry, the booth, the restaurant.

"For one thing, you're very pretty," he said. "I also thought you'd be an interesting person to know. What more can I say? If you want me to leave, I'll leave."

15

Margaret was flustered. She lowered her eyes and found herself looking at his shirt. It was blue. The top button was undone; she could see the hollow of his throat.

Harry suddenly yawned loudly. "You're not leaving, pal," he said to Ted. "I'm the one that's leaving."

Ted stood up to let him out. "Thanks, Harry," he said.

"For what?" said Harry, and he ambled away, leaving them mired in an awkward moment.

A waitress hurried past the booth, jostling Ted, who was still standing.

"Sit down," said Margaret, "before you get run over."

He sat.

They eyed one another across the table warily. They felt alert and self-protective, as people do in moments of crisis.

"Well," said Margaret. "Tell me about yourself."

Her voice delighted him. It was rich, and low, and complex, and seemed filled with many sounds other than speech. He didn't remember hearing it sound like that from the stage.

"I start teaching at U.B.C. next week," he said casually.

"Teaching what?"

"English."

"That's nice," said Margaret politely.

Ted would have preferred a more enthusiastic response. He looked at her across the table, a stranger who saw him as a stranger, too.

"What did Harry tell you about me?" he said.

"Nothing, really. He said I'd probably like you."

"Do you?" said Ted. Her hair was thick, the gold-brown color of old-fashioned honey; her skin was tanned; she had a slight overbite which he thought looked delicious. His hands on the table felt large and clumsy. He felt bereft of logic and good sense, both of which he prized.

"I don't know yet," she said.

"I don't know if I like you yet either," he said, and they observed one another remotely. "But since we're here, we might as well have lunch."

They frowned at the menus, holding them cautiously in front of their faces. Innocent and hostile, they stumbled through the last moments in which they might have decided to go their separate ways.

"What do you do," said Ted, when they had ordered, "when you're not acting?"

"I'm a stenographer."

Ted was astonished at the extent of his disappointment. He tried to imagine her answering telephones and typing letters. "Where?" he said finally.

"Until the end of June I worked for a moving company," said Margaret.

"A moving company?" He could hardly believe it.

"I quit to go to summer school," said Margaret. "Now I'm looking for another job."

"As a stenographer?" said Ted.

"Yes, as a stenographer," said Margaret briskly.

"Do you like that kind of work?" he said, as a club sandwich was placed in front of him.

"Of course I don't like it," said Margaret, and he felt that he'd been lightly jostled by a porcupine. She started to eat her soup and toast.

"Then why do you do it?"

"Because it doesn't take much out of me. I can go in at eight o'clock and do that job with no trouble at all, even when I've done a show the night before."

"You mean, you do this all the time?" said Ted, amazed. "I thought you were in that play just for fun."

Margaret looked at him. "You don't quit your job and go to summer school just for fun," she said. "You ought to know that, for heaven's sake."

"Then you're serious about it," said Ted. "You really want to be an actress." The idea was almost incomprehensible to him.

"I *am* an actress," Margaret corrected him. "I thought you were supposed to be intelligent." Her voice made his teeth ache.

He opened his mouth, but no words came out.

"It's like anything else, you know," said Margaret. "It's a career. You're a little further along in your career than I am in mine, but then, you're a little bit older than I am." She sat back and folded her arms in front of her, protectively. He was irritating, because he made her feel defensive, but she was acutely aware of his physical presence. "How do you happen to know Harry?" she said.

17

# THE FAVORITE

"We were in some of the same classes at U.B.C. He belonged to the Players' Club. He dragged me out to some shows."

" 'Dragged' you out?"

"I liked them, I enjoyed myself," he said hastily, and then grinned at her. "I was curious to see what he'd gotten himself involved with."

"Were you surprised when he stayed involved with it?"

"Yeah. I was. The whole business didn't seem very real to me." He glanced at her. "Sorry."

"It's a common enough opinion. My parents feel the same way."

"I thought you were very good, though, last night. When you died, I was very upset." He wanted to smooth her furrowed forehead with his fingers. He took a deep breath. What the hell, he thought. He said, "I was getting infatuated all the time I watched that damn play."

Margaret watched his hand reach across the table, and watched her own turn over, soft and submissive, fingers gently spread. When their palms met, her fingers closed tentatively around his hand, which was warm and strong. She looked up to see him smiling. Her gaze fluttered from the startling blueness of his eyes to their two hands, firmly interlocked, resting on the tabletop.

Ahhh . . . thought Margaret.

She didn't want to let go of his hand.

Margaret had decided by now that she could allow herself to go to bed with someone to whom she was not married, but only if she and this person were engaged. Before she met Ted, she had never been engaged. But their relationship developed rapidly, and very soon had reached the point at which she had to outline to Ted her philosophy about sex. She could see that it dismayed him. She accused him of assuming that since she was an actress she automatically must have a permissive attitude. He admitted this, and she railed at him for a while about stereotypical thinking. But she eventually realized that although he was disappointed that they wouldn't be immediately tumbling into bed together, he was also glad to learn that she hadn't yet done this with anybody else.

18

Very soon he was talking about marriage, which took Margaret by surprise; she hadn't thought it likely that he would go so far just to sleep with her. When he had convinced her of his earnestness, she became solemn. These were serious matters, and she wasn't about to leap the final hurdle into total engagement without giving it a great deal of thought.

It did occur to her that honestly believing oneself to be engaged was, for these purposes, equally good as actually ending up getting married; but she brutally thrust that temptation from her mind. She would not sleep with Ted until she was absolutely sure that she wanted to be married to him. Forever.

Meanwhile, other aspects of their lives had to be lived. Margaret found another job, at a salary of $235 a month. Since her rent was only $14 a week, she was satisfied. She didn't look for fulfillment in her job, anyway—that she got from acting, and now from Ted, as well. She had found another play to do, an amateur production, but she was more absorbed in Ted, and in whether they were actually contemplating marriage.

Ted was given an office at U.B.C. (really half an office) with a tall, narrow window. Next to this window someone had put an enormous plant which was growing with such extraordinary vigor that it threatened to block out the light entirely. Ted gazed at it, shaken, and wondered if Margaret knew anything about plants.

He had already made out a reading list for his English 200 classes which included, in the first term, Chaucer, *Hamlet,* and a gaggle of sixteenth- and seventeenth-century poets. He planned his lectures carefully, borrowing liberally from those he had given over the past four years, and arranged for his students to see Olivier's *Hamlet* early in the term. But it was *King Lear,* scheduled for the second term, which he most looked forward to; the only unplayable Shakespearean play, some people called it. He would discuss that with Margaret, who, as an actress, ought to have some strong opinions—assuming that she had read it, of course.

They saw each other almost every day, and wispy strands of commitment began to wrap around them both, innocuous but stubborn.

# Chapter 3

ALMOST AS SOON AS SHE MET TED, MARGARET WANTED TO
tell Moira about him. Things didn't feel fully dealt with until
she had told Moira about them, because they had discussed
with one another most of the things that went on in their
lives ever since junior high school. It was a friendship that
was important to them both, and they tended it carefully. An
event as important as having met Ted was something that
Margaret absolutely must tell Moira about.

But it was difficult to find an opportunity. Their lunch
hours didn't coincide, which left only evenings and week-
ends, and much of this time was taken up with Margaret's
rehearsals. What was left, she wanted to spend with Ted.

Finally she phoned Moira.

"I've met a man," she blurted, sitting tensely on her sofa
and wishing she could see Moira's face.

"Glad to hear it," said Moira. "I hope he's better than the
last one."

Margaret couldn't remember for a minute who the last one
had been. Then, "Oh, him," she said weakly. He was a tall,
pimply-faced boy whom she and Moira had gone to school
with. She had encountered him unexpectedly one rainy day
in early spring while waiting for the pedestrian signal at

Georgia and Granville to change, and had been so startled to
see someone from her past that she agreed to share his
umbrella. Moira had thought it hilarious that Margaret,
trapped in wretched courtesy, actually went out with him
twice, once to the Cave and once to the car show at the
Exhibition grounds, because she didn't want to embarrass
him by saying no.

"Moira, don't be snide," said Margaret now. "But as it
happens," she added with dignity, "he's a great deal better."

"Is he an actor?"

"He teaches. English. At U.B.C."

"Good," said Moira cheerfully. "A little more education
won't do you a bit of harm."

Margaret sighed. "Look, Moira," she said, "I haven't
been home for weeks and neither have you. Why don't we
go out there on Sunday?"

Their parents lived in Haney, a small town on the north
side of the Fraser River about thirty miles east of Vancouver. Margaret had been born there, and Moira's family had
moved there when she was eleven.

"In my car, I suppose," said Moira.

"I'll give you a dollar for the damn gas. I want to talk to
you."

"If that's all you want," said Moira reasonably, "why
don't we do it here?"

"Because if I stay here I'll end up seeing this guy instead
of seeing you!" said Margaret angrily, her patience gone.

There was a short silence. "Okay," said Moira. "I'll pick
you up at noon."

Moira drove a two-tone green 1947 Pontiac coupe, a gift
from her father which was much admired by everyone who
rode in it because of the state of its preservation. On the dot
of noon the following Sunday she swept up in her car in front
of the big, rambling old brown house on Thurlow Street, just
up from the beach, where Margaret rented two rooms and
shared a bath with the landlord and his wife. Margaret,
watching from her window, ran out and climbed in beside
Moira and they headed for the White Spot restaurant on
Georgia Street to fortify themselves for the trip.

The world that September was lush and still mostly green;
roses bloomed on in front gardens and the sun was dry and

hot. "We should have gone to the beach," said Margaret, letting her arm drift out of the open window.

"Everybody in the world will be on the beach," said Moira, and drove firmly away from the sea. "On days like this the whole damn West End gets dumped on the beach. Every house, every apartment building upended; every person in them dumped on the beach." She glanced at Margaret. "Besides, if we stayed here you'd rush off to that fellow. You told me you would."

Margaret glared at her.

The car billowed along with a regality derived from its deficient shock absorbers. Margaret's good spirits returned as they approached the White Spot parking lot. "Let's eat in the car, okay? Hey, look, there's somebody leaving," she said, pointing.

"I see him, I see him," said Moira. She maneuvered the Pontiac into one of the parking spaces reserved for drive-in customers, turned off the motor and switched on the head-lights until the carhop had come to take their order.

"Jesus, it's hot," said Moira, fanning her face with her hand. She pushed her sunglasses on top of her head. She was tall and square, with black hair cupping her jaw, and she wore sandals and a flowered muumuu with a dark blue background. She didn't care about getting tanned in the summer, because her complexion was olive to begin with. Margaret, who loved to toast herself in the sun, had brushed her hair back and tied it in a ponytail, and had put on white shorts and a white sleeveless blouse.

"My eyes hurt just looking at you," Moira complained, and lowered her enormous sunglasses.

The carhop came back and jockeyed into the car a long narrow tray laden with two hamburgers, two containers of french fries, two Cokes, napkins and cutlery, salt and pepper, and a glass bottle of vinegar.

"Every time I come here," said Margaret happily, "I think I'm going to have something else, but I never do." She sniffed the scents of food and vinegar.

"Me too," said Moira, her mouth already full of ham-burger. She chewed, swallowed, took a sip of Coke. "So how's your boyfriend?" she said.

Margaret's heart lurched. "He has a very strong effect on me," she said.

22

"Hmmm," said Moira, waiting for more.

Margaret was horrified to discover that she had nothing more to say. Quite unexpectedly, now that the moment had come she didn't want to talk about Ted at all. She couldn't understand it. She looked out the window into the noisy car in the next space; it was crammed with two adults, two small children, and a dog. Margaret suddenly didn't want to be there. She felt estranged and distant from the friend beside her, the parents whom she was going to visit. She wanted only to be with Ted, to close her eyes and feel his arms tight around her. She started to eat french fries, quickly, gobbling them down, not tasting them.

"Hey, Maggie," said Moira, astonished.

"I think I'm going to marry him," said Margaret, her mouth and her hands full of french fries. She started to cry.

"Maggie, Maggie," said Moira. She fished around in her huge handbag and brought out several Kleenexes. "Shhh, shhh," she said, thrusting the Kleenexes at Margaret with one hand and patting her shoulder with the other.

Margaret wiped at her eyes, aware that all sounds from the crowded car beside her had stopped. She shifted on the plush gray upholstery of the Pontiac so that the people next to them could see only her back. "I don't know what's the matter with me, really," she said to Moira. She was angry and embarrassed, but at least she felt like herself again, which was a relief.

"I understand it's quite an emotional experience, deciding to get married," said Moira. "I'm feeling pretty peculiar myself, and it's not even me who's getting married."

Margaret shook her head violently, trying not to cry again. "I haven't absolutely decided," she said. "Not for sure."

"Well, is he a nice person?" said Moira politely.

Margaret couldn't help but smile.

"I mean, is he decent?" said Moira. "Well-mannered? I know he's gainfully employed, you've already told me that."

"Yes," said Margaret. "He's decent. And well-mannered."

"Tell me then," said Moira, staring thoughtfully up at the ceiling of the car, "is he—attractive? Young? Old? Slack-shouldered? What?"

Margaret considered. "He's about five feet ten inches tall," she said clinically, "and he has dark brown hair, and

23

extremely blue eyes, and he's rather serious but he can be funny, too." She thought for a minute, suddenly dreamy. "Moira . . . don't you think, Moira, that there's something about the way men are—put together—that's really very sexy?"

Moira giggled, and nodded, and finished off her Coke.

"No, listen. I mean from the back."

Moira giggled again.

"Come on, Moira, I'm serious, are you going to be serious?"

Moira nodded, and frowned.

Margaret's hands made a V in the air. "See, they're wide across the top, across the shoulders, and then they get narrow down here, around the waist." She dropped her hands into her lap and sighed. "There's something terribly—substantial, about them."

"Sexy. That's what you said first."

"Yeah. And strong. It makes you want to put your arms around them, and lean against them."

"And pat their little buns."

Margaret looked at her. She felt a flicker of guilt. "Yeah," she said, and grinned.

"Well, well," said Moira. "You are really hot to trot for this guy, aren't you?"

Margaret shifted in her seat again; the angle of the sun had changed. "My leg's being fried," she said. "We'd better get going anyway."

Once they got out on the highway Moira said, over the noise of the wind and the road, "At least he's not an actor."

"What's wrong with actors," said Margaret loudly, "that isn't also wrong with artists?" She closed her window, reducing the racket in the car.

"Oh God, Margaret, I'd never marry an artist, it's bad enough to be one."

Three cars passed the Pontiac, which surged along at a sedate fifty miles an hour. Moira's father had warned her that even though the car was in mint condition, those worn-out shock absorbers deserved her attention.

"How long have you known him?" said Moira casually.

"Six weeks," said Margaret. She looked at Moira suspiciously. "I can hear you thinking, Moira. I know it's not

very long, I don't need you to tell me that, because I ...
know it."

Moira turned to grin at her. "What the hell," she said.

Margaret stared out of her window, watching trees pass
and hoping for a glimpse of the river. "Are you going to
come and see *Look Homeward, Angel?*" she said. She had
been cast as Laura. The show was scheduled to open at the
end of the month.

"What's it about? Maybe I'd be bored."

"You won't come to be entertained. You'll come because
I am in it. It's from a novel by Thomas Wolfe. You'll like it."
Then she added thoughtfully, "The guy who plays Eugene is
very good."

"Will your professor be going to see it?"

Margaret looked at her irritably. "Maybe you can go
together. Talk about me behind your hands."

"When does it open, this Eugene O'Neill thing?"

"The name of the play is *Look Homeward, Angel*. It was
written by Ketti Frings. It has nothing to do with Eugene
O'Neill. You're very ignorant."

"Tell me about Matisse, tell me about Rembrandt, tell me
about Jackson Pollock, why don't you."

"Okay, okay."

They drove in silence for a while. Beyond the low, green
mountains to the north were remoter ones, much higher,
which always wore some snow. In the forests that clung to
the hillsides and often crept close to the highway Margaret
could see there were now some splotches of gold.

"How's your painting?" she said. Moira never let her
watch her work, and seldom let Margaret see any of her
finished paintings. She said that at this stage, nothing she did
was ever finished.

"What am I supposed to say to that? It's good, it's great,
I'm a very talented person." Moira shrugged. "I just keep
plugging away." She had been working as a secretary in a
Vancouver law office and saving her money for art school
ever since leaving high school. Now she had enough, and
had just enrolled in the fall program.

"I've got a piece of news for you," said Margaret as they
approached Haney and the Pontiac slowed to thirty.

Moira, remembering Margaret's tears, was filled with
dread. "Oh God, don't tell me you're pregnant."

25

"Moira!" said Margaret. "I haven't even—" She stopped, blushing. Moira started to laugh. "No, don't be so—God, Moira. No. I've got a television job." As she said it, she began to smile, and soon her whole face was beaming.

Moira whooped, and reached across the seat to grab her hand.

"It's only a little one," said Margaret apologetically, still beaming. "But they're actually going to *pay* me." She sank back against the seat. "My God, Moira. They're actually going to pay me." She shook her head wonderingly.

Margaret decided then not to tell her parents about Ted that day. They might consider him a more important development in her life than the television job. After all, she couldn't expect them to see her priorities as clearly as she and Moira saw them.

# Chapter 4

MARGARET COULDN'T HELP BUT REST HER HOPES TOO heavily on the small television role she'd gotten. This was largely because when she told her parents about it, they were far more impressed than they should have been.

They had been going to see her in plays from the time she was in elementary school, but they had no more expected her to become an actress than the parents of seven-year-old hockey players expect them to end up with the Canadiens.

When she got to senior high school it was clear to them that the plays she was in were a little more difficult, a little more serious; but they only vaguely sensed that when Margaret stood up there on the stage, she was changed. They did realize that she could make them laugh or cry and that when they watched her they sometimes stopped remembering, for a minute or two, that it was Margaret they were watching.

But none of this had anything to do with real life, and when she announced that she was going to continue doing it after graduation, to the exclusion of a university education or even a career, Mr. and Mrs. Kennedy worked very hard to try to dissuade her.

Margaret's parents knew, of course, that there were people who made their livings acting, but those people were all

in Hollywood or New York or London and were very
different from ordinary people. When Margaret told them
there were also people in Vancouver and Toronto who acted
as a career her parents looked extremely doubtful. Who
would pay them? they wanted to know.

Margaret's father was a pharmacist and her mother had
been a very efficient secretary before she got married. Mrs.
Kennedy never considered going back to work—except
once, when Margaret went into junior high school and didn't
come home for lunch any more. Ivy seemed suddenly to
have a great deal less to do. So she thought about getting a
job, and even talked to Harold about it.

"I don't mind," he said in his deceptively slow way, "if
that's what you want. You'd have some catching up to do,
though, wouldn't you?"

Well, that was true. She'd have to go into Vancouver for
brush-up courses in typing and shorthand. When she tried to
work out the logistics of that, well, it was all just too much.
Certainly they didn't need the money, and certainly she
could find plenty of things to keep her busy if she put her
mind to it.

Ivy became an expert furniture finisher, buying old things
and stripping and sanding and polishing them. She made
drapes and slipcovers, and put up wallpaper; there was
always at least one room in the house that was being
redecorated. She tended her flowers, inside and out. She had
windows and rooms filled with plants, some of them hanging
from the ceilings, long before this became a fashionable
thing to do. She even became the leader of a Brownie pack,
much to Margaret's disgust. She also kept herself looking
good, and had had her hair tinted for years, just slightly
lighter than her natural blond color because God knew she
didn't want to look garish.

Margaret's parents had reluctantly accepted their daughter's ambitions, and drove dutifully in to Vancouver every
time she was in a play, which wasn't often. They continued
to urge her to go to university, for which they would gladly
have paid.

When she told them she was going to be on a television
program, they were flabbergasted and overjoyed. Television
was much more businesslike than the theater; and of course
they could tell all their friends to watch the show. It wasn't

Ed Sullivan or *I Love Lucy,* just one of those things for kids, but who could say where it might lead?

When Margaret walked with pounding heart into the studio the first thing she thought was that she was glad her parents couldn't see it. The place looked like something that should have been a railway station, or a warehouse. It looked as though it could have been designed with one of several purposes in mind. But it certainly did not look to Margaret like a television studio.

The ceilings seemed enormously high. There was white tape all over the floor. Some of it had been laid weeks, months, maybe years ago, and nobody had bothered to unstick it once its purpose had been served; they had just stuck some new whiter tape down on top of it. The whole barnlike place was sparsely occupied by absentminded, harassed people whose sole purpose seemed to be to rush from one corner of it to another. There were bits and pieces of furniture strewn forlornly around, and dusty shadows lurked dismally along the walls.

Margaret stood inside the door and looked around with rising dismay, her apprehension forgotten. She observed that one part of the room was brightly lit and that the rushing people appeared to have that area as their focus. They dashed about like water bugs, following a zigzagging pattern which, though invisible, seemed to have been laid down by a deity somewhere, and their point of reference was this brightly lit area.

Margaret watched them for a few seconds, amazed. They spoke abruptly at one another and ran about with an air of desperate intensity, but they didn't have anything in their hands, and Margaret could not see the point of their comings and goings.

She walked over to the lights, nervous again, trying to pretend as she went that she was an actress, trying to pull in her stomach and swing her legs just so. That worked, all right; but she couldn't seem to do anything with her arms. They hung from her shoulders like dead weights and caused her hands to thump uselessly against her thighs. Her script was clutched tightly in one hand, sticking to her fingers.

People looked up as she approached. *Everybody* looked

29

up as she approached. There was a little kid, about ten years old, she guessed, and he looked at her with mild interest but there was a shrewd gleam in his eye which she didn't much care for. There was an angular, aging actor whose face she recognized—he was one of the regulars on the program (which she had watched fervently for the last two weeks)—and he looked bored, but Margaret thought hopefully that he was probably kind. She wondered what had happened in his life since he'd been her age and had walked onto a television set for the first time. There was a fat, sulky-looking man, too, the other regular, dressed in a pair of overalls and some knee-high rubber boots. He played the comic role, she remembered, but looking at his face she couldn't imagine how he was going to bring it off this week.

And then there was the director. Producer, she corrected herself. He looked very tired, but he came immediately to greet her, shook her hand politely and introduced her to the rest of the cast. She hoped that none of them would ask her any questions like "What have you done?" and they didn't. It seemed there was no time for idle chitchat.

The set had a couple of chairs and a thing that looked vaguely like it was supposed to represent the inside of a boat. It seemed a very small area in the expanse of gloom that was the full studio, and Margaret realized with a shock that what the small screen showed was nothing more or less than what was actually there.

She was told to wait, and she waited, and she watched, anxious to pick up as much as she could before it was her turn.

The producer murmured for a while with the three actors. Then he walked off the set and said something quietly to one of the self-consciously frenzied people and the lights came on, blindingly bright and hot, and someone yelled "Quiet!" so loudly that Margaret jumped and then looked quickly around to see whether anyone had noticed, but nobody had.

There was silence.

The producer asked the cameraman if he was ready and Margaret for the first time saw the camera. It was huge, and it was pointed right at the actors. It occurred to her that she had been told to learn her lines before she came because there weren't going to be any real rehearsals. She had spent a lot of time on the script, and she knew the lines; but there wasn't much in them to indicate what kind of a person her character was. She had been counting on the rehearsals to help her make this character her own. She began to feel a certain amount of desperation.

The voices of the actors on the set occupied a conversational level in the stillness. The angular man with the graying hair spoke lazily, kindly. Margaret couldn't distinguish his words; her mind wouldn't register words, it was too absorbed with its own panic. The kid spoke like a chirping bird, drawing Margaret's eyes to his face—and she was astonished to see real tears there, glinting on his cheeks in the harsh lights. She stared at him, frowning; the aging actor was leaning over the boy, comforting him; the fat man was sitting close to them and he looked doleful, heartbroken. Had she *missed* the rehearsals? But someone would have told her . . .

As she watched the written script came crashing into her brain. This must be the scene just before hers. The kid's lost, these two have found him, they're trying to comfort him, find out where he lives, what his name is—the producer said a quiet "Cut." My God, thought Margaret dazedly, they really do say that; and then he was beckoning to her.

Her heart stopped beating.

She knew the lines, all right, but she was definitely not prepared for this, for that camera to point itself at her; she didn't even *know* this girl she was supposed to play.

Her script fell to the floor. The actors on the set turned to look at her. She picked up the script, bending from the waist, and put it on a chair. She walked around the camera to where the producer stood, patiently, one arm raised toward her, waiting.

"You know the script?" he said courteously as she reached the half circle formed by his upraised arm. She nodded. He brought his arm down, giving her shoulder an absentminded pat as he did so. "You haven't done any television before, is that right?"

"Right," said Margaret in a whisper. She cleared her throat. "Have I, uh, do I have the right clothes on? They said just normal clothes," she said, fumbling for courage.

He looked at her briefly. "They're just fine. One thing you have to remember. Television is much smaller than the stage."

Margaret squinted at the set. "Uh-huh," she said, nodding.

"You have to be much, smaller," he said carefully, showing her with his hands, which measured in the air a distance of about nine inches across.

Just about nine inches, she thought conscientiously. "Is my makeup all right? They said just normal street makeup." *I am not ready for this.*

The producer looked at her in surprise; then looked more carefully and smiled, very slightly. "Your makeup is fine, Margaret. May I call you Margaret?"

"Oh yes, sure, Margaret."

"Your costume is fine. Your makeup is fine. You've got nothing to be nervous about." He patted her shoulder again. "I'm sure you're a fine actress."

*Fine actress*, thought Margaret.

"You'll do just fine," he said. "The only thing you've got to remember is to make. it. small. Okay?"

"Okay," said Margaret. "Small."

He pointed to the newest strips of white tape which spread themselves over this part of the floor. He showed her where she was to go. He told her what she was to do.

"Now the scene starts with Jamie over there crying. Henry has a line, 'but, kid, blah blah blah,' then Cornie—" He stopped at Margaret's expression of bewilderment. "Jeff. He's Jeff in the script. Jeff says, 'But what're we going to do with him?' Then you come in. You've got to start moving as soon as Jeff begins that line.

"You enter the set here," he said, pointing to a white X on the floor, "and go along there; you spot the boy, run over to him, and—what's your first line?"

" 'Bobo,' " said Margaret apologetically. "It's 'Bobo.' Then 'Bobo' again. Then 'It's really you.' So what I say is, 'Bobo, Bobo, it's really you.' "

"Right," said the producer with another small smile. He started over to the camera.

"Why do I say that, by the way?" *I wouldn't have had to ask, if we'd had a rehearsal.*

He stopped, turned around. "I beg your pardon?"

"Why do I say 'Bobo,' do you think?" said Margaret.

The producer walked back to her. "That's what you call him," he said patiently.

"I know. But why do I call him that? Doesn't he have a name? Couldn't I call him by his name?" I have to know these things, she thought desperately.

She heard giggles from the kid on the set, and an exasperated mutter from someone else.

"No, never mind," she said, "I'm sorry . . ."

"No, that's quite all right." The producer stared thoughtfully at the floor. "You call him that because it sounds like 'baby brother,' I think." He looked at her. "That's the only reason I can think of. I didn't write the script." He smiled. "Thank God." He looked at her questioningly. "Are you ready?" Margaret nodded. He walked over to the camera.

Margaret wiped her hands on her skirt, tried to clear her throat silently. (Bobo Bobo it's really you.) Somebody yelled, "Quiet!" There was murmuring, murmuring—I'll never hear my cue, she thought distractedly.

"But what're we going to do with him?"

Margaret raced across the X mark, scurried down the white tape, lifted her head, spotted the kid. "Bobo!" she yelled, and lunged for him. "Bobo! It's really you!" she said, smothering the child in her arms.

"Cut," said the producer.

He beckoned her off the set and walked toward the center of the enormous almost empty studio, a finger to his lips. He half turned as she came up behind him, stopped, stared at the floor. He clasped his hands behind him and raised his head to look quizzically at her.

"I don't think you quite understood me," he said, "when I talked about 'small.' "

Three hours later Margaret staggered out of the studio, down the hall, past the reception desk and into the street.

She was somewhat surprised to find that it was still day.

She found a restaurant, sat in a booth and ordered coffee. She hadn't eaten all day, but she wasn't aware of that yet.

She sipped her coffee and tried to decide which hurt most, her pride or her self-esteem.

She tried to think of somebody she could go to and cry in front of—she thought of course of Ted, and of Moira, but neither of them would be able to understand her present very specific kind of mortification.

Gloomy and suffering, she looked at the clock on the wall and decided she had better eat something, because she had a performance of *Look Homeward, Angel* in a couple of hours. The thought of the performance made her feel slightly better.

She ate.

She kept reliving those awful moments when she had tried to get smaller, all the while convinced that if she got any more small her entire character would disappear.

There's a trick to it, she told herself. It's just a question of doing it often enough. But how, she thought wonderingly, do actors switch back and forth between stage and television, between big and small, without cracking up?

She wondered if she shouldn't try to get into the National Theater School after all. Or even major in theater at U.B.C.—go anyplace where people could teach her things.

But she knew she would never audition for the National Theater School, not now that she had met Ted; Montreal was too far away. And she didn't much like the idea of becoming a student on the campus where he was teaching.

She sighed, and got up to pay her bill.

She would learn by doing, she thought. It was a perfectly good way of going about things.

# Chapter 5

It wasn't the first theater party Ted had been to but it still made him uneasy, because by and large theater people made him uneasy. It should not be so simple for them to pretend they were someone else. He didn't think it bothered him unduly to think about Margaret doing this, but he was apprehensive about being in a no-holds-barred party situation with a whole lot of people who made it their day-to-day business to pretend to be someone else. Or to aid, in one way or another, in that pretense.

"What kind of a party do you think it's going to be, for heaven's sake?" Margaret had asked him, when he was obviously less than enthusiastic about going. And he had been unable to tell her.

He had been putting off mixing with her friends and he knew it was time he gave in. He knew he would have to learn to be comfortable in Margaret's life, as she would have to learn to be comfortable in his.

He watched the last performance of *Look Homeward, Angel* with Harry and with Margaret's friend Moira, whom he had not met before that evening. He was wary of her at first because she had known Margaret for such a long time, and was bound to know a lot of things about her that Ted had yet to learn. But she turned out to be pleasant and polite as they waited for the play to begin. She also dealt efficiently with Harry's advances, apparently understanding that they were delivered almost automatically to any young, reasonably attractive woman he chanced to meet. Ted found, too, that Moira was interested in many things, which surprised him.

By the end of the first act Ted was somewhat preoccupied. He had not enjoyed watching Margaret kissing and caressing someone else, and he was busy trying to come to terms with that. He would have liked to talk to someone about it. In the lobby he glanced over at Harry, who was still giving Moira his insistent attention. A lot of people, Ted told himself, are married to actors and actresses. They must get used to it; maybe they learn to pretend just as enthusiastically as their spouses that it's all make-believe. Then, more grimly, he thought that maybe they just never went to plays their husbands or wives were in.

He was relieved when the performance was over.

When they got to the party he was rattled and very much out of his element. The house was already filled with people. They stopped in the hall and he helped Margaret take off her coat. She reached up to put her arms around his neck and kissed him on the mouth; he was surprised, but his arms went around her waist. He wanted to tear off her dress. He was excited by her public teasing, but it angered him, too. He took hold of her wrists and pulled her arms away from him.

"Let's go somewhere," he said into her ear.

She put her hand on his cheek and pulled his head down to whisper, "I love you," and then she took him by the hand and they went into the living room.

Harry had plunged into the crowd but Moira was still at their heels, muttering. Ted had a feeling that Margaret might go winging off like a butterfly and he was relieved that he would have Moira to keep him company: she didn't seem to know anybody at the party, either.

The living room was smoky and noisy. Music played raucously from the stereo and people had spread themselves in groups whose membership kept changing. Margaret introduced him to everybody—they were all in the cast, or part of the production crew, or had come with someone from the show—and Ted repeated names knowing he wouldn't remember them. Someone asked what they wanted to drink and soon they had bottles of beer in their hands.

"Beer, Christ," said Moira, and she looked so baffled that Ted laughed and felt a lot better.

"What would you like?" he said, reaching for her beer. He was relieved to be taking charge of something.

"Scotch, if you can find some," said Moira.

Ted turned to Margaret, but she had disappeared. He pushed through the crowd to the kitchen and eventually returned with two scotches and sat on a cushion on the floor next to Moira.

"Quite a party," said Moira, and then someone asked her to dance.

When she had gone off, Ted looked around for Margaret. She was coming toward him, and her green dress showed a lot of her neck and shoulders and made her hazel eyes look green, and her hair swung and shimmered like gold. Ted got to his feet and held out his arms to her. They danced together in the dining room, where furniture had been moved out of the way, and after two dances Ted took her by the shoulders and led her to a corner. He had taken off his jacket. She reached up to loosen his tie; he kissed her temple.

"I would like to take you to my place," he said into her ear, "and take off your dress." His hands on her back moved slowly up from her waist. "Ah. A zipper. There's a zipper all the way up the back of this thing . . ."

Someone tapped him on the back. He looked over his shoulder at the actor who had played Eugene—Paul something-or-other.

"Excuse me," said Paul. His face was gleaming through a thin layer of perspiration.

Ted felt hot and rumpled, looking over his shoulder almost furtively at the actor, whose head was covered with brown curls; Ted had thought it was a wig, when he saw it in the play, but apparently it was his real hair. Ted stared at it. The actor was grinning at Margaret. He had very white, very straight teeth and there was a dimple in his cheek. Ted would have dismissed him as effeminate except for the breadth of his shoulders and the size of the muscles in his arms, which

37

he could see clearly because the guy was wearing a skin-tight shirt—Ted couldn't imagine where he had found such a thing—which was open almost to his goddamn navel, exposing the curly hair on his chest. He was also wearing extremely tight blue jeans. Ted disliked him instantly.

"May I dance one last time with my Laura?" said Paul.

Jesus, thought Ted in disgust, and stood back. Margaret kissed his cheek, patted his arm, and moved off with Paul. Ted watched them go.

My Laura, he thought, shoving his hands into his pockets. What crap.

He went back to the living room, where Moira was talking to a couple of people and Harry was leaning drunkenly over a laughing redhead in the corner.

Ted helped himself to another drink and wandered around listening to bits of conversation. He was sure that if he could listen to one of them all the way through he'd probably be fascinated, but it was like trying to isolate one tiny pattern from the jumble of shrieking light and color in a kaleidoscope. When he saw Moira standing alone, he joined her.

"Where's Margaret?" she asked.

"Dancing," said Ted. "Would you like to dance?"

"Oh no, let's just sit down someplace." When they had sat, she looked at him appraisingly. "Margaret says you're going to get married."

"Yup," he said, stretching out his legs, trying to be casual as he looked around the room.

"That was fast," said Moira, and she sounded amused.

Ted didn't resent her curiosity because he knew she cared a lot about Margaret. "Yes," he said. "It was fast."

"You don't have any doubts?"

"Sure I've got doubts," he said, and smiled. "So does Margaret. But I don't think we'd have any fewer doubts if we waited six months—or a year, or ten years."

He found himself wanting to explain it to her. He sat up and rested his elbows on his knees, concentrating. "I think at some point people are just ready to get married," he said. "I think it happens suddenly. It's probably biological," he said, grinning again, "having to do with the continuation of the species."

"Hmmmm," said Moira, noncommittal.

"And when you get to that point, your attitudes change; you're not looking for the same things any more."

"Like a quick roll in the hay," said Moira.

He looked at her coolly. "Right," he said, after a minute's pause. "You've got it. I want"—he enunciated clearly—"much more than a fast fuck."

She finished her drink and swished the ice around in the glass. "I'm sorry," she said. "Sometimes I have a big mouth."

Ted stood up and took her glass. "I'll get you another drink," he said, and made his way toward the kitchen. The sounds of the party were very loud; the music and the laughter were giving him a headache. And he didn't know what he thought of Moira. He knew it was important to Margaret that they like one another, and he admitted to himself reluctantly that they probably would, but right now he was still angry with her. He decided that when he'd delivered her drink he would find Margaret and suggest that they leave. They'd go somewhere else, just the two of them.

He walked into the kitchen and saw Margaret and the actor, Paul.

At first he couldn't make out what was going on. He thought incongruously, they must be rehearsing; and then he remembered that the show was over.

The actor had pushed Margaret up against the refrigerator and Margaret's arms were locked around his neck and they were kissing each other, moaning in their throats. Their eyes were closed and their bodies were pressed hard against each other. The actor's hands were around Margaret's waist, pulling her close to him; they were moving against one another.

Ted watched them blankly. You couldn't get a toothpick between them, he thought. He had another instant of calm, in which he wondered what the hell they thought they were doing, going at each other where anybody could wander in and see. Then he was gripped and shaken by a tremendous rage, and he turned abruptly and walked out of the kitchen, knowing he would have to get out of the house quickly.

He thrust the empty glass into Moira's hand as he passed her, not looking at her; he thought of her, and of Harry, as conspirators, even though he knew that was not rational. He got outside and climbed into his elderly red sports car and drove away, and the strength of his anger and his jealousy amazed and sickened him. He roared off down the street gripping the steering wheel hard, hating himself for the sense of bitter betrayal that possessed him, hating Margaret more.


Moira watched from the doorway as the car disappeared down the street. Then she went to the kitchen.

"Ted's left," she said loudly.

Dismay stumbled across Margaret's lipstick-smeared face as Paul released her. He backed away into the living room.

"He saw us, I guess," said Margaret.

"It's a good thing I brought my car. Jesus. What got into you, anyway?" said Moira.

"Did he say anything?"

"Nope, he just left. Jesus, Maggie. I've never seen you do anything like that."

"Did he look—upset?"

"You could say that. Actually he looked furious. His face was kind of white. It was very interesting."

"Oh God. What am I going to do?"

Moira sighed. "I don't have a clue. Wait, I guess. If you don't hear from him in a few days, call him."

"To hell with that. Why should I wait for him to call me? Whose fault is this, anyhow? Maybe I should go to his place right now."

"I wouldn't do that."

"Why not?"

"I think you should give him a chance to cool off. Besides, you'd have to go home first and put your makeup on all over again."

Margaret glared at her furiously.


Several days went by before she was able to get him on the phone.

"I would like to see you," she said, thrusting at him all the dignity she had.

"I don't know if I want to see you," he said, and when there was a pause he thought she had hung up.

"It would be courteous of you to see me," she said finally, "even if you don't want to."

He remained angry, but in his apartment where she couldn't see him, he smiled. "It would, yes."

"I like a lot of things about you," she said evenly. "I especially like your politeness."

He smiled again. His politeness was a thing he used to keep people away from him. "I wouldn't like to end our relationship by disappointing you," he said.

"Can we meet somewhere?" said Margaret briskly.

He began collecting anger to form it into a huge rock with which to bash her head open. "Why don't you come here?" he said silkily, and waited.

"Of course," said Margaret, and the words rippled from the telephone through his ear and straight into his head, dissolving his anger.

He dusted the whole apartment, feverishly. He even washed out the glass in the bathroom. He hesitated for a long, agonizing moment and then stripped the bed and put on clean sheets, pretending he was just doing his laundry. Then he raced out to his car and drove off to get some flowers.

He divided them into two piles. He put half of them into the coffeepot and dumped out a jar of mayonnaise and washed it and put the rest of the flowers into the jar. He put the coffeepot on a table in the living room and put the jar in the bedroom, defiantly.

He was amazed at himself, and felt himself becoming angry again. He didn't know what would happen and tried not to think about it, but he was humiliated that he had gone to all this trouble, as though he had been at fault, and not Margaret.

He threw himself into a chair, ripped open a package of cigarettes, and began smoking one after another. When she knocked on the door he refused to let himself get up. He called out, "Come in."

She came in and sat down opposite him, without taking off her coat.

"I don't want us to waste time," she said. "I am extremely sorry about my behavior the other night."

He squinted at her through the cigarette smoke. He thought she looked pale, and less attractive than usual. Her voice, however, had the texture and sweetness of cream.

He told himself that he might as well see if he could get her into bed. They had been engaged for three weeks; he figured she owed it to him.

"Mmmmm," he said.

"I've never behaved that way before, in public," said Margaret. "Not in private, either, not since I met you. But I can't guarantee that it won't happen again."

He had been sure she had come to guarantee that very thing, and realized that he had intended to believe her.

"Why?" he said, shocked. His mind busily sketched alarming pictures of Margaret in various stages of arousal and intercourse with a variety of men, all of whom wore the face of that actor.

"Because I think it happened because of you."

"Just a minute," he said, standing up. He put his cigarette in an ashtray which he noticed already contained a great many butts. "Because of me." He put his hands in his pockets and began walking around the room. He stopped. "Would you like a drink?" he said politely.

"Yes, please."

"Scotch, or brandy, or beer?"

"Brandy, please." She folded her hands in her lap until he came back with two snifters and handed her one. "Thank you."

"Because of me," he said again. "Jesus. I don't follow you, Margaret." He shook his head, his anger returning.

"I don't mean that it's your fault."

"Well, that's a relief. Thanks a hell of a lot."

"It's my fault, of course it is. I let myself feel trapped."

"Trapped. By me?"

"Yes."

He took a large swallow of his drink and put the glass down on the table, hard. "You are not trapped, lady. You are most definitely not trapped."

"Oh, Ted, listen. Just try to listen. It's very hard. . . . Because of my philosophy—you know about my philosophy. . . ." She took a deep breath and started again. "In order to go to bed with you, I have to marry you. I *want* to

42

go to bed with you. So how can I be sure that's not the only reason I want to marry you? Do you see?"

Ted stared at her.

"Oh God, it's all so complicated."

He sat on the arm of a chair.

She drank some brandy.

"I think I've been wrong," said Margaret. "I think I have to keep them separate. Going to bed with you, and marrying you."

He thought about this.

"What's that—actor got to do with it?"

"I don't know," said Margaret wearily. "I was feeling restless." She sighed. "The thing is, I think I should do something. To keep the things separate." She looked him full in the face and his heart began to pound.

"I'm not sure I know what you mean," he said carefully.

"I think we should go to bed together," she said, and blushed, but refused to look away. "And then see if we still want to get married." The blush deepened, spreading to her throat.

Ted's mouth was dry and he thought he should be angry, or at least amused, but he was only excited.

"Oh God," she said, and stood up. She reached blindly for her purse.

"Maggie, Maggie." Ted pushed himself off the chair and put his arms around her. "Don't do this, please don't." He turned her around and she cried into his shoulder. "Look, we'll work it out. I love you, Maggie; we can work it out."

"I love you, too," she said, still crying.

"Hey, look at that," he said, and when she opened her eyes he waved toward the flowers in the coffeepot. "I got them for you."

"They're awful," said Margaret. "I hate asters."

Ted looked at them in surprise. "Is that what they are?" He turned back to her. "There's some more of them in the bedroom."

"Ha."

"I changed the sheets."

"You bastard." She looked up at him. "Oh, you bastard." Her heart was thudding. She thought she might panic and run out of the apartment. "You probably *had* to change them, God knows who's been in there, I just gave somebody one little kiss . . ." He picked her up and staggered toward the bedroom with her. ". . . God knows what you've been up to . . ."

"Nobody's been in here," he panted, "nobody but me."

He lurched into the bedroom and dropped her on the bed. She lay there feeling like a bundle of laundry and screamed to herself that she was not ready, but as it happened, she was.

# Chapter 6

MARGARET AND TED HAD BEEN MARRIED FOR ALMOST
three years when they had their first child. It was long
enough to have gotten to know each other, and to have
decided (as much as these things can ever be decided) that
they were glad they had gotten married.

Margaret left her job soon after the wedding. They didn't
really need the money, and she found that she actually
enjoyed spending the time necessary to take care of another
person as well as herself. She continued to do the occasional
show; she didn't give up acting. But she gave up certain
elements of her determination, because she saw things differently, married. She saw that Ted had his priorities and she
had hers, but that together they had had to form a whole new
set of them. It was a procedure so delicate and complex that
it took quite a while to work out, but once this was accom-
plished Margaret was not surprised that her acting was not at
the top of their joint list. The fact of their togetherness was
what had floated up there. And while Ted's work did not
suffer from this, Margaret's did, which made her wistful, and
occasionally resentful. Still, she figured that, all things considered, she had made a pretty good deal. She began to think

of herself not as an actress, but as a person who sometimes acted.

It was at a rehearsal that she first suspected she was pregnant.

The Playhouse Theatre Company was now in operation, but although several of Margaret's acquaintances were getting work on that stage she didn't feel she had enough experience to audition there. In the spring of 1964, however, she did try out for another company, and got the part of Lady Anne in a production of *Richard III*. This company was struggling hard to survive as at least a somewhat professional theater, and had recklessly chosen to do Shakespeare in the hope of attracting high school audiences dragged in by their English teachers. The students came, but not in sufficient numbers to make up for the virtually empty houses at night. Margaret didn't think the company was going to make it, and she was right; it lasted only two seasons. But at least she got to play Lady Anne. They performed in an old movie theater. The dressing room was the furnace room in the basement. No one got paid. There was at first some hope that they might all share in the profits once the show opened. Unfortunately, there weren't any.

One of the people involved was Harry Innes, who admired the five actors who ran the company simply because they were stubbornly blind to the impossibility of success. He also liked the idea of working with Margaret.

One day during rehearsal she was slumped in an aisle seat in the house, a jacket around her shoulders, fast asleep. She wakened slowly, her mind crowded and gluey. Her shoulder was being shaken.

"Can't hack it, eh, kid?" said Harry, down on one knee beside her. "Marriage still keeping you up at nights, eh? Jesus, it's disgusting." Harry was thinking about getting married himself, to a girl he had met the previous summer who was pretty and easily amused.

Margaret shook off his hand. "I just dozed off," she said. "I must be tired." But she was dozing off every day, no matter how much sleep she got at night.

"It's time for your big scene," said Harry, standing up. He reached down to haul her to her feet. "I was dispatched to find you. Next time I'll bring a bucket of water." He grinned, and watched her hurry away. She ran up the steps onto the stage, where the director and the other actors in the scene waited. He heard her apologizing, and saw the director wave his hand impatiently, and gesture to her to take her place by the makeshift coffin at center stage. Harry wondered if she was going to be any good.

A few days later Margaret went to her doctor. He was jovial during the examination—surely, she thought resentfully, a misplaced characteristic in so young a man—and he told her that although he could not be certain, he thought she was probably pregnant, and that she should call in two days for the results of the test. She stared at him and decided he looked like a slightly overweight rodent, except for his glasses.

When she phoned his office at the end of the week, the nurse told her the results were positive.

Margaret sat holding the telephone receiver. "What does that mean?" she said finally. "Does it mean I'm positively pregnant, or positively not?"

"Positively pregnant," said the nurse, with a trace of supercilious amusement.

Well, how am I supposed to know, thought Margaret.

She hung up the phone slowly and looked around the living room. She was glad that women found out they were pregnant so early. The idea of giving birth staggered her; she would need as much time as possible to get used to it. She shuffled out of her mind the prospect of great pain, extending over many hours, but it left little tracks there, small furrows of dread.

She stood up and looked aimlessly around. They lived in a one-bedroom apartment in the West End which although it was too far away from English Bay to offer a view, even from the fourth floor, at least faced in that direction.

Margaret began to pace, and eventually found herself staring down at a large plant which her mother had given them. Mrs. Kennedy was still buying old pieces of furniture and refinishing them—every time Margaret visited her parents' house it was more and more crowded, and harder and harder to find the objects she remembered lovingly from childhood. Her mother had wanted to give Margaret some of these pieces for the apartment, but Margaret had persuaded her to wait until they got a house, which she visualized as being about ten years down the road. So Mrs. Kennedy sighed and scanned her large collection of plants, and triumphantly presented this one to Margaret and Ted. It stood four feet tall in a corner of the living room near a window, and it had lived and even grown throughout the more than two years of their marriage. Margaret stroked its huge, thick leaves. She went to the kitchen and wet a cloth under the tap and wrung it out and returned to the plant, to wipe the dust from each of its leaves, gently. She wondered how much longer she could go on working until being pregnant interfered with being in plays. She figured the baby would be born in December.

She left the wet cloth on the arm of the tweed sofa she and Ted had bought secondhand, and went over to the desk, which sat under a window in the opposite corner. Margaret watched the late-afternoon sun flood through the glass and aim itself at the surface of the desk. She blew, and tiny specks of dust whisked into the air and trembled back down onto the top of the desk.

She really ought to call Ted, and her parents. It was very odd, being the only person in the world who knew she was going to have a baby. Except the nurse, who didn't count.

I'm pregnant, she said to herself, and said it out loud a couple of times. It didn't sound like the right kind of word for what was happening. She stood up straight and put a hand on her very flat stomach, looking down as if to spot movements of the fetus bumping around in there. But it wasn't a fetus yet, she realized; only a fertilized egg. She wondered how tiny it was—and what it would turn out to be. She wondered how many other babies would be born in 1964, and what they would all turn out to be.

She sat down on the desk chair, bewildered. She thought she knew herself reasonably well as a person, and as a wife, and as a sometimes actress. Now it seemed she was a couple of other things as well—a female creature, and a mother—and it was confusing to wrestle with these concepts, which were suddenly not merely concepts any more.

Margaret wondered if one of the new aspects of herself would eventually push one of the old ones out. How much room is there in a single person, how many things can a single person be, and how does a person learn to switch from one to another? Perhaps they all bleed into one another, she thought; but if that were true, how could she hope to call upon just one of them at a time and throw herself into it, cleanly and purely?

She sat in the desk chair, her back straight, holding herself alert and cautious, staring out the window through the leaves of a tree at the windows of the apartment building across the street, and somewhere beyond the great mass of ugly apartment buildings that tumbled across the West End was the sea, and that's where she wished she could be, at that moment, on the beach, watching the sea.

Eventually she got up and combed her hair and put on a jacket and left a note for Ted and left the apartment. She would go to the ocean and eat fish and chips in a café somewhere near the beach until it was time to go to the theater.

That night the actor playing the corpse of King Henry VI lay quietly backstage as usual, waiting to be carried into the play, and Margaret stood quietly by, since she made her entrance at the same time.

He was a very convincing corpse. Margaret liked to take a good close look at him before the wooing scene, carefully examining the gashes in his shirt, the red-smeared skin; this was a corpse that had not been tidied up for burial.

She checked him over this night, satisfying herself that he was as dead as he could possibly be. Then she flicked the veil down from the headdress; it covered her face like a thick, black spider's web. She felt the weight of it, and the black weight of her costume, and the sleeves of her dress tight around her forearms and wrists. She bowed her head and clasped her hands in front of her and closed her eyes, and began a gentle concentrated search for the center of herself.

She felt herself poking and prodding, tenderly, respectfully, not hurrying. Part of her consciousness was alert and alive to the place where she stood, the scene taking place on the stage, the actors clustered in the wings waiting to go on, the ticking away of time. But the rest of her curled and swirled languorously around the center of herself, warming it, urging it to open and make itself available; if she were to do everything just right, it would flood through her performance, bringing to it things she didn't know she had.

The smell of dust and of sweat and of makeup surrounded her, and the sounds of breathing exercises and whispered lines all a-jumble, and the rustling of costumes and the muted clanking of swords and the dry squeaking of the floor. Margaret pulled in slow deep breaths, expanding her diaphragm, letting each breath out slowly, fully. As she concentrated on what was being said onstage, she began to feel the beginnings of perfect balance, when it felt that all four of her limbs were precisely the right length and her head was precisely the right size and her neck was long and slim and that all the parts of her body moved in a swirling perfection controlled by a mechanism that was part of the exact center of herself. From this center came discipline and control, and from it also came courage and imagination, sometimes in a rusty hesitant trickle and sometimes in a swelling flood.

She stood with eyes closed, head bent, hands clasped, breathing strong deep regular breaths, feeling the beginnings of exultation. The timing was almost completely right; she was almost completely ready; just a few more lines from the stage and she would hear her cue and she would be ready. Her hands lifted and began stroking one another, lightly, lightly. She kept her eyes closed and her fingers felt longer than usual, slimmer than her own; the dress and the tall headdress had settled onto her body, they felt like her own clothes; she drew herself up tall, opened her eyes and looked down at the corpse, felt sorrow swell behind her eyes, and hatred, too, very cold, for of course she knew who had done this to him. Her hands pressed hard against her belly as she thought of him, Richard . . .

I am pregnant, thought Margaret clearly. I am pregnant.

Anne retreated from her.

Her hands whipped out in front of her.

She heard Richard, onstage: "For then I'll marry Warwick's youngest daughter. What though I kill'd her husband and her father? . . ."

The coffin bearers lifted the corpse. Margaret could see the glimmer at the bottoms of his eyes, which half opened as they hoisted him.

"When they are gone," said Richard, "then must I count my gains. . . ."

Margaret saw her hands gleaming white against the black of her skirts, and a small red line beneath one fingernail, where she had cut herself the day before, opening a can: they were definitely her own hands, Margaret's hands. On the stage, Richard's shadow scrabbled huge into the opposite wings.

The guards moved slowly onto the stage, the men followed bearing the corpse and Margaret stepped in behind them, black skirt swishing against her legs, hair hidden under the towering headpiece. The veil brushed her face, she heard a board creak, felt the blaze of the light like a silent explosion as she walked into it.

She was acutely aware of it all; the lights, the stage, the live corpse, the shadowed wings, the breathing audience.

She called out to the bearers as they reached center stage: "Set down, set down your honourable load." She heard her voice clearly, and knew that at least she would not forget her lines. She clutched the black folds of her skirt where it covered her belly, and went on with the scene.

After the show Margaret laughed in the dressing room with the other women in the cast, helping them with headdresses and buttons. Then they left for the cast party, and Margaret waved them out the door, saying she and Ted would join them later. After they had gone she sprawled in costume, a billowing black cloud, on a chair against the wall.

When Ted came in she unpinned her headdress and wrapped a scarf around her thick blond hair.

"Help me out of this, will you?" she said, turning her back so he could undo her dress. She slipped out of it and hung it up and put on an old bathrobe. She sat down at one of the makeshift makeup mirrors and began smearing cold cream all over her face and throat.

"You were good," said Ted, straddling a chair. "I love to watch you do that," he added, smiling.

"I was not good," said Margaret, slowly and distinctly, as she swiped at her face with Kleenexes.

"Well," said Ted after a moment, "not as good as opening night. But you didn't fall down, or forget your words."

She glared at him in the mirror. He had rested his chin on his hands, which were clasped on the back of the chair. He wasn't actually smiling, but she could see laughter in his eyes. She opened her mouth to tell him about the baby, then snapped it shut.

"There's a party, isn't there?" said Ted. She wished he would go home so she could go to the party by herself, and maybe flirt.

Margaret screwed the top on the jar of cold cream, took off her scarf and brushed her hair. "I wish you hadn't been there tonight. Once ought to be enough," she said, brushing energetically. "Nobody should sit through *Richard III* twice in the space of a week." She slammed the brush down on the table. "I'm not even getting paid, for God's sake."

"You're doing it for the experience. That's what you said."

"Why did you come, anyway?" she said, staring at him in the mirror.

"I don't know," said Ted, exasperated. "Is there any reason I shouldn't have come? Didn't you want me to come? You should have said so in your note."

"I wasn't any good!" she shouted at him.

She felt she had caught him observing her doing something extremely private, which was ridiculous, since she'd been doing it in full view of the thirty-five people in the audience, not to mention the entire cast.

It's all right when you're good, she thought. You don't mind what people find out about you, because you've used it to make something new, something nobody else could have made. But when you are *not* good, thought Margaret, remembering the distance between herself and her lines; the woodenness she had struggled with; when you are *not* good, then the whole thing is excruciatingly embarrassing.

She looked at herself in the mirror. Tawny hair, hazel eyes with long lashes, freckles spattered across the nose and the tops of the cheeks, full lips. That's a mother I'm looking at, she said to herself, and watched her eyebrows lift in faint astonishment.

"What is it, Margaret?" said Ted softly. He got up and came to stand behind her, kneading the muscles in her shoulders, gently. "I was a little worried when I read your note. I was going to go down to the beach to look for you, but I decided you might not like it." He bent to kiss her cheek, with some hesitancy.

"We're going to have a baby," she said, and watched his face in the mirror until she didn't trust it, and then she turned to look at him closely.

They had not talked much of having children, and she realized in the silence which had dropped so suddenly that she didn't really know whether he wanted any.

He was very still, half crouched over her, as though running the words through his head again. Then he put one large, square, long-fingered hand on her stomach; it looked peculiar, resting on the faded green of her old dressing gown. She watched his hand and waited.

He pulled her to her feet and put his arms around her, and she turned her head so that her cheek was in the hollow of his throat; she could feel the pulse through the cotton of his shirt.

He took her face in his hands. "It's going to be a girl," he said, gentle triumph in his eyes, which were extremely blue, and for a flickering second Margaret felt absurdly like a Christmas cake tin.

# Chapter 7

SOMETIMES, WHILE SHE WAS PREGNANT, MARGARET wished fervently that she was at an earlier stage in her life. She would squeeze her eyes shut and imagine herself hiking jauntily with Moira through a patch of woods to a street in Haney where there was a grocery store and a bakery and a drugstore and a post office. They used to spend their allowances on this street, buying comic books and Cokes and glazed doughnuts. They did it almost every Saturday all year long, but whenever Margaret imagined herself back there the day was summer hot and the lane down which they walked was dusty. She could hear the whine of mosquitoes and feel the sun on her back and see the nettles that grew along the edge of the lane and smell the blackberries that grew there as well. She remembered scuffling her feet in the dust, and that the trip home always seemed longer, as they hurried to get to her back yard or Moira's before their Cokes got too warm.

This was a day like those remembered ones, hot and slumbrous, and Ted was teaching summer school and Margaret was on her way to have lunch with Moira, aiming her recently acquired secondhand Volkswagen toward West Vancouver.

She wanted to be convinced that her life would not turn

completely inside out and upside down just because she was going to have a baby. And Moira ought to know, having one of her own. Margaret hadn't noticed any substantial changes in her, except that she was no longer free to go places and do things whenever she wanted to. It didn't seem to bother her. But then it was hard to tell, sometimes, whether Moira was bothered.

Even with all the windows open Margaret was sweaty and uncomfortable in the heat as the car inched along through Stanley Park. But the traffic speeded up as it reached the Lions Gate Bridge. She looked left and right, quickly, trying as always to imprint the harbor forever upon her eyes. The water was silky, flecked with sailboats, and the breeze from it was cool.

At the end of the bridge she swung around the circle that took her onto Marine Drive heading west, and a few minutes later pulled into the driveway of the small house Moira and Jason were renting. She parked beside the old Pontiac, which Moira didn't drive much any more. It had lost its reliability, though it looked as well preserved as ever.

When Moira answered the door Margaret stared at her. "Moira," she said. "Are you pregnant again?"

Moira's face became cool and expressionless. "Come in," she said, stepping back from the doorway.

"Moira," said Margaret. "So am I."

Moira shook her head slowly. "Well, it happens to the best of us," she said. She started for the living room, then stopped and turned back to Margaret. "Will you tell me something?" she asked. "Why aren't we on that bloody pill?"

Margaret shrugged. "My doctor fumbled with his pen and mumbled something about unclear research."

"Mine talked about cancer, and maybe my left leg would drop off. I think he was making a joke, but you never know, with doctors."

They looked at each other and began to laugh.

"You do look just a bit thicker around the waist," said Moira. "Shit." She went into the living room, and Margaret followed.

The living room was full of Moira's paintings. Margaret didn't know how good they were, and couldn't tell how much they had changed from the work Moira had done before she went to art school. But they gave Margaret feelings of warmth and exultation. They filled the living room with lusty energy. You live with Moira, she thought, and you live with her work. She walked slowly around the room, peering at the paintings. She wondered where in the house Jason kept himself.

Moira came in from the kitchen carrying her son.

"My God," said Margaret, turning. "He's huge."

"He should be. He's a year old, just about."

Margaret sat down and regarded the child with a new and intense interest. He watched her warily, hanging on to Moira's pant leg. "He walks," said Margaret, astonished.

"He's just been walking for a couple of weeks. Sometimes I wish he'd put it off for a while longer."

"Why?"

"Because he gets into everything," said Moira, and sat down. The child wedged himself in between her legs, still staring at Margaret.

"Mine's supposed to be born in about five months," said Margaret. "What about yours?" She wasn't enjoying the conversation. She wanted to throw her arms around, and yell.

"October," said Moira, smiling faintly, stroking the baby's hair. "You got a good review for *Richard III*. I wish I'd seen it."

"One good one, one not-so-good one. I guess we're lucky they even bothered to come."

Moira watched the baby totter a few steps across the room. "I guess you're going to put all that aside for a while, now," she said. The baby had an eye on some stacking toys lying on the rug, not far from Margaret's foot. "Kick those over here, will you, Maggie?"

Margaret watched her sandaled foot nudge the toys across the rug. She had gotten used to the signs of a baby in Moira's house—a laundry basket filled with clean diapers to be folded, bizarrely tiny garments hanging on Moira's outside wash line, bottles of formula beside bottles of beer in her fridge and now, lately, toys, made of plastic and without sharp edges. She supposed that five months from now all these accouterments of babyhood would be cluttering up her own apartment.

"I don't mind giving up being in plays for a while," she said, watching the child plop down upon the floor among the blocks. "Maybe the whole thing will turn out to be useful. I remember when I was in *Dark of the Moon*, Barbara Allen was supposed to be pregnant in Act Two and I knew there must be things she would have felt that I didn't have a clue about. It was very frustrating. You need to know as much as you possibly can. And I don't think it helps, with things like being pregnant, and giving birth, and making love, to have somebody tell you what it feels like."

They watched the baby, who was pushing the blocks around with sudden, uncoordinated movements and making occasional honks of triumph when he got one to sit briefly, totteringly, upon another.

"Still," said Moira, "you haven't done it on purpose, have you?"

"No," said Margaret.

"You sound very staunch and cheerful about it," said Moira. "Are you trying to make the best of a bad thing, or what?"

"At first all I could think about was the pain," said Margaret, her eyes on the child.

Moira glanced at her son. "Just remember," she said, "that he was a hell of a lot smaller than that the first time you saw him, and even smaller when he popped out of me."

Margaret looked up and saw that she was smiling.

"Are you going to go to classes, do your exercises, all that sort of thing?" said Moira.

"Should I?"

"Oh yeah. You should. It's all that preparation that gets it done right—not your doctor, for Christ's sake, he just stands there and watches until practically the last minute."

Margaret sighed. "The other thing I wonder about is whether I'll be different, afterward. Not physically," she added hastily. "Not that, so much. Just—different."

Moira looked at her, measuring the gulf between them. It had already narrowed slightly, and she supposed that when Margaret's child was born it would be crossable again, and for that she was glad. "Oh, Maggie. What can I say? Am *I* different?"

"Yes, sure you are." Margaret waved toward the baby.

"There's somebody in your life all of a sudden who seems more important to you than anybody else, and I hardly know him at all. You're—concentrated on him."

"Yeah," said Moira.

"But, Moira, what about your painting? I never thought anything could come along that would be more important than your painting."

"He isn't," said Moira, stroking the baby's hair. "But the painting can wait for me, and he can't. It won't be like this forever. As soon as he's four, I'm shipping him off to nursery school, lickety split—aren't I, love?" she said, picking him up and holding him above her with outstretched arms. "And then kindergarten, and then, glory be he'll be in school all day, won't you, love?" she said, shaking him gently, and giggles fell from him, high-pitched ripples of laughter. She put him gently back on the floor, smiling, her face flushed. "I love the little bastard." She looked at Margaret. "That's the thing, you see, Maggie," she said. "That's where they really get you. You might resent them while you're pregnant, especially at first, when you can't really tell there's anything in there that's alive and growing."

Margaret nodded vigorously.

"But you just can't help it, Maggie, so don't worry about that. The minute you see him, you'll love him." She shrugged and patted her stomach. "This one, too. It put me somewhat off my stride, believe me, when I found out about him. It means putting my life on hold for longer than I'd expected." She shook her head. Grimly, she said, "I'm having no more after this one, you can bet your *life* on that, Maggie, I'll get those damn pills if I have to go to every doctor in town." She sighed, and sat back in her chair. "What the hell. It'll be rough, at first, they'll only be fifteen months apart. Jesus." She thought about that, as she obviously had before. "But at least I'll get the whole family over with in the shortest time possible."

"Is Jason glad you're having another one?"

"Oh, Jason," said Moira, pushing herself to her feet. "Jason figures the more the merrier." She laughed. "Why shouldn't he? He doesn't have much to do with the kid—not so far, anyway. He just likes the *idea* of being a father."

They went into the kitchen, where Moira put the baby into

a high chair and loaded the tray with carrot sticks and pieces
of bread and peanut butter.

It had never occurred to Moira that anything would ever
stand in the way of her painting that she couldn't jump over
or walk around or, if necessary, smash to pieces. And then,
a year after Margaret had married Ted, Moira met Jason.

He fascinated her because of his colors, which were all
silvery and gleaming, like a monochromatic work of art, and
when she went to bed with him she had a better time than
she had ever dreamed of having. And she got pregnant,
which was the kind of stupid mistake she had never even
considered.

Jason had already said he wanted to marry her. Moira had
been trying to decide how to put him off without losing him,
because, truly, he was very good in bed: she loved that. And
she loved, too, the way he talked about his work. He was a
beginning lawyer and the whole business of the law enraptured him. He became animated when he talked to her about
it, and glittered, then, not only gleamed.

When she became pregnant, there was nobody she could
think of to talk it over with. Margaret would be horrified,
and, being married herself, would of course tell Moira that's
what she ought to do. Her mother, thought Moira, shivering,
would die of a stroke—but not before she'd screamed many
terrible things. Her father would get smaller and grayer and
more stooped and sicker-looking as she watched.

She ticked off her alternatives, lying awake in her bed one
night. She could have the baby and never see it and put it up
for adoption. But she wasn't about to leave art school, and
she knew she would not be able to make herself attend
classes while pregnant and unwed.

She could have an abortion.

Or she could get married.

She didn't know how to go about having an abortion, but
she knew that someone at school could put her on to
somebody. She had heard awful, terrible things about abor-
tions; about going to crummy seedy little holes in the wall in
the Birks Building and coming out thinking you were going
to die.

And besides all that, thought Moira, shit; it was a person

in her, and what if that person turned out to be a painter? Could one artist go about having another artist butchered before she/he ever got going?

Eventually she told Jason; this would do it, she thought. She didn't know whether she was disappointed or relieved when he insisted that he was happy about it, and that now they would have to get married right away.

They had gotten married, and Moira had stayed on at art school and finished that second and last year before the baby was born.

And now he sat in a high chair and Margaret watched him, fascinated.

He seemed happy enough, waving carrots in the air, smearing his mouth with peanut butter, and occasionally banging the tray and shrieking imperiously.

What seemed remarkable to Margaret was that Moira had learned what to do with him. But you can learn anything, if you have to, she thought.

"Have a sandwich," said Moira, pushing a platter across the kitchen table. "How does Ted like the idea of being a father?"

"He loves it," said Margaret. "It's amazing. I've never seen him so happy about anything."

She saw that Moira had done a lot of work in the house. The kitchen was wallpapered in brown and gold. Chunky yellow canisters sat on the counter and the window had a yellow blind, pulled up now to admit the sun. Plants covered the top of the hutch which sat on a chest in the kitchen's small eating area. It was a pretty kitchen; a pretty house. If the living room felt stuffy after you'd been sitting in it for a while, it was because of the trumpeting defiance of Moira's paintings, flashing their brilliance from the walls. Perhaps the room wasn't large enough to hold sufficient oxygen for the paintings and for people,too.

She cleaned up the kitchen while Moira put the baby to bed. She discovered bits of carrot and bread and peanut butter on the floor, as well as all over the high chair.

Margaret went to the window and looked out at a railed porch, whose steps led to a back yard which was untended, weedy, unfenced, and dribbled away into some trees. She could see the back yards of the houses on either side of Moira's and they didn't seem to be in any better shape.

She pulled her shirt away from her body, feeling the sticky heat of the day again. She put her hands on her stomach and wondered what was growing in there. She amused herself for a moment imagining that it might be a tree, or a lilac bush, or a teddy bear. But she wanted it to be a boy. Maybe Moira would have another son, and the three boys would grow up to be friends.

Moira came back and said, "Let's go out on the porch," and they sat in two wobbly chairs, but there was a breeze.

"Jason says we're going to buy a house next year," said Moira.

Margaret felt desire for a house stir in her, too; it was a completely new sensation. She decided that it must be having babies that made people want houses of their own.

"Do you paint while he's asleep?" she asked.

"Yeah. Except when I'm too tired. It's been better lately. But now I guess I have to go through the whole thing again." She shrugged, and grinned at Margaret. "Never mind, kid. It's just a temporary setback. For you, too."

"Do you enjoy him? Are you really glad you had him?" It was imperative that she know; she leaned forward in the wobbly chair to watch Moira as she decided what to say.

But Moira didn't have to think about it at all. "Of course I'm glad," she said, "I told you, I love the little bastard."

Soon Margaret got up to leave. At the front door she hugged Moira, and felt the swelling of her friend's belly, and the tentative swelling of her own. She stepped back quickly, threatened by melancholy. Things change so, she thought, looking at Moira's face. It held within it the face of the olive-skinned, overweight kid with braids who had once helped Margaret shove a mutual enemy into a patch of nettles; who had led the way the evening they climbed a cherry tree in the orchard of their elderly music teacher and hooted at her house like bucolic ghosts until she suddenly appeared in the dark waving a lantern and looking convincingly ghostlike herself in a long, old-fashioned nightgown. It was the same Moira, she thought, smiling at her. But there was more to her, now, and Margaret no longer felt that she knew all the things that Moira was. She kissed her cheek. "We must never lose touch with one another, Moira," she said. "That's very important."

"We never will, Maggie," said Moira. "Not really."

# Chapter 8

SHE HAD BEEN IN THE WINGS, WAITING FOR HER CUE. THEN there was someone behind her with an axe. She knew that if she could get onstage and start to say her lines she would be all right, the man with the axe wouldn't notice her. But her cue wouldn't come, the actors in the scene seemed to be speaking in circles, avoiding the words which brought Margaret's character into the play. Closer and closer came the man with the axe. Margaret couldn't hiss at the actors onstage because then the axeman would hear and notice her for sure. Finally she heard her cue and rushed onstage and opened her mouth; but she couldn't remember her lines, the actors turned to her expectantly, silently, and she couldn't say anything, and the axeman's eyes gleamed from the wings and he stretched out his hand and the axe caught light and cracked it and Margaret thought she would just say anything, anything at all, he didn't know the play and wouldn't know that she had forgotten her lines; so she opened her mouth but nothing came out, nothing, she could not speak, and the axeman stepped upon the stage, holding his weapon high and smiling . . .

` . . . Margaret's eyes opened wide, trying to get her out of her dream. Her heart was pounding, sweat was a sheen over her body; she lay tense and still in a puddle of fear.

She felt the warmth of Ted's body in the bed and considered turning over to get close to him; but she didn't want to make any movement at all, and if she turned over she would leave her back exposed.

If he's lying there sleeping, she thought, there can't be anything in the room with us. But whatever was in the room might have silently disposed of Ted while he slept, before it had wakened her; she might be lying right now beside a corpse with its head cut off.

This was ridiculous, and if she had dared to think it in daylight she would have jeered at herself. But it wasn't daylight, and all things are possible in the dark, in the aftermath of a nightmare.

I should turn over and shake him awake, she thought, or turn on my lamp, or get up and go to the bathroom. But she lay still and pretended to breathe slowly and evenly so that nobody could tell she was not asleep.

Finally she reached a hand out behind her, cautiously, and poked him with a finger; he moved a bit, she poked him again, and he grunted, still alive.

Soon she had some courage and she thrust herself up in bed and turned on her lamp. The room was filled with fleeing things which she could not see. They fled through the half-open window, through the bedroom door which stood open a few inches; she sensed the flickering tails of them escaping. Let them go change themselves into somebody else's personal demons, she thought, and haunt them; let them go anywhere, as long as they go. She got out of bed angrily, turned off her lamp and stomped down the hall to the bathroom.

She shut herself in and put on the robe that hung from the back of the door. She splashed water on her face and looked in the mirror. Her hair was tangled, and she thought her eyes looked smaller than usual.

She went to the kitchen to get herself some cocoa and a couple of cookies. In the living room she turned on all the lights so as to kill shadows in corners and sat in a big chair with her cookies and cocoa, her feet curled up under her.

There was no point in going back to bed, she thought

glumly, drinking and munching. She was too wide awake. And in less than two hours the alarm clock would ring and she would get breakfast and watch Ted leave for his eight o'clock class.

He hurried out to his car every morning with his arms full of books, briefcase, and maybe a lunch, or letters to be mailed. He always looked up at the sky, even if it was raining, and if his face got splattered by raindrops she would see him shake his head before ducking into the car.

Just then he came through the door from the kitchen, looking bewildered. "What are you doing out here?" he said, his voice fuzzy with astonishment and sleep.

"You're going to get cold," said Margaret. He stood with one hand in his hair, his face screwed up against the light, wearing only the bottoms of his pajamas.

"What are you doing?" he said again. "It's only five-thirty."

"I couldn't sleep," she said.

Ted came in and sat in a chair opposite her, leaning his arms on his knees, his bare feet curling into the carpet. "What woke you up?" He shivered.

"I told you you'd get cold."

Ted's mouth settled into a straight line. "You're the one who's going to have the baby. I said, what woke you up?"

"I just woke up, that's all, and I couldn't get back to sleep." He shivered again. "Oh, go back to bed, Ted, my God."

He got up and went out of the room, but returned a minute later tying his robe around him. He had put on slippers, too, and brought hers, which he dropped on the floor in front of her.

"There's no point in both of us not sleeping," she said.

"What have you got in that cup? Is there any more?"

"No, there isn't any more," said Margaret. "I just made enough for me. I didn't know we were going to be having a meeting in here."

He got a glass of milk and settled into the chair, ankle crossed over his knee. He looked at her interestedly. "What shall we talk about?"

Margaret shifted position. Her legs were aching. Reluctantly she lowered them and put her slippers on, shoved herself back in the chair and crossed her arms in front of her.

"I've been offered a part in a children's show in September."

He peered at her stomach. "How big will you be by then?" he asked hopefully.

"It doesn't matter. I'm playing an old woman. It's okay if she's fat."

"You've decided to do it, then?"

"I thought I'd ask you what you think about it," she said sullenly, picking at the tie belt of her robe.

"I think it's a good idea. As long as you don't have to turn cartwheels, or hang from a trapeze."

She looked at him in disgust, but he was grinning.

"It'll be my last show, before the baby comes," she said, and Ted nodded. She felt thunderous with anger. "I might as well make breakfast," she said, and trudged into the kitchen.

"What're we going to have?" said Ted, following.

"What do you want?" said Margaret, staring into the fridge.

"I'd like the works—bacon and eggs and juice and bran muffins or something."

"I should make you get your own damn breakfast."

"I'll help," said Ted, looking eagerly around the kitchen. "Just tell me what to do."

"Sit down, for God's sake. Make some coffee and then sit down."

He got out the coffee, turned on the cold water tap, began to sing.

"Shut up, you'll wake the neighbors."

"It's time they were up, for Christ's sake," said Ted, "it's a quarter to six," and he sang louder.

Margaret stood still and looked vaguely at the clock above the sink. "What're we doing?" she said, dismayed, and let weariness catch up with her. "It's only a quarter to six."

"You're not doing anything," said Ted briskly, "I'm going to do it all. Sit down. You just instruct me. Now. Where do I start?"

"Ted, this is ridiculous."

"I don't know about you," he said, getting eggs and bacon out of the fridge, "but I'm starving. How shall I do these eggs, you want them fried or scrambled? Maybe I could try an omelet," he said, turning to her. "What do you say, should I try an omelet?"

65

"Ted, you'll never get all this done by seven-thirty. Forget it. Just warm up some muffins." Margaret buried her head in her arms on the table.

"I can be pretty efficient when I want to," said Ted, "but actually it doesn't matter, since it's Saturday."

Margaret looked up in astonishment. Ted was measuring coffee into the percolator.

"Now this I can do good," he said. "I make terrific coffee."

"Is it really Saturday?"

He turned to her, smiling, and nodded, and turned back to the sink to put cold water in the coffeepot.

Margaret was suddenly very happy. She got up to embrace him, to taste the underside of his lips with her tongue. She ran her hands beneath his robe and spread them, fingers wide, across his back, and pressed herself against him, hard, her breasts flattening against his chest.

"Just wait 'til you've had these eggs," he said, holding her tightly. "Then we can get amorous." He pushed her gently into a chair.

She sat down and watched him break eggs into a bowl. "Scrambled," he muttered.

"I saw Moira the other day," said Margaret.

"Yeah? How is she?" He dropped an eggshell into the garbage, bashed another egg on the side of the bowl.

"She's going to have another baby."

Ted gazed at her for a minute, the eggshell in his hand dripping slimy stuff onto the counter. "Yeah?" Margaret nodded. Ted got rid of the shell and started beating the eggs vigorously. "What else do I put in here? No, don't tell me, I'll improvise." He poured in some milk, added salt and pepper, hesitated, poured in a lot of grated cheese from a Kraft container.

"Ted, why do you want a girl?"

"I don't know," said Ted, beating. "Maybe because I want another one of you," he said, and smiled at her. He abandoned the eggs to peel strips of bacon from the package and throw them into a frying pan. "We ought to get ourselves a house."

Margaret laughed, delighted.

Ted stood at arm's length from the frying pan, poking the

bacon. His hand sprang back and he cursed as some flying fat hit him.

"I think," said Margaret helpfully, "that you've got the heat on a little too high under that."

Ted was whistling. He stopped, and said, "Christ, forgot the toast."

"I'll do it," said Margaret, about to get up.

"Sit the hell down," said Ted, harassed. "We're going to have bran muffins, that's it, where are they?"

"In the freezer part of the fridge."

"Freezer? They're frozen?" He looked appalled.

"You just wrap them up in foil and put them in the oven to warm."

Ted turned on the oven as high as it would go, whipped out the muffins, wrapped them up and tossed them in. "There," he muttered. He dumped margarine into a second frying pan.

Margaret rested her chin in her hands and watched him beat the eggs furiously, then pour the mixture into the pan. She sat up and touched her stomach, gingerly. She was swelling out a bit around her waist now, no doubt about it. Ted flipped the bacon out upon paper towels.

"Can I set the table?" said Margaret.

"Yeah, sure," said Ted. "That's woman's work anyway. I'll stick to the creative stuff."

She grabbed one end of his belt and pulled. Ted straightened himself with dignity, tied the robe tightly around him.

"Control yourself," he said. He peered at the eggs. "Do I turn this over, or what?"

"Or what," said Margaret. He glared at her. "Do whatever feels most creative," she said, grinning.

A few minutes later Ted put laden plates in front of them.

"I don't know why I don't do this more often," he said smugly.

"I don't, either," said Margaret. "I guess you get bored easily."

The kitchen was warm, fragrant with breakfast. She watched Ted cut open a muffin. He buttered it and gave half to Margaret. As he held it out to her she looked up at his face, and it was suddenly the realest thing she had ever seen. It was all of a piece, each part of it—dark brown hair falling over his forehead, thick eyebrows, long, narrow nose, slightly thrust-out chin, mouth full of scrambled eggs, and the eyes, a deep and steady blue—each part fit perfectly with all the other parts; there was not another face in the world, she thought, so absolutely in tune with itself. He winked, and she took the muffin from his hand.

"Ted," she said, "what do you think of my acting?"

"I think you're pretty good," he said promptly.

"But what do you think about the fact that I *do* it, I mean?"

He looked amazed. "I think it's fine. I think it's great," he said, and went on eating.

"I don't want to lose it," said Margaret. "Not completely. It's important to me."

He nodded, reaching for another muffin. "I know it is."

"It's important to have something that's just my own, you know? Like your teaching is just your own. Do you understand?"

He looked at her curiously. "Of course I understand, Margaret. I probably wouldn't have been interested in you in the first place if there hadn't been things that were important to you."

"Then why," she said, crashing her cup into its saucer, *"why* do I feel that my acting doesn't matter to you at *all?"*

"Because it doesn't," he said quietly. He took her hand. "Look, Maggie. What I teach to those kids every day doesn't mean a hell of a lot to you. Why should it? I'm the one who does it, not you. So why should you need my constant, eager intrusion into what you're doing to be able to get total satisfaction from doing it? That doesn't make any sense, now does it?" He got up for the coffeepot and refilled their cups.

"When the baby's a few months old," she said sullenly, "I'll probably want to go back to work."

"Sure."

"I don't want to just sit down and do nothing all my life."

"Sure. I understand." He put the pot back on the stove and sat down. "Of course I don't think people with babies get much chance to sit around and do nothing. It's probably easier for your friend Moira—she can at least do her painting in her own home."

"I may have to put my life on hold," she said dismally, thinking of Moira.

He dragged her over and sat her on his knee. "Not all of your life. Maggie," he said, his face in her neck, his hand under her nightgown, cupped around her breast. "Do you realize, you're going to get even bigger up here? Not all of your life on hold—just one small part of it. And there'll be other things, new things . . ."

"Baby things," said Margaret, trying to sound doleful, but she arched back in his arms, wanting his hands to move down across her belly, down to stroke the insides of her thighs.

"What are we going to do today," he said into her throat. "Before we go out and look at some houses. What are we going to do first?" He stood up and led her to the bedroom.

# Chapter 9

By Christmas, Margaret knew the meaning of the phrase "heavy with child." She scoffed at metaphors like sailing ships and balloons, for they were light and fleet and she was swollen and cumbersome and very heavy with her child.

The child should have come by Christmas, according to her doctor, but what the hell do they know, grumbled Margaret to herself.

Her disposition had become snarly. She took black delight in watching her in-laws and her parents trip over each other as they prepared Christmas dinner.

"Now just you sit down there with your daughter, Ivy, and let me tend to this," said Kathleen Griffin soothingly, attempting to maneuver herself around in Margaret's galley kitchen.

"I couldn't possibly, Kathleen," said Mrs. Kennedy firmly. "Why don't we divide things up."

Eventually they did. Margaret's mother sat at the table making stuffing and salad, while Ted's mother prepared the turkey and the vegetables in the kitchen.

In the living room Margaret and the three men looked uncomfortably at each other. Ted was tense, watching Margaret for any sign that the birth of his child was imminent, waiting for his mother to finish what she was doing in the kitchen, wondering whether his father and his father-in-law would find anything to talk about.

Margaret was tense, too. She hated to be watched, even by Ted, and she knew the whole damn apartmentful of people was watching, hoping to be present at the moment when it all began. She saw them not as individuals at all, as they sat there waiting for dinner; just felt them as a lot of eagerly breathing Peeping Toms.

Once at the table, though, and forced by proximity to look each of them in the face, she began to relax. Her mother was obviously more concerned about not losing her temper with Kathleen Griffin than paying undue attention to Margaret. Her father had become very friendly with Ted's father, William. And Kathleen—well, Kathleen just talked and talked, as usual, and Ted became more and more quiet.

After dinner they opened presents. Everybody had given something to the unborn grandchild. Kathleen frowned and shook her head and said that was bad luck, even though she hadn't been able to resist, either. But Mrs. Kennedy said, "Nonsense," briskly. And Mr. Griffin snorted and nodded, and Mr. Kennedy polished his glasses and said what a beautiful Christmas it was.

Then they all had more wine, although Kathleen said, "I'm not at all sure, Margaret, that it's a good idea for you, it may be that one glass is all you should have." But Mrs. Kennedy said, "Nonsense," again, and Margaret, smiling, had another glass, as her mother, watching, added uncertainly, "It will help her sleep."

Then they put on their coats to go back to their hotels. All four were leaving for home the next morning, two to Haney and two to Kelowna. As she prepared to leave, Kathleen took Margaret's face in her hands and kissed her forehead and said, "Bless you," which was the shortest sentence Margaret could recall ever having heard from Kathleen; she felt a surge of affection and hugged her mother-in-law, as best she could, and ended up hugging all four of them, and when they had left she turned to Ted and burst into tears.

Late on Boxing Day it began to snow. It snowed all through that night, and by the next morning the skies had cleared and Vancouver was blindingly bright. Margaret and

Ted went to a small park and pushed, laughing, through the snow, which was thick and moist and heavy and which they knew would not last.

And that night it started, lazily, with a tightening in her back. She lay awake for three or four hours, calm, knowing it had begun.

She had devoured information from books and worked and studied as though preparing her body for a role in a strenuous play, and as she exercised her way through the weeks and months she traveled through fear into readiness. The grumpiness of the last week or so was due to her having prepared herself as well as she possibly could for an opening night which kept backing away from her. And now it was here.

She lay quietly, being alone with it, becoming warily acquainted with the almost gentle sensations which would eventually tauten into pain.

At seven she woke Ted and enjoyed his consternation. He called the doctor. Margaret had a warm bath. She watched the rippling of her distended belly, blue-veined and mysterious, and thought it might be nice to have the baby right there; except that the porcelain bottom of the tub began to feel rather hard after a while.

By the time she was out of the bath and getting dressed, contractions were gathering strength, although they were still more than fifteen minutes apart.

"Here, come," she said, laughing shallowly, bent over, pausing in the act of putting on a shoe, holding her hand out toward him. "Come."

"My God, Christ, what?" said Ted, and dropped her overnight bag, which had been packed for days, and rushed to her.

"Just, nothing," she said, gasping, exultant, and she leaned heavily on his shoulder, waiting. "I think we better get going," she said, and she was excited. It was good to know that all those experts were there waiting for her.

At the hospital she was shaved, which her reading (but not her doctor) had warned her about; but even the books had neglected to mention the coldness of the liquid soap poured upon her by nurses whose third fingers left hand, she noticed, were ringless. There must be some married nurses in the obstetrics ward, she thought; but they weren't around just then.

Ted sat next to her as she lay in the labor room. She was tranquilized enough to doze off between contractions but not enough to prevent her from coming fully awake and breathing properly when they occurred. Except sometimes. Those times were dreadful. She had wanted no drugs at all, and when she dozed through the first seconds of a contraction her breathing got all out of whack and her outraged body poured grinding pain. "Not necessary, not necessary," she whimpered through clenched teeth, furious.

"How much longer?" she asked the doctor when he examined her at 10 A.M. She suddenly remembered, incongruously, that his first name was Monty, and felt a giggle deep inside her, far beneath the activity in her uterus, much too far away to reach. It was a name so wildly incompatible with the man himself that she had always wanted to use it, since he had called her Margaret with no compunction at all from the first time she'd been in to see him.

"Oh my, not until evening," he said cheerfully, his glasses bouncing off the tops of his cheeks.

I don't see what's so goddamn funny, thought Margaret.

"These things can't be rushed," he said, and patted her arm, and left.

"Oh my God I can't stand it, I can't do it," she said, and turned her glistening face away from Ted as another contraction gathered itself together.

"What do you think I'm here for?" he said. "Of course you can do it. Breathe right, I'll help you, I'll count for you, why do you think I'm here?"

Three hours later Margaret shot awake. "Tell that nurse to come in here."

Ted ran to get the nurse.

"I'm in the second stage of labor," Margaret announced, but the nurse laughed and said that wasn't possible and disappeared. "Goddamn," said Margaret, gritting her teeth.

"Relax, Margaret," said Ted, "relax, breathe."

She did, and carried several more contractions; many more contractions. "Get that damn nurse in here," she hollered half an hour later. "You tell that damn nurse to get in here."

The nurse came in, smiling.

"You better take a look," said Margaret.

The nurse took a look. "My goodness," she murmured.

They put her on a stretcher and wheeled her into the delivery room and bundled her onto a table and put her feet in the stirrups she had read about. Everything was occurring just as the books had predicted. She thought no more about Ted, who hadn't been allowed in the delivery room.

She panted very well. The doctor was pleased. He was more acceptable with a mask over the lower half of his face. When he said, "Push!" Margaret remembered the books she had read and called upon whatever gods there were and in direct contradiction of what she wanted to do, which was scream, she pushed, with the pain; it was sure to kill her . . .

. . . but it didn't; the pain vanished and became power, and the earth split open and turned inside out, and Margaret was astride eternity; she was part of an explosion in the universe, tumbling through space, and when it became too strong, when she knew she was traveling too far to come back, it faded, and she rested, and then it began again . . .

And as it went on, the final volcanic stage of birth, panic sometimes threatened to seize her; but always a small part of her mind said firmly, "Push, push, go with the pain and it will disappear."

This was not pain at all. "Pain" was a soft, listless, droopy word that came nowhere near describing this. This was elemental, inexorable, nothing human at all; it was the thin stream of molten life that is never seen and never vanquished; maybe this is what death is like, she thought, as she pushed, and the pain metamorphosed again into that power, so vast and uncontainable . . .

. . . and then, there was a baby. Her hair soggy with sweat, Margaret looked at the baby. It had been there all the time, first inside of her and then tumbling with her on that terrible, magnificent ride into life. She could tell looking at it that it had been there, although she had not seen it; it seemed to wear Margaret's skin, its eyes were squished closed as Margaret's had been, its limbs were jerking still, it did not know that it had arrived; it lay there on her stomach, roaring out its terror . . . oh, baby, I wish I could have told you what it would be like but I didn't know, I wish I could have held you close, all I can do now is make you forget . . .

She took the baby into her arms as the nurses held her up and she looked it over carefully. Its eyes stayed squeezed shut and its small chest heaved rapidly, rhythmically. Moira had been right. Margaret marveled at how harshly, how strongly she loved it; she had expected to love it later; she had not expected to love it so immediately.

They called her Sarah.

When Ted saw her for the first time, he recognized her.

He was certain that he could have picked her out for himself from the vast number of babies behind the glass, because when they showed her to him, when they put her bundled in a blanket in his arms, he looked at her and he recognized her.

It wasn't love that he felt—not then. He just knew her, as he knew his own hand. He was not at all surprised to see her there, lying in his arms, squiggly soft-boned limbs waving jerkily. He knew that he had been waiting for her, and that his life was changed now that she had arrived.

Throughout the rest of her life an image from that day remained stark and frozen in Margaret's mind.

It was of Ted holding Sarah, swaddled and almost invisible, in his arms.

He had stood beside Margaret's hospital bed, looking intently into the tiny, wizened face of his daughter. Margaret had reached up to touch him and Ted, absorbed, had shifted his position, turning his body, and the blanketed baby, just slightly away from her, out of her reach. He did this undeliberately, without taking his eyes from Sarah's face.

No matter how many times after that Margaret looked him full in the face, in conversation or while making love, she was never able to completely banish the irritating notion that his proximity to her had been slightly, indelibly, eternally altered.

His daughter turned out to be tawny-haired, like Margaret, with eyes as blue as his own.

Margaret had no idea what was required of a parent until she had become one. It meant being constantly on call, sleeping only when the baby felt like sleeping, and somehow managing to find time between naps to do laundry and prepare formula and sterilize bottles. She couldn't imagine, those first weeks, ever again having either the time or the energy to clean the house or make a real meal, let alone go to a movie, take a trip, or be in a show. If it hadn't been for Ted she didn't think she would have survived, because in addition to requiring a great deal of care Sarah was a fractious baby and Margaret frequently felt, to her horror, like throwing her away with the trash just so as not to hear her cry. But Ted had limitless patience. Sarah's crying bothered him only as a sign that something was bothering her. Margaret thought he was positively saintlike and sometimes resented him for it—but not often; usually she was too grateful.

Later, when the baby had actually begun to sleep through the night, Margaret was able to look around and notice that the world had continued to turn, the seasons had progressed through winter to spring, and Sarah had become portable. So she resumed her friendship with Moira, who now had two sons and whose house, so used to babies, Margaret found was one of the few in which she could feel relaxed with Sarah. These visits were very good for her soul. She also began to think of trying to get into a show, but she didn't know exactly how to go about this, having been out of commission for several months. Her new freedom to do simple things like sleep, and go shopping, and visit Moira, and take Sarah out to Haney to see her grandparents was so luxurious that summer slipped away, and fall; and then, when Sarah was almost a year old, she and Ted began looking seriously at houses again, and soon after Christmas they found one. It was a small white stucco house not far from the university, on Sixteenth Avenue, and across the street was a forested section of the university endowment lands. "Look," said Ted, pointing. "Woods for the kid to play in." Margaret thought that was thinking a bit far ahead, since Sarah had just begun to walk, but those woods made her nostalgic for her own childhood and for the first time she thought of the pleasure she would find in watching her daughter grow to, and through, ages that she herself could still remember living. She hugged Ted's arm. They bought the house.

Moving took up all her extra time for the next couple of months. And then there was painting and wallpapering to be

done. Her mother came in eagerly to help with this, or to
watch over Sarah while Margaret did it. And then it was
spring, and the garden had to be put in order, and one of the
first things Ted did was build a fence to enclose the back
yard.

The summer before Sarah's third birthday, Margaret
wanted the two of them to go away somewhere for a holiday.
"The only problem we've got," she said to Ted, "is deciding
whose parents are going to get to look after Sarah. Maybe
they could share her. She could stay a week in Kelowna with
your parents and a week in Haney with mine."

"I've got a better idea," he said. "Why don't we take her
with us?"

Margaret looked at him in dismay. "But the whole point is
that we can be together by ourselves."

"But why, Margaret?" he said. "Half the fun of going
somewhere is taking Sarah."

"She's got lots of time to go places," said Margaret coldly.
"Are you telling me that we are never, ever, going to be
alone together again?"

"We're alone right now," said Ted, grinning, and he
reached for her. His parents had come down to stay for the
weekend, and had taken Sarah away for the afternoon to
show her off to some old friends who still considered the
Griffins too young to be grandparents.

Margaret slapped his hand away. "Jesus, Ted, I don't
understand you. You're going to spoil that kid, don't you
know that? We've got to go off by ourselves now and then,
it's important to us, don't you see that?"

"No, I don't see that. How long will we have her?
Seventeen years? Eighteen? Almost three of them are already gone. We've got each other forever, Maggie; but we
won't have Sarah forever, not living with us."

She looked at him incredulously. "You mean, for the next
fifteen years that child comes first? For the next fifteen
years, you and I don't do anything without that child?"

"No, of course that's not what I mean," he said angrily.
"Christ, Margaret." He waved his hands around, searching
for a way to explain it to her. "We're a family, goddamnit.
First we were a family of just you and me, now we've got

77

three people in our family and I'm goddamned if I'm ever going to leave one of us out if I don't have to!"

That evening Margaret went into Sarah's room. The blinds were drawn, but evening light squeezed in around them. A few years from now, thought Margaret, she'll be outside on an evening like this, maybe skinning her shins climbing down trees, her hands stained with stolen cherries. She had a feeling that these things wouldn't be as funny for her as a mother as they had been for her and Moira as children.

Her child slept with total concentration, as she did everything. She slept so soundly that she even looked heavier than she was during the day. Her golden hair clung to her forehead—Margaret quietly opened one of the windows, to let in some fresh air, and the evening caroling of the birds. She touched Sarah's cheek, knowing that she wouldn't awaken. It felt like the petal of a flower. Her eyes were closed; long lashes lay motionless against her cheeks. Her mouth was partly open. She lay on her side, with one chubby hand near her face. She wore only a sleeveless undershirt and diapers and some rubber panties, just in case, and the covers were pushed away from her body. Suddenly Margaret wished Sarah would open her eyes, her dark blue almost violet eyes, and smile at her, and reach out her arms to her. Margaret loved it when she did that; loved the unexpected strength of Sarah's arms around her neck. She reached down and kissed her damp forehead, but Sarah didn't awaken. Margaret thought that if Ted had kissed her in her sleep, Sarah would have awakened. "Good night, baby," she said, and went out and quietly closed the door.

In the spring of 1968, Margaret discovered that she was pregnant again.

"It'll be kind of nice to have another kid," said Ted, but Margaret could see that he was astonished, that this was something he had never expected to happen.

When she told Moira she was pregnant, Moira smiled and said, "Now you'll each have a little hand to hold."

"You're being sarcastic," said Margaret sharply.

"Nope," said Moira.

Margaret resignedly dug out her exercises and determinedly did them, and the following October her second child was born. Margaret had hoped very much to have a boy this time—until she saw her. Of course, she thought, looking at her, listening to her cry; of course. Just as with Sarah, this baby was so immediately known to her that she was amazed she had not seen its face in her dreams throughout her pregnancy.

Margaret chose her name—Glynis.

Ted welcomed her—but he had not recognized her at birth.

The theater seemed to retreat from Margaret more and more rapidly over the next few years. Actor friends whose progress she had eagerly followed disappeared from her life. Some of them had given up the theater—Margaret did not yet consider herself one of these. Others had wandered off to Toronto, or to school in London or New York or Montreal, and some, still in Vancouver, now appeared regularly on the Playhouse stage. Margaret never saw them, although sometimes she sent them opening-night telegrams. None of them, as far as she knew, had any babies. Hardly any of them were even married.

It wasn't that her life was devoid of joy and satisfaction. Sarah fascinated her, intent as she was on the exploration of her widening world, her ambitions always half a step beyond her capacity. And Glynis, extremely quiet during her first months of life (which fostered in Margaret a fervent gratitude), once she began to walk revealed an exuberance that propelled her through each day in a series of gentle explosions. She wasn't yet pretty, as Sarah had always been, but she had great energy and poured out love with a reckless generosity. Her biggest frustration was in trying to keep up with Sarah, who treated her with those doses of consideration and contempt which are often administered by the strong to the less able.

Margaret could see no real resemblance between her children and herself, though she was often told that Sarah looked like her. When Margaret searched for this likeness she couldn't get past Sarah's eyes, which were her father's eyes. And Sarah and Ted were alike in other ways, too. They shared a reserve, a seriousness, a restlessness which Margaret didn't possess, and doubted that Glynis would.

She felt differently toward each of her children, and this at first surprised her. She had assumed that that mythical thing called maternal instinct would cause the distinctions between her offspring to be blurred in her own mind. But they each arrived in the world as a unique person, and she, as another separate person, found herself reacting to each quite differently. She didn't think she loved one of them more than the other—but she certainly loved them differently.

She refrained from discussing this with Ted, because she was already afraid that Glynis was going to end up being cheated by her father. Ted liked Glynis, she often made him laugh, and Margaret was sure that he loved her, too. But his closeness to Sarah was a larger part of his life than whatever he felt for his other daughter.

Meanwhile, Margaret alternated between reading, and refusing to read, everything in the entertainment sections of the *Sun* and the *Province* that had anything at all to do with the theater; between seeing every play produced at every theater in town, and avoiding all of them; between envying Moira for her dedication to her work, and pitying her for not seeing that she was wearing herself out and neglecting her family. She was, in her confusion, becoming bitter.

Then, one afternoon when Moira had come to visit, and the four children were for the moment scattered happily across the back yard, Margaret heard her friend say casually, "I got a commission the other day." They were sitting on the lawn, which was warm and fragrant from the sun. "Some guy's asked me to do a mural."

"What guy? What mural?" said Margaret. She remembered telling Moira when she got that job in the children's television show; it seemed a hundred years ago.

"One of Jason's clients," said Moira. "He saw a couple of my things in Jason's office."

"What kind of a guy is he, though? I mean, what does he want you to do a mural of?"

"I'm supposed to go look at his living room this weekend, and he says I should do whatever I think will look best."

"Moira! That's great!" Margaret thought her voice sounded tinny. "That's really great," she said, squeezing Moira's hand.

"Yeah," said Moira with a grin. "Of course, I think having a mural painted on your living-room wall is a pretty shitty idea, but it's not my wall, thank God."

"And just think, he could have asked you to do an African scene, or a pine forest."

They giggled. "Nope," said Moira, sighing. "Whatever I want."

"You're a working artist, then," said Margaret with awe. "You are actually a real working artist."

Moira looked at her and slowly smiled a splendid smile.

That night Margaret lay in bed, awake, morose and aching somewhere. She knew, lying there, her hands under her head, that *not* doing something, whatever the reason, is also a decision.

Beside her Ted lay quiet, quietly breathing.

# PART II

# Chapter 10

It was the Monday after Ted's funeral, and Sarah was having a hard time deciding what to wear on her first day back to school. She looked for a long time into her closet, aware of ritual; but she didn't seem to own anything that was appropriate.

And even worse, all the clothes she did have were connected in one way or another with Michael.

There was a blue sweater: he said it made her eyes look like the ocean on a sunny day. Or her black pants: they ought to be just the thing, except that he said they made her ass wink at him. She didn't want to go down the halls with her ass winking, not today.

She realized as she stood looking into her closet that she was terribly weary, and terribly confused, and not just about what clothes to wear.

Her wardrobe seemed to get smaller as she pawed through it. She *must* wear the right thing. I'm only seventeen, she thought angrily. How am I supposed to know what to do?

She pushed things back and forth; a brown and white checked dress (she certainly couldn't wear a dress to school, that would be going too far), the ass-winking black pants, some brown ones she had never liked, white frilly blouses

85

she had never worn—except sometimes on Sundays, when she was filled with an urge to come to the dinner table wearing her long skirt of cobalt blue, and her blond hair tied atop her head with a matching ribbon. There was a pink sweater she liked very much, and it was baggy, too, which would be good; but it looked like spring and smelled of Michael's favorite perfume and she shoved it to the side.

I need to ask my father what to do, she thought. She listened to herself think it, waited to see what would happen, but nothing much happened until her knees began to shake. She sat down on the edge of her bed and looked at her knees curiously. The shaking did not show.

What's going on here, anyway? she asked herself, and then snorted a little, reminding herself of her grandfather. He never really laughed out loud, just made these little snorting noises, usually at something his wife, Kathleen, had said, and if it weren't for the way his pale blue eyes scrunched up and the fact that his mouth smiled, you'd never know that the snort meant he'd been amused.

Let's face it, she told herself, still sitting on the bed with her hands on her pajama'd knees. I very badly need my father to tell me what to wear.

She had once thought it literally true that he was the only person in the world who knew everything. Gradually it dawned on her, as she grew up from being a child, that he didn't actually know everything. But even then, for a long time she had remained convinced that he knew everything of any importance. It seemed that she believed this again, now that he was gone, which to Sarah didn't seem quite fair.

She shut her eyes and tried to think what he would say to her, if she could ask him. She'd known him for a long time, after all; for all of her life. She ought to be able to guess pretty accurately what he would say. But all she could hear was some faint faraway laughter that tingled in her ear where it was born, and she felt bitter resentment; and then she saw him lying in his coffin under the earth. He couldn't be laughing, not from down there, surely he wouldn't be laughing, not he, and she doubled herself over, holding on to her stomach.

"That is going to be just great," she said, "if every time I ask you something all you do is laugh."

Her eyes ached.

She got up and put on a pair of jeans and the blue sweater and some blue socks and her blue sneakers. Her father didn't like her in jeans. Her father didn't like a lot of things; but that's his problem, thought Sarah. She struck her thigh, hard, with the edge of her hand.

Sarah walked to school alone that morning. It didn't occur to her to tell anybody she was going back. As she neared the school other kids appeared heading in the same direction, but it was a very large school with many hundreds of students and she didn't see anyone she knew. They might have been there on the sidewalk near her, but she didn't see them.

A reasonably large part of her mind was functioning more or less as usual, observing things and reporting on them. But the rest of her mind wasn't terribly interested. Sarah became more and more angry as she approached the school. This surprised her, but she welcomed the anger and recognized it as strength. It absolved her of responsibility. She stalked into the school, up the steps through crowds of noisy kids, down the hall to her locker. She noticed that she had remembered the combination, and decided it must be a thing like breathing or going to the bathroom, not to be forgotten just because somebody had died.

She went to her homeroom and sat at her desk and wondered why she had spent any time at all worrying about the embarrassment of this moment. There wasn't any embarrassment—at least, not for her: other people obviously felt some. She watched them through telescopic eyes as they stopped laughing and yelling when she entered the room. She sat down easily, no strain at all, put her books on the desk. She watched herself fold her hands in her lap, as though they were a pair of gloves; watched the hands lie there slumbering; then looked up and watched the kids in the room steadily.

They will have thought about this, she thought, and was interested to see what they would do.

They came over to her desk, most of them, one at a time or in pairs, and mumbled that they were sorry, as though it had been their fault; apologies over with, they skittered hunchbacked to lean against blackboards or window ledges and talk confidingly in low tones or outright whispers with their friends.

# THE FAVORITE

I wonder if any of them have had anybody die, thought Sarah; but even if they have, it wouldn't be like this for them. That was an absolute certainty, the difference of this grief of hers from other griefs—it was grim, and purposeful, and did not hint of its conclusion. It was what created her aloneness and her anger and her strength. But she didn't think the strength would necessarily last; sometimes there was a trembling inside her somewhere.

At lunchtime in the thin spring sunshine she walked in the school grounds and saw Michael coming toward her, and she seemed to see her old self just behind him, wavery in the sunlight, faceless in the brilliance of the noontime sun, and she almost cried out from the wrenching in her chest. She reached out to touch her old self on the fingertips and touched Michael, instead, and as he pulled her close to him she watched the sunlit faceless shadow disappear. I will never see that me again, she thought, not anywhere, not ever.

She let Michael hold her. She even put her arms around him, limply, and as she rested her head against his cheek she felt the chasm of time that separated her from today in this school and the last day she'd been there. She never used to let Michael hold her like this at school. It had made her feel guilty and smudged, as though a muddy-pawed puppy had climbed into her lap and how would she get the marks out of her clothes before her mother saw them.

"Sarah, why didn't you tell me you were coming back today?" said Michael. "You poor kid, it must be hell for you. How did you get here, did your mother drive you?"

She pushed herself away from him and looked up into his seagreen eyes. He is genuinely concerned, she thought, and patted him on the back. "I walked. I'm fine."

Michael continued to look at her worriedly. "You sure?"

"Yes, sure, I'm fine."

She hadn't brought a lunch. This wasn't unusual. She often left her lunch at home on the hall table when she raced out the door, and then at noon she would clap her hand to her forehead dramatically and announce to Michael that today she would have to eat at the café down the street. She loved the dry hamburgers and the greasy french fries they made at that place.

But this morning she hadn't forgotten her lunch. She had

88

looked around for it, but it hadn't been there. She hadn't given it another thought; had kissed her mother on the forehead and left the house.

Michael gave her a cheese sandwich. She looked at it curiously and chewed a few mouthfuls and then sighed. Still couldn't taste anything.

She thought for a second of the body lying in the coffin which lay beneath the earth and wondered how long it would feed inertly upon itself before it started to crumble.

I don't mind imagining skeletons, she thought, but I do not want to be imagining rot.

"I can't eat any more of this, Michael." She crumpled up the sandwich between the palms of her hands and threw the bits and pieces onto the grass for the birds.

"Can you go out tonight?" said Michael.

She thought about it. "No."

"At least I'll drive you home from school," said Michael, rubbing the back of her neck. She resented the possessiveness of that hand.

Sarah stood up. "No," she said. "I'm going home now, and I don't want anyone to drive me." She walked off toward the sidewalk.

Michael scrambled to his feet and ran after her. "Hey, what's the matter, don't you feel well? Sarah, hey, stop!"

She kept on walking, hiding her fury. It seemed shockingly wrong that he should be so real, so healthy. She had had that thought before.

"I'm fine. I just feel like going home," she called back over her shoulder. "Don't worry, Michael. I'll see you tomorrow."

He caught her by the shoulders and turned her around. "Sarah, Jesus. You came back too soon." He hugged her. "Let me drive you."

Sarah broke away. "I don't want you to. I want to walk. See you tomorrow."

She felt him watching as she walked over the grass to the sidewalk and across the street to the bus stop, where she stopped and glanced back at the school. Michael was still watching her. She waved, and he waved back, and then he turned reluctantly and walked away around the side of the building.

Sarah stood alone in an empty moment, looking at the

school, and tried to remember that it was important in her
life. She was supposed to graduate from it in three months.
That ceremony flashed into her head, frozen as if in the
photograph that would be taken. She couldn't see herself in
it.

She walked around a corner and down a couple of blocks
and sat down on some grass, pulled up her knees, leaned
against somebody's fence. She was looking up into the sun,
which glowed at her through a haze of cloud that had drifted
over it.

The sky was fuzzy, light blue, cool, lit dreamily by a
shrouded sun. She heard traffic on the street in front of her,
and when now and then no cars or trucks or buses came by
she could hear the pale breeze rustling bushes in the yard
behind her. She closed her eyes, and rested.

After a while she heard a busy click-clicking, and turned
her head and saw a small dog approaching. It was golden
brown with white paws and a white chest and a black mark
around one of its eyes. It wore a collar, and one of its ears
stood straight up and one of them drooped. It bustled and
clicked along the street toward Sarah, stopping to sniff at a
fire hydrant, and a light post, and the edge of the fence
against which Sarah was leaning. While it sniffed the fence
its eyes darted up to Sarah's face, and then away, and then
back again. It leaped away from the fence and looked at her,
and then suddenly pawed the earth with great energy and
speed, all the time watching her. Sarah heard herself laugh.
The dog, alarmed, bounced back a few steps, and turned
around and scurried away, its claws click-clicking hastily on
the sidewalk. A couple of times it looked back over its
shoulder at her; then it turned a corner and disappeared.

Sarah rested her forehead on her knees and closed her
eyes. She had completely forgotten, for a few seconds.
Obviously a dangerous lapse. She would have to pay for
every single moment of pleasure from now on. The whole
thing would keep crashing down on her head again and
again, just as it had the first time, whenever she allowed
herself to forget. You would really think one time would be
enough, and then a person could just try to get used to it but
no, every single time you forget about it, even for a second,
when you remember again it's as though it's happening all

over again, just as bad as the first time. People's fathers die all the time, every day, it's not so unusual. People get over it, they do, I know they do; why am I so sure I will never ever get over it? . . .

At first she had thought everybody had a father like him. She thought that was what a father was; the person in your life from whom you had no distance, the person who knew you better than you knew yourself, who helped you from the very beginning to kind of zoom up above yourself and look down on yourself and see yourself clearly, the person who gave to you, without your knowing it, the conviction—not just the belief, or the faith, but the *conviction*—that you could do anything you wanted with your life, that you were unique, that you were special . . . that's what she had thought was meant by "father."

But Sarah began to realize that this was not a common thing when Glynis got to be five or six years old and started taking potshots at a neighbor's garage window with rocks. The neighbor caught her and hauled her home and her father had been extremely angry. Sarah had thought it funny, and had admired both Glynis' choice of target and her aim.

But their father had not seen anything amusing in it at all. While her mother stood around with tears shaking in her eyes, her father took Glynis into her bedroom and actually spanked her, three times. She yelled, but Sarah didn't think it had hurt all that much. Glynis sounded more surprised than anything else. Sarah tried to imagine how it would feel to have her father hit her, but she couldn't. He had never hit her, and he never did. He'd never even gotten terribly angry with her (not then—but later, later . . .).

But her mother had. Sarah remembered her mother hitting her on the rear end with a flyswat once, and another time with her father's belt, which had seemed to Sarah unnecessarily nasty. She couldn't remember what she had done. Her mother obviously thought that if Glynis was going to get spanked for doing something wrong, then Sarah should be, too. Sarah had privately agreed, it did seem fair, and it had to be her mother who did it, because they both knew her father never would.

Sarah lifted her head from her knees. She was feeling more visible, more aware of the people who occasionally passed her on the sidewalk and must surely wonder what she was doing, sitting there with her head on her knees. She got to her feet and dusted off the seat of her jeans and started walking toward a bus stop.

Gradually she had come to see a kind of structure in their family that set her mother and Glynis on one side and Sarah and her father on the other. It wasn't that they didn't all four love one another, because they did. And often Sarah would go somewhere with her mother or do something with her and be very happy; she liked trying to please her mother.

She did not try to please her father, because she didn't have to; she knew that she pleased him, just as she was, that they pleased each other. It was quite a different relationship than Glynis had with him, or her friends had with their fathers.

One of her friends had a father whom Sarah never ever saw, though apparently he was there. Her friend's mother worked as a teacher, which the friend (whose name was Janet) said was okay because she wasn't in the same school as her mother. "That would be awful, can you imagine?" said Janet, shuddering.

But evidently there was a father there, too. Sarah used to think he was some kind of invalid, which would have been terribly interesting. She could never go to Janet's house to play. Janet's face would begin to shift around and she would mumble, "My father . . ." and they would go somewhere else. All the years Sarah knew Janet, she never once went into her house. She would call on Janet at a specified time and hang around out by her front gate waiting for her to come out. The house looked cozy and warm, huddled down among the trees, and every time Sarah thought about it she saw it in her mind at night, with lights glowing in its windows. It looked like a very nice house. But she never got inside it.

Later she found out from someone else that Janet's father was an alcoholic, and she wondered how they kept him in there. She had heard that drunken people lurched about a lot, and she didn't see how the house could have been big enough for him. Then she thought maybe there was a room in there with steel walls and they kept him locked up in it, sliding trays of food through a slit in the padlocked door.

Eventually he died, but by then Sarah and Janet were going to different schools and never saw each other any more.

Another friend, Pat, had a father who never said very much, although his smile was slow and pleasant. He walked around rather slowly, his shoulders slightly hunched. Sarah went into their house quite often. Pat spoke to her father warmly, but there was distance between them. Everybody seemed to have distances between themselves and other people—Sarah had them herself, with everybody in her life except her father.

A bus pulled up to the stop and Sarah got on.

It was almost a half-hour trip to the cemetery, where she got off the bus and walked through the gates and headed for her father's grave.

The ground rolled around her in low hills and shallow valleys, and a stunted forest of gravestones grew in orderly rows. There were splotches of flowers here and there, resting bright dying heads against the gray stone markers. Wide paths cut neat, flowing swaths through the area and birds sang from far away and from somewhere—the place was huge, she couldn't see all of it—from somewhere came the sound of a lawn mower. It was an aberration, but then Sarah thought the whole place was pretty queer. Death, a well-organized phenomenon, with places on the earth all staked out ready to receive its victims.

Sarah found the rectangle of ground in which her father had been buried. At the head of it was a temporary white wooden cross on which was written only his name and the dates of his birth and death.

It was like the bracelets they put on people in the hospital, she thought, remembering the plastic one (reusable) that had encircled her father's wrist. Temporary identification, so nobody could get people mixed up, whether they were dying in a hospital or dead under the ground.

She knelt down and tried, peering into the dug-up earth, to see through it, through the top of the coffin, into what lay there.

Does he lie restlessly, does he toss his hands about, do his feet twitch, do his eyes open?

She stared very hard at the earth but could see nothing, and she felt nothing, either, no vibrations, no nothing; and she wondered if he was really there after all. Maybe he was lying in another dug-up part of the graveyard, or maybe he wasn't anywhere; maybe he'd just disappeared.

She knew, though, that he had not disappeared. She knew it.

She looked around the graveyard, which was very quiet; she could no longer hear the lawn mower, the birds had flown away. But she saw a breeze that ruffled nearby grass almost silver, and smelled the rich, acrid scent of freshly dug earth.

She stared again into the clods of dirt and saw a slight movement; an ant running around in there. She could now smell the flowers that somebody had dumped on the grave next door. Sarah wondered if the occupants of all these graves yawned and stretched and came up for air some-times—it would have to be at night, she supposed—and looked around critically and compared tombstones, and the flowers left on their gravestones; and if some of them then descended back into their coffins grumpy, or depressed, or sad, because nobody had come to see them at all, or had come and left only dandelions.

Sarah crouched beside the grave, arms hugging her shins, listening for breathing under the earth.

"I can sit here forever, Daddy, if you need me," she said. "I will sit here forever and when you're ready, let me know, and I will dig you up."

She couldn't imagine how he had gotten himself into this mess.

He was a person not meant to die at all, and how he'd gotten himself dead and buried under the earth she could not fathom.

Sarah stood up and looked down on the grave with a sigh of frustration, her fingers pushing her locket back and forth along its chain. She raised her head and swept her eyes across the expanse of gravestones, the rolling lawns, to the trees which edged the cemetery, and far off she saw glints of sunlight on windshields as cars sped along the highway, and still farther off she thought she might see the sea if she cared to look hard enough. The sun warmed her back, and the air held the scents of moist dirt and grass and roses from the grave next door.

On her way down the paved path to the gates of the

cemetery Sarah stopped sometimes and looked back, but the newly dug earth lay quietly on the green lawn, and the white cross remained immobile.

When she arrived home she stood at the bottom of the driveway, which sloped up slightly to a two-car garage. A brick walk led down from the front door. Shrubs were planted beneath the living-room windows. At the side of the house opposite the garage there was a dogwood tree, and at the front, by the sidewalk, more shrubs and a flower garden. The crocuses had already come and gone, the daffodils were blooming now, and next would come the tulips, and the lilies of the valley.

She turned to look at the house. A lot of Sarahs had lived in that house, yet they had all been the same person. It seemed unreasonable to expect one Sarah to grow naturally into a new, older one unless there were at least some threads there stretching back into a younger Sarah. She was desperately afraid that every single one of her threads had been snapped, and all the ends were now aching and quivering and reaching back blindly and that all of them were quickly running out of life.

And where are you now, eh? she thought, stalking up the walk to the front door, gathering her fury into her heart. Where are you now, my daddy, when I really need you; sulking, even now, still sulking, wherever you are, damn you, God damn you . . .

# Chapter 11

On five-year-old Sarah's first day of school, in the first week of September 1970, Margaret wakened suddenly, feeling inexplicably content and magnanimous, a good dream fading to a warm spot in the center of her. The room was light, but not bright enough to herald a sunny day. She turned in bed and cuddled next to Ted, who made a sound between a groan and a grunt. She wiggled up until her head was near his, and kissed his ear. He groaned and turned onto his back, his eyes still closed.

"We've got twenty minutes," she said, breathing into his ear.

He threw himself on top of her. "Until what?" he whispered.

"Until the alarm goes off."

He rolled away, smiling, eyes still closed, hair mussed, and began fumbling with the drawstring on his pajamas.

"Here," said Margaret, "let me do that. . . ."

Sarah had been allowed to start school while she was still five because her sixth birthday would occur before the end of the calendar year. She liked the idea of going to school, because she was impatient to learn more things and because

96

if she didn't go she'd be left almost alone in the neighborhood, except for the babies like Glynis. On the other hand, though, she *didn't* like the idea, because mysteries made her uneasy, and that school was a mystery, all right. She thought about it a lot. And her parents thought about it too, marveling that their first child could have come so far, so fast. Margaret was struck by the realization that a day would certainly come when her life would be mostly her own again. She had tasted this thought shyly, then tenderly, finding increasing sweetness in it, as the last days of summer spun themselves out.

Breakfast on the first day of school was a flurry of activity, since they were all going out that morning and the household wasn't used to this. Sarah picked gloomily at her cereal, urged on by Margaret, while Glynis banged her bowl with her spoon and whooped, imperious. Ted hurriedly ate a piece of toast and excused himself from the table, giving Sarah a kiss on the forehead as he passed her. He went into the bedroom to finish dressing, and looked up and smiled a few minutes later when he heard her at the doorway.

"I don't really want to go, Daddy," said Sarah.

"Come on in, chicken. I meant to tell you, you look very pretty. Are those your new school clothes?"

"Yeah," she said, spreading her arms and looking down at brown cords and a yellow sweater. She let her arms fall. "But I don't think I want to go after all."

Ted finished buttoning the cuffs of his shirt. "Help me pick out a tie." He pulled a handful from the closet.

"That one," said Sarah, pointing to a tie that was mostly blue.

Ted began to put it on. "Why do you think you don't want to go?"

"I don't know."

"I remember, I was very scared on my first day of school," said Ted, watching in the mirror as he adjusted his tie.

"What were you scared of?"

"Nothing in particular. It was just that I'd never been there before. I didn't know what it would be like. Maybe I'd hate it."

"I know about school."

"Good. Will you help me polish my shoes?"

"Sure."

Ted got out shoe polish, a cloth and a brush. "I'll put the polish on and you brush, okay?"

"Okay. Did you hate it?"

"We'll just do the toes this time." He handed her the first shoe and she started to brush, slowly. "No, I don't think I ever hated school. Sometimes it was boring, that's all."

"Didn't you learn anything there?" The leather began to glow, and she brushed harder, to make it shine.

"Oh sure, I learned lots of things."

"Didn't you like the other kids?"

"Oh sure, most of them I liked a lot." He handed her the other shoe. "How are you doing?"

Sarah gave the first shoe a final swipe and handed it to him and picked up the other one.

Ted got his jacket and put it on. "How do I look?"

"Fine. You look good." She drew the brush back and forth, sniffing the smells of leather and polish, which was getting less sticky now, the brush was passing over the shoe more easily, she could see the shine peeking out from underneath the polish.

"Well? What do you think?" said Ted, putting on the first shoe.

Sarah continued to brush. "I might try it, anyway."

"Good," he said, smiling at her.

The school was a large stone building plunked down in the middle of a dusty playground, a fortress whose grounds were cleared the better to spot invading armies from the cupola on top; Ted scoffed at himself as they approached it, but that's what it looked like to him. It was old, like the schools of his own youth. He didn't want to take her in there.

They marched down the path toward the front of the building, all four of them, Margaret in brown slacks and a tweed jacket carrying Glynis. The dirty gray doors were inset with small windows placed too high for children's eyes; Ted imagined teachers' nervous faces peering suspiciously through the glass, barricading children in, parents out.

"I've changed my mind again, Dad," said Sarah, tugging at his hand. They stopped halfway up the path. "It doesn't look like a good place. I've changed my mind."

"It's probably better inside," said Ted.

"I'll bet your school didn't look like that," said Sarah.

98

"As a matter of fact, I'll bet it did," said Margaret cheerfully. "Come on, you two, don't be silly. Sarah, you'd be bored to death at home with all the other kids at school."

"Evvie's not at school. She doesn't go until next year." Sarah gazed fixedly at the door. "I think I'll wait and go next year, too."

"You'd better at least go inside and take a look," said Ted. "There'll be books, and a blackboard, and chalk. You'll learn bigger words—"

"I can learn bigger words at home."

"—and how to do arithmetic—"

"Ugh."

"Sarah, come along," said Margaret, heading for the door. "We're going to be late."

"Look, I couldn't even open this door," Sarah muttered. "It's too big and heavy."

"They have side doors for the children," said Margaret. "You'll be able to open them."

"How do you know that?" said Ted, amazed.

"I remember," said Margaret.

As they stepped inside a rush of memory engulfed him, too, with the scent of resin and wax and the squeals and shrieks of children. He looked dazedly at Margaret, who laughed, and put Glynis down, and took her hand.

"This isn't so bad, eh?" he whispered hopefully to the top of Sarah's head, but she refused to look anywhere but straight ahead. She marched like one of a captured miniature army, separated from her comrades, a prisoner of war.

The gymnasium was filled with rows of elderly metal chairs. They found seats among the crowd of mothers hanging on to their children. There were few fathers there. Ted wondered indignantly where the hell they all were, on such an important day.

Sarah scrunched down in her chair, folded her hands in her lap and stared stubbornly at the floor. The adults squirmed surreptitiously in the hard metal chairs. Older, bigger children gathered in fluttering noisy clusters at the door to the gymnasium. They whispered excitedly to one another behind hands or sheets of hair, stared triumphantly at the newcomers miserable in the shiny-floored gymnasium.

Where the hell are all the teachers, thought Ted, and heard an adult voice in the hall outside the gym, then hands clapping briskly. The shrieking stopped and was replaced by a busy hum like the sound from a monstrous beehive.

"All right, children," said a severe voice, "line up, please, come on now, look lively."

A middle-aged man with a cane limped across the platform at the front of the gym.

A small girl in the row ahead turned around to observe Sarah. "Psst," she said, and Sarah's head came up warily. "Are you going to stay all day?"

"I haven't decided yet," said Sarah clearly.

Right, thought Ted.

The principal in a soft wheezy voice told them the rules and welcomed the children to the school. They were assigned alphabetically to one of three Grade One classrooms, and the parents were asked to deliver them. The crowd stood up. Some mothers, those to whom this was not a new experience, bustled off quickly. Others milled about clumsily, hanging on to a child with one hand and a purse with the other.

Margaret, carrying Glynis, led Ted and Sarah out of the gym and down the corridor, checking the numbers on the classroom doors. Sarah walked stiffly in her new corduroy pants, watching her new Buster Brown shoes gleam as they approached and passed beneath each of the light fixtures hanging above.

"Now, Sarah," said Margaret, stopping at Room 2, "this is your classroom." She put Glynis down and hugged Sarah. "You're going to have a good time here," she said softly. Sarah's eyes were huge. "I know, it's strange at first but don't worry," said Margaret, suddenly not wanting to let her go, "it's only a short day today, only 'til lunchtime, so you'll have a chance to get used to things before you go back and really start learning, tomorrow." She smoothed Sarah's hair from her forehead and stood up, feeling helpless.

Sarah turned to Ted. "How am I supposed to get home?" she said. "How do I know when to go home, and how do I get there? I don't like this place."

"I'll come and get you," said Ted. "You've got nothing to worry about. I'll be here to get you." She threw her arms around his waist. He kissed the top of her head. She pulled back and turned around and walked into the classroom like one surrendering, but not defeated.

THE FAVORITE

Ted and Margaret peeked around the corner. Sarah had burrowed herself into a desk in the back row. In front of her, a girl with brown curly hair had collapsed in tears on her desk. Her sobbing intensified. The other children turned to stare with great interest, their own tears drying inside their eyes. Sarah ignored the girl and lifted the top of her desk to look into the cavity there.

A small round woman pushed past Ted and Margaret. "Excuse me," she said distractedly, and with small steps hurried into the classroom. "My, my, what have we here," she said softly, stopping beside the desk of the crying child. As Margaret swung the door closed they saw the teacher's gray head bend down, saw her small hand rest gently upon the girl's shoulder. Sarah continued to stare into the inside of her desk. The door closed with a clunk.

Ted carried Glynis as they walked down the echoey hallway, the sound of their footsteps alien and specific, through the smell of wax and old dust, through the murmuring of children who had not yet let go of summer and whose voices seeped restlessly through the walls, through closed classroom doors.

They went out of the school through one of the side doors, and the grooves worn in the stairs which led down to the playground were too small to fit their feet.

# Chapter 12

By the time Sarah started school, Margaret was thirty. Ted had hurdled this milestone seven years earlier, but even with his good example she stumbled and cracked a shin upon it when it was her turn. She spent more time than usual staring at herself in the mirror, looking for gray hairs among the long blond ones and not finding them, looking for a slight deepening of the fine lines around her eyes, and finding those. Even reasonably close up, though, she decided finally, she didn't look thirty. Ted, however, was definitely thickening around the waist, and there were a few traces of silver in his hair. She liked the gray hairs, but worried about his waist. She sometimes tried to persuade him to get more exercise, but he was impatient with that.

Right out of the blue, Margaret that autumn began to flirt with the idea of employment. The more she thought about it, the more excited she became.

"But why, for God's sake?" said Ted in exasperation when she told him. "If you want to do something, why the hell don't you act again? I can see why you'd want to do that, but a *job*. Jesus."

Margaret didn't understand it very well herself. But she liked, very much, the fact that an actual job would require

her to be in another place for a specific portion of each and
every day. Right now, that's what it seemed she wanted—to
have another place she had to go to, every day. Everybody
understands and respects the requirements of a regular job,
she said to herself—even Ted.

And of course she'd get paid for it.

"But, Margaret," said Ted, with studied patience, "we
don't *need* any money from you."

"*We* don't need it, Ted," she said, "But I think *I* do."

She knew she had hurt him, although she had not wanted
to. It was his pride again. He kept up with most things going
on in the world, but he hadn't come to terms with what was
going on with women. She didn't feel it was her right or her
responsibility to instruct him in this matter—but she did
often wonder, smiling faintly to herself, how he was going to
handle himself when his daughters got older. There was no
way they were going to avoid growing up liberated. Not if I
have anything to do with it, she thought with a sudden
ferocity which surprised her.

"I do believe," she said to Moira, "that I'm pretty liberated myself, despite it all."

"Sure you are," said Moira. "You've made some choices
our braless sisters mightn't approve of—but they've been
your own choices."

Margaret thought about that. "Well, I love him, you see,"
she said.

"He does kind of live in the Dark Ages, though," said
Moira, and Margaret, recalling the shocked indignation with
which he had thrust *The Second Sex* back at her after
reading only three chapters, had to agree.

"This is a bunch of bullshit," he had said. "You are not
and never have been 'the Other' to me. What a total bunch
of crap."

This had occurred early in their marriage and had dismayed her, until she decided that she could continue to love
him, and need him, and at the same time read and change,
privately. But it was a shame that she couldn't share with
him the revelations she got over the years from Simone de
Beauvoir, and Gloria Steinem, and Kate Millett. It would
have been exciting to discuss with Ted the books she read,
and her halting speculations, and finally the new truths that
became as much a part of her as were her love of her

husband and children and her wistful nostalgia for the stage. But she couldn't. He was mired in the nineteenth-century novel, she thought affectionately. At least he'd finally gotten to teach it.

Eventually, with Ted's grudging acceptance if not his approval, Margaret enrolled in a night school class to brush up the typing and shorthand skills she had learned in high school and with which she had supported herself for four years after her graduation. It was hard work, and frustrating. She remembered how quickly her fingers had once sped across the typewriter keys, and that she had once not had to translate spoken words into shorthand before putting them down on paper. But she persevered, and by the end of Sarah's first year in school Margaret considered herself once more employable.

She agreed to wait until after the summer holidays to look for a job.

By the end of the next September she had one, as a secretary in a small public relations firm. She had also found a housekeeper who would clean and do laundry as well as look after Glynis, and Sarah, too, when she got home from school.

The housekeeper's name was Muriel Aspen. She had been deserted by two men and had left a third, all in a space of ten years, all because of alcohol, and although Ted did not appear to be a drinker he was a man and so she didn't completely trust him. She reluctantly acknowledged his devotion to his family, but to Muriel, it wasn't seemly that he should be more devoted to them than to his work, which she judged to be of tremendous importance because he did it at the university. His work was the thing that helped Muriel distinguish him as being different from and therefore superior to her own three men.

Muriel knew that Mrs. Griffin's work was far less important than her husband's, but she understood why Margaret was doing it. She, Muriel, would obviously not be looking after a house and children all day if there was anything else she could do better. She liked doing it, though, because she didn't have any children of her own, and because she knew that at the end of the day she could go home to her quiet basement apartment on Harwood Street in the West End where she left the front window open just a smidgen while she was at work so that her black cat with the white chest could go in and out at will. Muriel didn't believe in thieves. Not in thieves who would want to steal from her, anyway.

She was a small, bony woman who seemed to live in a state of constant alertness. She was also clean, efficient, briskly affectionate with the children and uncannily attuned to things they might do to try to put one over on her. She had been working for the Griffins for close to two years when Sarah had what Muriel later called her Bad Time in the Playground.

It was a warm but cloudy day in May. Sarah was meandering across the playground on her way home from school, when suddenly a girl shouted at her.

"You're a retarded pig, a fat retarded pig!" said the girl.

Sarah stared at her, incredulous.

The girl wouldn't shut up. Sarah didn't understand it. She didn't know how it had begun, and she didn't know why. She tried to ignore the girl, but the girl wouldn't be ignored. When Sarah tried to walk away, the girl ran past her, and hopping backwards, her face clenched, she kept on saying it: "You're a pig, a fat retarded pig!"

Sarah knew that she wasn't fat, or retarded, or a pig; she could not comprehend what was going on.

"What's the matter with you?" she demanded shrilly.

She was eight, and almost through Grade Three. The girl was the same age only bigger, stronger, with short pigtails that stuck out from the sides of her head and a raspy voice and arms that swelled out from under the sleeves of her T-shirt and ended in round fists made of iron. The girl's mouth was in a sneer as it spat out words at Sarah. There were more girls hanging around the edges of Sarah's vision, and maybe a couple of boys as well.

"Go home!" she said to the girl, whose name was Kelly. "Leave me alone!" She waved her hand industriously in the air, as though trying to wipe the girl's image from a blackboard.

"Baby baby baby," said Kelly. "You suck cocks!" she said triumphantly.

Sarah thought wildly, trying to separate and understand the stings. "I am not a baby," she said. "Shut up! Shut up!" she hollered. "And let me go home!"

"Baby, baby, wants to go home," Kelly taunted, "just like a baby, 'let me go home!' " she whined, mocking. Then she crouched, shot her fists up. "Fight me!" she said. "Go ahead, fight me, you baby, great big baby!"

Sarah's foot lashed out and kicked Kelly in the calf of her leg. Sarah was at first horrified. Satisfaction had just begun to make itself felt (that'll fix her, she started to think) when she found herself in the air, but before she got a chance to notice the sky she pounded down on her back in the dust of the playground and Kelly was beating on her face with her fists. Sarah lay with eyes scrunched closed, wondering if this were really happening.

The girl leaped off her. Sarah opened her eyes. Kelly stood above her, legs enormous, wide and tall, her head a long way off against the sky. She stood there, waiting. Sarah heard no sounds from any of the children gathered around. She heard nothing but the thick beating of her beaten heart, the scuffling of her shoes as she dragged herself upright. Now I'll go home, she thought, I won't cry until I get there. But Kelly stood before her, blocking her way. When Sarah tried to go around her, Kelly moved so that she couldn't.

"Cry, baby, come on, cry, little baby; you suck cocks," she said, and Sarah swung her arm, helplessly, and hit her in the shoulder, and almost with resignation felt herself fly energetically through the air and land on her back in the dust. Kelly hit her about the arms and shoulders and once on the side of the head; then stood back, and waited.

Wearily, Sarah pulled herself to her feet, started toward the edge of the playground, the sidewalk, heard Kelly say "baby . . . sucks cocks," hit her again (got her head this time, anyway, she thought, reeling), and plummeted to earth again; got hit again; again staggered up; again . . . she stood feeling small on the playground, blood running slowly from her nose, a bruise on the side of her head, ragged with dust, hair full of it, tangled and wild. She looked at Kelly, who didn't move, and she didn't even wait for Kelly's mouth to open, she swung her arm back and let it land against the side of the other girl's neck.

Sarah squeezed her eyes shut, hunched up her body, and waited. Nothing happened.

She opened one eye and peered out.

The girl was wandering off, followed by a jumping, sud-

denly yelling group of other girls. Sarah opened her eyes all
the way and looked around her. Other kids were heading off
in other directions, jackets slung over their shoulders or tied
around their waists, as they walked or trotted or skipped.

Sarah aimed herself toward the sidewalk and started to
move her feet, one after the other. She knew her body must
be broken into hundreds of pieces. It wasn't falling apart
because of her skin. She was grateful to her skin. It would
have been awful if her whole body had fallen apart right
there on the public sidewalk.

She struggled up the street and past the neighbors' houses
and if she saw anybody she knew, she didn't remember it
later. But a big black dog came running out of somebody's
yard, barking. It came to her and sniffed at her and followed
her home quietly. She thought that was very nice of it. She
wished that dog had been around on the playground.

She walked up to her front door and hoped Muriel would
know what to do about something like this. She knew her
father would know what to do, but he was at work, and so
was her mother. She put her hand out to take hold of the
doorknob and saw that her hand was shaking, her whole
body was shaking, she thought her skin wouldn't be able to
hold in all the broken pieces if it kept on being shaken
around like that and she opened the door and started to
scream.

The telephone on her desk rang, and when Margaret
picked it up Muriel was already talking.

"Now, Mrs. Griffin, I don't want you to get yourself all
upset, these things happen, but Sarah's had a kind of an
accident and I think you ought to get yourself on home early
today."

"My God, what kind of an accident, where is she?"

"Heavens, there's scarcely a mark on her, a bleeding nose
is about all that's wrong, that and a lot of dirt all over her,
and she's been crying some, wants her daddy, she does, or
her mommy, and I figured best to call you and not bother
Professor Griffin up there at the university."

Margaret was looking at the top of her desk and seeing
Muriel, who would be clutching the phone with one hand
and the skirt of her bibbed apron with the other, her red-
brown hair in tight curls, tucked carefully under a hairnet.

"What happened?" said Margaret, feeling the grittiness of dust between her teeth.

"I'm not too clear on that, Mrs. Griffin, something at school is all I know. She's bundled up on your bed, calming down some now, but I told her I'd telephone you, so here I am doing it. She wants to know if you could maybe come on over here and I said I would ask you that, so here I am."

"Of course I'll come, tell her I'm leaving right away."

When she got home, the front door opened before Margaret could get her hand on the knob. Muriel stood there, stiff with importance. She had finally had an occasion to rise to; she had been there when minor disaster struck and had tidied up the chaos, and at last felt that she had earned her pay.

"She's upstairs, Mrs. Griffin, perfectly fine, don't you worry," she offered comfortingly as Margaret streaked past her. She wagged her head, watching Margaret take the stairs two at a time, and bustled into the kitchen to make a pot of coffee.

Margaret raced along the upstairs hall without pausing to think. She didn't want any more time in which to wonder if she was afraid to see Sarah. What if there was blood? But she knew Muriel would have cleaned all that up.

Sarah lay small in the center of her parents' big double bed. Margaret could see the memory of recent tears resting in the bottoms of her eyes. She sat down and pulled Sarah close, rocking her and murmuring. Finally she said, "What happened, honey? What happened to you?"

Sarah shook her head against Margaret's breasts. "A girl beat me up, I don't know why," she said, and began to cry again.

"*What* girl?"

"Just a girl, a kid. I don't know her. When will Daddy be home?" said Sarah, holding on to her mother and crying.

"Where the hell were the goddamn teachers?" said Ted later. He wanted to get hold of that kid and break her in two.

"It happened after school," said Margaret. "You can't expect them to watch every single kid every single minute. It's just one of the things that happen to kids, Ted, there's no reason for it."

"Goddamnit, she's been beaten up, Margaret! She's an

eight-year-old kid and she's been beaten up!" He couldn't sit still. He walked up and down while Margaret watched him from the living-room sofa. "I'm going to find that kid, I'm going to break her goddamn neck." Margaret didn't want to get close to him in case she got singed. "Goddamnit!" he roared, turning to face her. "You send your kid off to school, you don't expect her to get beaten up by some goddamn eight-year-old hoodlum!"

"Ted. Don't."

"Let me tell you," he said, coming close to her, his eyes burning. "I don't like that job of yours." He leaned down, stared into her face. "I don't like it," he said, and her cheeks stung. He straightened up, his face pale, his mouth set.

"Ted, God, it wouldn't have made any difference if I'd been home—"

"Of course it would have made a difference," he said coldly. "*You* would have opened the door to her. *You* would have held her. *You* would have cleaned the blood and the dirt from her face. *You* would have done it. If you had been here."

She felt each word as a soft blow to her chest. "You have never spoken to me like that before," she said.

"My daughter has never been beaten up before," he said with cold precision, and left the room.

Ted held a wet cloth to the bruise beside Sarah's eye.

"There's nothing much wrong with you, chicken," he said, and she tried to reconcile the gentleness of his voice with the thin white lines around the edges of his nostrils and his mouth.

"Yeah. I thought I was breaking into little pieces," she said, and laughed a little, scornfully. His eyes were more gray than blue, she noticed, and knew that he was very angry, but not with her.

After a while he tucked her into her own bed and kissed her good night.

A few minutes later four-year-old Glynis tiptoed into Sarah's room.

"What're you doing here? You're supposed to be asleep," said Sarah, irritated.

"What happened to you, Sarah?"

Sarah felt very old, much, much older than Glynis; even

older, for the moment, than her mother. "A girl beat me up."

"What for?"

"I don't know. She's a stupid girl."

"Is Daddy going to fix her?"

"Sure he is."

"Will I get beat up, when I go to school?"

Glynis had come right up beside Sarah's bed and stood there clutching her hands. She still looked a little like a baby; she was chubby, and there were a lot of things she didn't know about yet.

"I don't know," said Sarah wearily. "I'm the only person I know that it's happened to. Probably not."

Glynis stared at her for another minute. "Daddy'll fix her," she said finally, and went back to bed.

Sarah didn't know what she wanted her father to do. She knew she couldn't ask him to take her to school and pick her up afterward—then she really would be a baby, just as Kelly had said. —

He couldn't go and see the teacher, either. Sarah thought that would probably get her into even more trouble.

It was a very complex problem. As she went to sleep, today was already changing into tomorrow, and she was deeply afraid of tomorrow. She tried to cry, because sometimes crying made her feel better, but she was too frightened to cry. There didn't seem to be anything left in her life, in the whole world, except tomorrow.


Ted came home for lunch the next day. Muriel was not glad to see him. That he should arrive home in the middle of the day was shockingly inappropriate, not to mention completely unnecessary.

"I been looking after your girls for pretty near two years now," she muttered, banging soup cans around in the kitchen cupboard.

"I know, Muriel," said Ted.

"No need for you to be hanging around here," said Muriel, throwing cutlery onto the kitchen table.

"I know there isn't."

"Won't help, having you hang around here," said Muriel, slicing bread viciously.

"Just today," Ted said, and retreated to the front porch to watch for Sarah.

Muriel opened the door and stuck her head outside, frowning. "She won't be here for half an hour yet," she said, and banged the door.

Ted respected Muriel, but had never allowed himself to become fond of her. He did not like to think of her as a permanent, though live-out, addition to the family. He resented Margaret's delight in Muriel's efficiency, and he resented Glynis' love for her. But he respected her. He couldn't help it, because he had to admit that neither of the children appeared to have suffered as a result of Margaret's job, and this was wholly because of Muriel.

He knew, though, that as much as Sarah liked Muriel and felt comfortable with her, that hadn't been enough yesterday and it wouldn't be enough today. It wouldn't be enough ever again; not for him.

He had stood there on the porch in the morning and watched until Sarah was out of sight, a small slim child with yellow hair dressed in jeans and battered sandals and a pink blouse, wearing a cardigan. She had seemed to be trotting along with her usual nonchalance, shoulders straight, head turning so she could look at the front yards she passed. Ted sucked in his breath between his teeth. He wanted badly to go with her. But he hadn't offered, and she hadn't asked; it seemed clear that this was a thing she had to do by herself.

Sarah, fearful and wary, didn't tell anyone at school what had happened to her, and nobody asked her about the bruise on the side of her face, except teachers. She told them she had fallen down. Nobody said anything about the fight in the schoolyard, not even some of the kids in her class who she was pretty sure had watched it.

Kelly ignored her all morning—until they met going out of the school at lunchtime.

Sarah saw her approaching.

She remembered her father watching her from the porch that morning, his hands in his pockets, his shoulders hunched a little. The blue blaze of his eyes had followed her down the sidewalk; it had made her back warm.

She thought, watching Kelly getting nearer, that he must have armed her in some way. She had a superwoman's strength now; she felt it pulsing in the upper parts of her skinny arms; all of her father's strength plus the little bit that was her own.

111

She watched Kelly coming closer and closer.

She would reach down and pick Kelly up by her ankles and swing her up into the air and down, bashing her head against the dirt of the playground, and then she would drape her over her shoulder and march home, maybe with other kids skedaddling behind to watch as she presented Kelly, bruised and bleeding, to her father like a prize.

Kelly came nearer and nearer and Sarah waited, tense and almost eager, for something to tell her when to attack.

Kelly clapped her on the shoulder. "Hi, kid," she said, and sauntered off across the playground, surrounded by a small group of bouncing friends.

Sarah watched her walk away. Then she went home, easily, lithely, strong and painless.

She was excited by the mysteriousness of it all.

Her father was standing on the porch as she approached the house. When he saw her he sat down on the top step.

"Well? How did it go?" he said, smiling.

Sarah saw that he already knew. He must have been momentarily distracted the day before or that Kelly girl would never have been able to get her. Even so, she reminded herself, he had stepped in just in time to end it before Sarah started to cry.

"I don't think she's going to do it any more," said Sarah.

Her father nodded. "You're a brave girl," he said.

"I didn't try to be. I don't even know what you're supposed to do to be brave. Except not cry." She sat down next to him. "There are a lot of things I don't know."

Her father hugged her. "There are a lot of things nobody knows," he said, but Sarah smiled to herself, and didn't believe him.

# Chapter 13

ALMOST IMMEDIATELY AFTER THE INCIDENT IN THE PLAY-
ground Margaret resigned from her job with the public
relations firm, creating considerable bewilderment there.
She said, looking grim and untouchable, only that she had to
leave. She gave them two weeks' notice. It made her sick
with frustration and shame. It also made her furious. Her
anger with Ted, on whom she at first piled the full responsibility for her resignation, had built slowly, having to wait
until his own had subsided, but once under way had gathered
strength until by the time she told her office she was quitting
it was a cold and dreadful thing. She refused, at first, to let
him know that she had succumbed.

He didn't know how to treat her. He had made it clear
what he wanted her to do. Sometimes, away from her and
Sarah, he felt pangs of guilt about having actually seemed to
order her to do something. But he had what he thought were
such good reasons for it, namely the welfare of his children,
that he smothered the guilt until eventually it expired from
lack of nourishment. Then he waited for Margaret to bring
the subject up again. But she didn't. Her behavior was
unusual. She was very quiet around the house, very controlled. She was not interested in making love. Each morning she went off to work as though sailing bravely into

martyrdom. That could mean, he thought busily as he drove off in the mornings, either that she was determined to keep her job despite an unfeeling, selfish husband or that she was going to give up something she deeply enjoyed (God only knew why) on behalf of that same bastard. Ted couldn't help but notice that Sarah had completely recovered from her experience in the playground, and left for school each day quite happily. She had said nothing that might indicate she wished Margaret, instead of Muriel, was puttering around in the kitchen when she got home. He began to feel dismayed, powerless. Of the three of them, it seemed he was the only one who was afraid some other bad thing might happen to his daughter.

As the days left to her at work dwindled to nine, eight, seven, Margaret was shaken by the conviction that she should not have resigned. She was disgusted with herself. Ted had not called the firm and withdrawn her services—she had done that deed herself. There must be more to this than wanting to make Ted feel guilty, she thought—there must be. Maybe she *did* share his belief that she, not Muriel, ought to be home with Glynis, home to greet Sarah. She gnawed over this, trying to concentrate, listening intently for a chime within her head that would signify she had stumbled on a truth. But her mind was quiet. She remained convinced that in this world of working mothers she was not different from the rest, no less deserving of the intangible freedoms, the space to stretch, the pay packet, that work provides.

Defiantly, she told Ted that a week from Friday would be her last day at work. She looked him in the eye as she said it, in the privacy of their bedroom, just before breakfast, and watched for his reaction. First, relief; then, love. She pulled away fastidiously when he made to embrace her. His relief offended her, and she didn't want his love back yet.

On the evening of her first day as an unemployed person Margaret and Ted had a party. They had one every year, on the last Saturday in May, and Margaret usually looked forward to it eagerly. Not this year. But she gathered flowers from the garden and put them in vases throughout the house; prepared the food; and dressed herself for the occasion with rather more care than usual.

"Did I tell you," she said casually to Moira, when everyone had arrived, "that Sarah got beaten up the other day?" She was sitting on the arm of the sofa and swinging her leg, which flashed bare almost to the thigh through the slit in her dress, and working on her second martini.

"My God," said Moira from the sofa. "I would have thought that was something you didn't have to worry about, with girls."

"It was a girl who beat her up."

"At school? Why?"

Margaret shrugged. "Don't know. Sarah doesn't know either. Maybe the kid doesn't like the shoes she wears."

"How is she?"

"Oh, she's fine. Got dirty, mostly. And there was a nosebleed. And a bruise. That's all."

"And how's Ted?"

Margaret looked at her thoughtfully. "I've quit my job," she said.

Moira's brown eyes opened wide. She shook her head, slowly, her black hair swinging gently. "Oh, Margaret. Why do you do such dumb things?"

"I'm hoist on my own petard, Moira," said Margaret dramatically, and finished her drink. "What I'm really dreading is telling Muriel."

"We get what we want, you know," said Moira.

"Jesus, Moira," said Margaret coldly. "You can really piss me off."

Moira shrugged. "That's one of the things friends are for."

"He's coming over here now, I think, Ted is." Margaret turned to Moira, bemused. "Do you think he would have quit the university if *I'd* got beaten up?" She raised her eyebrows. They both thought it over, and bubbled over with sudden laughter.

"What are you two doing over here?" said Ted, slowing uncertainly as he approached. "Come on—mingle."

They laughed harder.

Ted looked bewildered, miserable. Margaret had hardly smiled for two weeks.

She stood up and put her hands on his shoulders, her eyes wet, her face still marked by laughter.

"I can see your whole damn leg in that thing," said Ted.

"I'm going to mingle," said Margaret to Moira, and went off, giggling.

She had a good time for a while, mingling, and refilling drinks. She liked seeing guests enjoying themselves in her house. But gradually she became restless: it was the prospect of Monday morning with no job to go to, she thought.

She became irritated with the people clotted around the fireplace, strewn around the entrance hall, cluttering up the makeshift bar in the dining room, creating a din in every corner of the house. She went into the hall and peered up the stairs, but all seemed quiet up there, the darkness was serene.

As she returned to the living room she saw Jason deep in conversation with somebody from the biology department and what a biologist and a lawyer could possibly have in common she did not know, unless it was racquetball. She watched Jason, whose hair was as gray as the suit he wore. He looked made out of pewter. She had never known what Moira saw in him. But their kids are nice, there must be something there, she sighed.

She went to the kitchen for another drink. "Out of the way, Harry," she said as she opened the refrigerator door and got out the pitcher of martinis.

"Ah, Margaret, where have you been, you glorious thing," he said, beaming at her. She glanced at him wearily, poured her drink, and put the pitcher back in the refrigerator.

"The olives are in the dining room," said Harry. He took her hand and led her in there, speared two olives on a plastic toothpick and dropped them in her glass.

"Such chivalry," said Margaret dryly. She found herself wishing that Harry was attractive. "Where's your wife?" she said to him, stepping back from the dining-room table and bumping into Jason, who was trying to ease his way in. "Sorry," she said, and he smiled, and she thought his gray eyes looked like fog and wondered what he saw with them.

"I feel sadly undereducated," she said, watching Jason, "in the midst of all these academicians."

Harry nodded pityingly. "It must be terrible for you," he said.

"You bastard," said Margaret, laughing.

"I'm not an academician," said Jason, pouring scotch into his glass.

"You're a professional man," said Margaret. "That's almost as bad."

Jason took a drink. "You used to be an actress," he said. "I think that's even worse."

"What do you mean, worse?"

He leaned against the sideboard, pushed aside a bowl of flowers, lifted his hip so as to half sit on it. It was an act of deliberate casualness; Margaret wondered if he behaved that way in a courtroom.

"Academicians think they understand what's happened in the past," said Jason. "Professional men try to deal with what's happening in the present. But 'artists' pretend they know the future."

"That's a gross oversimplification," said Margaret. She didn't understand how she could have gotten so angry so quickly. She smiled at him. "You have a superficial mind."

Jason, also smiling, leaned toward her. "You don't feel undereducated at all, do you?"

He doesn't like me, she thought. And that is quite a different thing from my not liking him, which I had thought was private. She tried to decide whether it made any difference, knowing that Jason didn't like her any more than she liked him.

She wanted to remind him, too, that although she wasn't an "artist" any more, Moira was.

"About my wife," said Harry, turning her around. "Now that's a mournful subject." He took her hand and led her to a corner of the room. "You asked me where my wife is." He looked around furtively. "I think she's going to leave me," he whispered.

"What makes you think so?" said Margaret.

"She said so."

He looked sad, and Margaret thought it only partially an act.

"Why is she going to leave you, Harry?"

"She says I'm too old for her, Margaret. Can you believe that? And me just barely forty, just easing into my prime."

Margaret frowned. "Harry. Are you putting me on?"

"No, no I am not. But if you detect some insincerity in me . . ." He looked at her humbly.

"I do, Harry. I do detect it."

He sighed. "I was getting tired of her anyway. I should never have gotten married. You were right."

"I never told you that. Not even the first time."

"Maybe I just wish somebody had told me." He took her hand and laced his fingers with hers.

"Harry, you can't be so cavalier about marriage."

"We don't find each other attractive any more. I think that's it."

She pulled her hand away.

"Do you find me attractive, Margaret? It does a thing to a man's ego, Margaret," he said, taking her hand back, "when a woman ceases to find him attractive. I'm looking for ego-reinforcement."

"You had girlfriends before and you'll have girlfriends again," said Margaret briskly.

"But not you."

"Don't be ridiculous," said Margaret, smiling, and she pushed past him. The thin strap of her yellow gown began to slip from her shoulder and as she quickly yanked it up she felt disheveled.

She saw Ted across the room explaining something to Jason. She supposed he must be good at it. She had never seen anyone look less than interested. Ted's presence seemed to grip people, whether they agreed with him or not. It was the blue snap of his eyes, she thought, and the harsh, joyous tension in him. She always had trouble, in his presence, remembering what her parents looked like; as though he had scooped up all of her past and held it within him, guarding it for her. Except for Moira, she thought, a flash of triumph.

She tried to see him objectively. Even in summer his skin was fair, almost pale. He bent toward Jason, one foot up on a footstool, one arm leaning on the upthrust knee, his other hand gesturing in the air. Jason stared thoughtfully at the carpet, nodding occasionally. Sometimes he said a sentence or two, hands in his pockets, rocking slightly on his heels. Ted had taken off his jacket and loosened his tie, but Jason was still clad head to toe, counting his pewter hair, in gray. Why the hell didn't he at least wear a brightly colored tie, Margaret fumed, watching. Ted stood up and picked up a glass from the mantelpiece, finished off his drink.

Margaret sighed and pushed back her hair, looking for

118

Moira. Someone smiled and waved at her. She waved back, and headed quickly for the hall and the bathroom there.

She turned on the light, locked the door, and scrutinized herself in the mirror. She cleaned off the makeup smudged beneath her eyes, tidied her hair, and put on more lipstick. Her reflection in the mirror looked unsubstantial, empty. She saw nothing there that suggested energy or purpose. She thought she looked lovely, but extraneous.

Back in the living room a man came up beside her; Joe Schriver, who was single and had come to the department the previous September from someplace in the United States. Margaret smiled at him. "Do you want to help me serve the food?" she said, looking up into his face, which was square and smooth.

"I'd love to," he said, and she took his hand and led him toward the kitchen.

When the food had been brought out and displayed on the dining-room table Margaret floated into the living room and looked for a place to sit.

"Let me get a plate for you," said Joe, taking her arm.

Margaret's body seemed to be straining against her dress. She put her hands on her thighs, as if to hold them in. Joe sat her down in the middle of the sofa and went back to the dining room.

Harry wandered in and settled himself at her feet, a plate of food in his lap, a fresh drink placed carefully on the floor beside him.

"Sit up here, for heaven's sake," said Margaret.

"I'm quite comfortable where I am," said Harry, his mouth already full.

Margaret leaned back, stretched her arms out along the top of the sofa, and closed her eyes.

"Here," said Joe, and she sat up and took a plate from him. He looked at her, and at Harry, and then sat down on the floor on the other side of her.

"For heaven's sake," said Margaret. "This is ridiculous."

Joe smiled up at her. "Eat," he said.

Margaret stared down at them, perplexed and embarrassed. Their heads were bent over the food. The light from the table lamp struck Joe's hair. She reached down to touch it; he turned and smiled at her.

"It's very soft," said Margaret apologetically, and Harry turned, too, and lifted his eyebrows.

Some potato salad clung to Harry's lower lip, making him look particularly reproachful, and Margaret burst out laughing. She laughed very hard, her hand on Harry's shoulder, and soon all three of them were laughing and Margaret felt effervescent and beautiful.

Ted came into the living room with two plates heaped high with cold meats and salads. He looked around for Margaret and saw her immediately, in the middle of the sofa, straight ahead of him. Most of the guests were still in the dining room. She bloomed there, golden-haired and lovely in her long yellow dress, and there were two men sitting at her feet, their faces uplifted to her, the plates on their laps forgotten. Her hand was on Harry's shoulder and her other hand fluttered somewhere near her face. Her head was thrown back and she was laughing. It was an extremely unpleasant sound, one which grated in his ears and made him flinch; there was coquettishness in it, and that jarred him.

He felt like a fool, standing there gawking, holding two plates, like a teenager at a picnic.

What the hell was the matter with her, she was a grown woman, Christ. There was a trembling in his stomach muscles and he realized he was attempting to physically control his anger.

Shit, he thought viciously, and walked back to the dining room to get rid of the plates.

He escaped out through the kitchen into the hall and upstairs, where he sat on the top step in the darkness and stared down into the empty lighted hall and listened for Margaret's laughter. I'm jealous, he thought coldly.

He sat there, hands between his knees, pulling at his fingers. He did not want to go back to the party. He wanted to disassociate himself from Margaret and Harry, Christ, what a goddamn idiot mooning around after her year after year, and from Joe who was much too young for Margaret, Christ. He grabbed his head and banged it a couple of times with the heel of his hand, trying to force some sense into it.

"Daddy?" said Sarah. "What's the matter?"

He looked up, and was struck by the immediacy of her presence. She was wearing pajamas with some kind of pattern all over them, and her hair was messy.

He took her hand and pulled her gently onto the step to sit beside him. He put his arm around her and leaned his head against hers, careful not to lean too hard, because his head was a lot bigger than hers, his neck a lot stronger than hers.

"Nothing, chicken. I've just got a little headache."

"It's very noisy down there," said Sarah. "Is that what gave you a headache?"

"Yeah, I think so."

"Who's down there, anyway?"

"Oh, a lot of people. Most of them you don't know."

"Do I know some of them?"

"Some of them. Moira and Jason. Harry's there." He kissed the bruise on the side of her face, lightly; it had almost disappeared. "There's some ginger ale down there, too," he said. I want to show off my kid, he thought. What's wrong with that?

She smiled up at him happily.

"I suppose if we woke you up," said Ted, "the least I can do is get you some ginger ale." He stood up and held out his hand.

"The party didn't wake me up." She took his hand and started down the stairs with him. "You woke me up. Sitting there."

When they got to the bottom of the stairs he picked her up and carried her through the kitchen and into the dining room.

He got her ginger ale in a glass, with ice cubes, and introduced her to people, enjoying their extravagant compliments and her restrained responses. When he saw that she was becoming uncomfortable he said, "You'd better say good night to your mom and let me get you back to bed."

He led her into the living room, toward the sofa. He was still angry with Margaret and knew that it showed on his face as he approached her, presenting Sarah like an accusation.

Sarah stopped and looked at her mother, amazed. She thought Margaret looked like a flower growing in somebody's garden. She could see one whole leg, although her mother's dress was long to the floor, and the leg looked like a golden stem, and her mother's golden head looked like a blossom. Sarah thought that her mother looked like a beautiful stranger. She was almost afraid to get any closer to her without some signal that her mother remembered her. Margaret was leaning down toward the men who were sitting on the floor, her hands outstretched to them as though she were blessing them, and she seemed to wave in the air as a flower waves when a breeze comes across the garden.

Sarah held on to her father's hand.

Margaret looked up and saw her and the smile on her face changed, grew slowly deeper, and warmer, and it was her mother's smile all right. Sarah was greatly relieved.

"Daddy got me some ginger ale," she said, holding out the glass so suddenly that a bit of the liquid slopped over the edge. She saw her mother look up at her father and didn't understand that look at all. She was intensely curious about it, and uneasy.

"Time for you to get back to bed, young lady," said her father, as if it hadn't been his idea in the first place to bring her down here.

When he tucked her into bed she hugged him and without thinking about it patted him on the back, comfortingly.

He left her door open a little when he went downstairs.

Much later, when all the people had left, saying goodbye and laughing loudly, and the record player had been turned off, she heard the muffled clattering of dishes for a while.

Finally her father came upstairs. She heard his heavy steps, and the squeaking of the banister when he leaned on it. He went into their bedroom, which was next to Sarah's, and after a while her mother came up. Her steps were lighter, she did not lean upon the banister, but her perfume preceded her down the hall. Again the bedroom door opened, and closed.

Sarah turned her face to the wall and strained to hear them, but she couldn't hear very much—only a faint murmuring, and that only when she lifted her head from the pillow so as to listen with both ears. She was uneasy, edgy, waiting to be soothed.

Occasionally the murmuring would take on a deeper tone—then she knew it was her father's voice. But mostly it was her mother's, moving heavy and cloudlike, brushing the other side of the wall.

Her parents' door opened. Sarah closed her eyes and knew when her mother pushed her door open wide and looked in at her. She lay very still, breathing her mother's scent. Then she heard her door being softly closed and when she opened her eyes it was at first pitch black, until the room stopped hoping for the door to be opened again and gradually allowed some light to enter through the window. Sarah never closed the curtains in her room, and when somebody else closed them for her she always got up and opened them again.

She turned over, to be able to see the window, and watched the white curtains draw light from outside and wondered if it was all from the streetlamp or if maybe there was a moon.

She was wondering this, and thinking about her mother, who she knew was now down the hall looking in at Glynis, probably tucking the covers around her, and thinking about that, feeling a little better, when she fell asleep.

In the morning she lay still, collecting the scattered remnants of dreams and tucking them away somewhere where they wouldn't bother her, and when she realized that the house was very quiet she remembered the party, and the strangeness of it, and wondered uneasily if things would be different today than yesterday.

But when it was finally breakfast time and all four of them had gathered around the kitchen table, she looked carefully at the faces of her parents and they were smooth and calm, and when a pair of eyes met hers, the person's face smiled.

# Chapter 14

FOUR YEARS LATER, WHEN SPRING WAS ALMOST SUMMER, Sarah said composedly one morning, "Mother, I really think it's time I had a bra."

Glynis stared, her cereal spoon dripping milk. "What for?" she said.

Sarah ignored her, but her face grew slightly pink.

"Well," said Margaret. "Well."

"Don't be silly," said Ted briskly, and looked at his watch and pushed his chair away from the table. Sarah's face got redder. She looked at him reproachfully. "Nobody turned on the radio this morning," he said.

The toaster popped and Margaret handed slices around. Ted wanted to eat his toast but felt the need to leave. He pulled his chair back up to the table and started buttering.

Immediately he was swept by nostalgia, a sickening lamentation for the loss of a place he'd never been. It was like being wrapped in a sticky, invisible cobweb. Triggered by hot buttered toast. He snorted to himself, slathered marmalade on the toast and took a cautious sniff. Nostalgia can be battled with marmalade, he thought. I must remember that.

"I think you're probably right," said Margaret to Sarah, her voice bumping against Ted's face like a velvet pillow. A dark red one, he thought, and wished fiercely that she'd stop throwing her voice around like that. It always seemed to happen at the wrong moments—no, at moments when I'm most sensitive to it, he reminded himself. Those voices of hers don't work except when I'm receptive, I've been all over that before. Sometimes he participated eagerly, luxuriating in the sensations she produced. But sometimes he was irritated—little scrapes on his psyche made more painful.

Glynis was giggling into her toast.

"Eat your breakfast," said Ted sharply. "You're going to be late for school." He got up and went upstairs to brush his teeth.

"What's the matter with him?" said Glynis.

"Nothing's the matter with him," said Margaret.

"He probably had a bad dream," said Sarah sympathetically.

That afternoon Margaret went over to see Moira, who still lived in West Vancouver but in a bigger house, on a hillside from which she could see the outer harbor. There was often a lot of low cloud there, and at certain times of the year a lot of fog. But when the skies were clear and the sun shone on the inlet, on Point Grey thrusting west, on Stanley Park, a mass of dark green leading north to the arched sweep of the Lions Gate Bridge, Moira would stare from her windows wondering if it was all real.

Margaret drove through the park, where in spring hundreds of daffodils waved in the breeze on either side of the causeway, and across the bridge, three lanes wide and a bottleneck in the rush hour; and as she drove she thought about all the bits of her past that littered this city. She knew they were still around. She caught glimpses of them sometimes, not with her eyes, but with some part of her which felt, rather than saw. There were a lot of separate things in the world which every now and then seemed to thwack together—only to spring lithely apart again, releasing bubbles of clear laughter. Margaret thought that anything in the world which moved, however imperceptibly, had this tendency, and that included among them were things that could not be seen.

It was only weeks ago that Sarah had summoned her into

the bathroom, and she had knelt in front of her daughter and had seen on the cushion between her thighs a short straight businesslike line of soft but bristly-looking fuzz. Maybe newborn porcupines look something like that, she thought, and had wanted to reach over and brush it off, so sure was she for a second or two that Sarah had gotten something mysteriously stuck to that plump firm triangle.

She had stood up abruptly, blood churning back into her legs, which had been holding their muscled breath.

"That's what it is, isn't it, Mom?" said Sarah, casualness barely covering her excitement.

"Guess so," said Margaret.

"I'm starting to become a woman," said Sarah with a flustered laugh, putting on the quilted robe that came half-way up her legs and was too short in the sleeves, too.

And now a bra.

Margaret shook her head, still gently incredulous, and in the car remembered that as her eyes had swept upward from Sarah's triangle they had caught and stumbled on her swelling breasts.

In Moira's living room she said thoughtfully, "Do you remember when you first started wearing a bra?"

Moira thought. "No," she said, surprised. "My God, I don't."

"I don't, either. And I've been trying. I don't remember when hair started to grow on me—you know—either."

Moira continued to look blank. "My God. Neither do I."

"You'd think that kind of thing would be so important we'd never forget," said Margaret. "I remember when I started to menstruate."

Moira began to laugh. "I do, too. I remember being closeted inside one of the stalls in the girls' washroom, with a Tampax, trying so frantically to shove it in. I couldn't understand why other kids could get them in, but I couldn't. You remember Annette and Billie?" Margaret nodded, smiling. "They stood outside the door, giving me directions. But it was no good; I couldn't do it. I don't remember anybody laughing about it, either. We were so grim."

"I didn't know you did that," said Margaret. "You never told me about that."

"I knew you didn't use Tampax either. I needed help from an expert."

Sunshine billowed into the room so strong, so golden, that Margaret was surprised that the curtains hung limply, sleepily by the windows and didn't thrust themselves forward over the billows of light, fluttering on the light, turning themselves over and over to catch the light on their every surface.

Moira served them coffee in cups, with saucers, and the sunshine flicked on the cups and saucers with bright translucent fingers.

"Sarah's about to start wearing a bra," said Margaret, and heard, saw, her voice bloom in the light like exotic flowers. "She seems awfully young for that. I'm sure I didn't need one when I was twelve."

"I didn't think kids did that any more," said Moira, pouring more coffee from a silver pot she had loved when a child, scorned as a teenager, and sweetly demanded from her mother as soon as she got married.

"I think they give them up later, once they've become casual about them," said Margaret, and they giggled.

"I think having girls makes you feel older faster than having boys," said Margaret, sighing.

"I doubt it," said Moira, amused.

"Do you worry about getting old?"

"No time for that." Moira grinned. She rubbed her hands together in a mild parody of eagerness. "I'm counting the years until the kids leave home. Now that's freedom."

"But freedom from what?" said Margaret.

The afternoon seemed serenely haunted, ghosts of the two of them scampering soundlessly, invisibly, in the trees behind Moira's house. Margaret imagined them sitting, all grown up, in an earlier era; they would have been two ladies in a summer garden, sitting in wooden swings, one in each, facing each other, the swings shaded by fringed canvas, ladies' stockinged legs beneath frilly flowered skirts, pushing themselves delicately back and forth with slippered feet.

"Jesus, Maggie," said Moira, disgusted, and she put a sneaker-clad foot up on the coffee table. "Not freedom *from,* freedom *for.* For doing whatever you want to do."

Margaret remembered the day in Grade Ten when Moira had gotten a C in an art class assignment. She had been furious, outraged, and had torn up the paper violently and sworn that the teacher didn't know his ass from a hole in the ground. It was then that Margaret realized how seriously Moira took this painting business.

"Well, for Christ's sake," said Moira, "you know what I mean, sitting there with a smirk all over your face." She sat up and leaned toward Margaret. "And what are you doing, may I ask, wasting your time keeping your house clean?"

Margaret examined her. There was some gray in her hair, which still swept down from a center part, thick and usually shining, to curl under slightly just above her shoulders. She was stouter, but the bones in her face were both definite and delicate. It was always hard to look below Moira's face, because all the good things about her were concentrated there.

"Obviously," said Margaret, "I do what I want to do. You've told me that. We do what we want to do."

Moira nodded. "You really should give some thought to it, though. To what you're going to do when your kids leave home."

"For heaven's sake, Moira, that's years away."

"But how many? I mean, I figure you count them gone once they leave high school. Even if they go on to university, by that time they're positively elderly and even if they keep on living at home they won't let you muck about in their affairs even if you want to. God forbid you should."

"Well, that's years. Five more for Sarah, nine for Glynis, for God's sake."

"Jesus," said Moira, subdued. "That long?" She shrugged. "Still, Maggie. It's going to happen."

"Yeah, well, I'll think about it when I can at least see it coming around the corner, if you don't mind."

Moira sighed, and poured more coffee. "Jamie's starting to phone girls," she said, speaking of her elder son. She grinned. "He asks them about homework. Next year he'll be asking them out."

Margaret sat very still, holding her coffee cup in mid-air. "My God," she said. "Really?"

"How do you think Ted's going to react when boys start calling Sarah?" said Moira.

"I don't know," said Margaret slowly. "I've thought about it. But not much." She put the cup down on its saucer. "Do you remember those Jolly Jumper things we had for our kids?"

"Yeah. Why?"

"Sarah used to sort of hang in it, and she'd poke her toes at the floor and bob up and down like a toy boat in a bathtub, dreaming. And after three or four minutes she'd start to frown, and hold out her arms to be taken out of it. Glynis, though . . . Glynis pounded up and down in it, shrieking, grinning all over her face . . ."

"What's the point of this tale, Maggie?" said Moira, smiling. She was very fond of Glynis.

Margaret looked at her. "I don't know. They're so different. I guess that's the point."

"Do you like one of them better than the other?"

"Is that a serious question?"

"Sure."

"I take it you figure that since Ted likes Sarah better, I must like Glynis better?"

"I don't think it's that simple."

"Good. Neither do I. Do you like one of your kids better?"

Moira pondered. "No. I like them differently. *Love* them differently."

"Right," said Margaret.

Moira grinned at her.

"I don't even think," said Margaret, reaching to touch the silver coffeepot with the tips of her fingers, "that Ted loves Sarah more than Glynis. Not really." She sat back and looked at Moira. "But there is certainly something—special between them."

"Are you jealous?"

The sunlight in the room was something joyous and strong, but although it would drench her in warmth and even comfort if she were to move to stand or sit directly within it, Margaret knew that its caresses were impersonal, intimate but uncaring. It is that which I must learn to love about the sun, she thought, and answered Moira: "Yes. I guess I am. But I don't know which one of them I'm jealous of."

That night Margaret and Ted went for a drive. They waved Glynis and Sarah off to a field to play baseball and got in the car and rolled down the windows and drove off.

They talked about going all the way out to Haney to see Margaret's parents, but that was too far.

129

They drove slowly, aimlessly, past Kitsilano Beach and Ted decided he wanted to do a tour of Stanley Park, so they went there. The fountain blew crystal high into the warm May evening and the park wrapped cool shady arms around them. When they had made the circle and come out at English Bay, they stopped to buy popcorn from one of the streetside vendors whose reappearance each year marked the start of summer.

Elderly men were lawn bowling across the street, the grass on which they played like black velvet where tree shadows lay. The beach was crowded with people, mostly kids. The air was filled with the scents of grass, and the sea, and popcorn, and vinegary fish and chips. Laughter floated from the sand and people shouted to one another and the traffic was heavy, the sounds of it often driving everything else away, so that the people on the beach seemed to be laughing and shouting noiselessly.

They got back in the car and Ted turned up Georgia Street. The day had begun its slow slide toward death, but what does a day care about that, Ted thought, and his body felt suddenly heavier. It just gets chased around the earth, it never really dies at all.

The car plodded along, stopping for red lights and carefree careless summer-drunk pedestrians, and as they got to Granville Street, where the tree-lined mall packed with movie theaters and restaurants sailed north and south, Margaret said, "When are we going to let Sarah go out with boys?" Her voice was an extension of the gathering warmth and long-lit days of summer.

Ted thought his lungs had stopped pumping, and he thought how odd it was that every part of his body took such an intense interest in conversation. Then his lungs gave a little ache and resumed their work.

He looked at Margaret sharply, shards of words in his mouth, ready to spit them into her neck. He was shocked by his reaction, and soothed by her face, which wore only contentment; there was perhaps a trace of something else in the droop of her shoulders.

He could ignore it, of course. He could pretend not to have understood.

"The kid's off playing baseball in a pair of dirty shorts," he said, and was pleased at the calm in his voice.

130

. . . and he remembered holding a bat huge in his hands, watching the ball plummet through buzzing summer air, lopsided soft-sided bat becoming a toothpick; crouched like a panther, he could feel it again, there at the makeshift home plate, swinging your toothpick, throwing yourself into the curve, the jar in the arms as the wood thwacks against leather; you drop the bat and pelt toward first base and you hear the skinny kid with braids and pretty eyes shrilling "Good hit!"—you land, panting, on first base, rest palms on knees slightly bent, breathe dust, feel it settle into the sweat on your face; and you wish you'd hit the ball hard enough to have made it all the way around, to see her jumping up and down, braids bouncing, as you slid gracefully into home plate . . .

"Don't be silly, Margaret," he said calmly. "There's no need to make decisions about things like that."

The pigtailed kid had sat three rows ahead of him. But after Grade Six he had never seen her again.

# Chapter 15

SARAH AND HER FAMILY SPENT PART OF EVERY SUMMER with her father's parents in Kelowna—not the largest of the towns in the Okanagan Valley, but certainly one of the prettiest. It had streets where matronly houses sat comfortably in big, bushy yards; and lots of tall old trees, whose leaves made green swishing sounds in the wind and cast great cool shadows. And right at the town's edge, the lake began. In the hot sunlight it was the color of ink. When Sarah was much younger, she had thought if she stayed in swimming long enough she'd come out dyed blue all over.

Sarah's grandmother didn't go to the lake in the summertime, because she said there were too many tourists around. She spent July and August tending her vegetable garden.

"She's talking to herself again, look at her," said Sarah, the summer she was fourteen. "She's crazy."

"You're just mad because she told me to pick the peas," said Glynis.

"I don't care about the damn peas. Mumbling away out there. It's embarrassing."

Glynis dragged the roaster out from the bottom cupboard in her grandmother's kitchen and went outside, letting the screen door bang behind her.

"Hi, Grandma," she said. "I'm going to pick the peas now." She lugged the roaster over to the vegetable garden and hunkered down.

"Make sure you put as many in that pan as you put in your stomach," said Kathleen. She straightened, groaning, digging her hands into the small of her back. The thick knot of gray hair pinned on top of her head was loosening, letting little tendrils fall around her neck. Glynis thought she looked hot out in the sun in her black dress, but then there was a lot of her, and the bigger you are, the hotter you get, probably. Certainly it always got a lot hotter in Kelowna than it ever did in Vancouver, too.

Glynis shut her eyes and threw her face toward the sun for a minute, letting it beat down on her. It was so strong it felt like it could melt her eyelids. She lowered her head and opened her eyes and blinked them rapidly when she heard the screen door slam; her grandmother had gone into the house. Glynis settled down to pick peas.

"And what are you doing here, young lady?" said Kathleen, panting slightly, as she came into the kitchen.

"Just sitting and thinking, Grandma," said Sarah.

"From the look of you it's not producing much. You've got sulk written all over your face."

"I'm not sulking, Grandma," said Sarah, mildly indignant.

Kathleen came closer. "What's that you've got all over your eyes?" she said, peering into Sarah's face.

"It's eye makeup, Grandma," said Sarah, flushing. Kathleen stood back and observed her. "I'm fourteen now," said Sarah, but that didn't seem to make much impression on her grandmother. Sarah could practically hear all the things Kathleen was thinking, but Kathleen said none of them, just shook her head and went over to the sink and turned on both taps full blast.

Sometimes Sarah thought her grandmother didn't like her much. But then Kathleen would do something or say something completely unexpected and Sarah would feel sure that her grandmother loved her a lot.

"And where's your dad, then?" said Kathleen, scrubbing her hands in the kitchen sink.

"I'm waiting for him. We're going to buy Grandpa his birthday present."

Kathleen turned off the water and shook her hands over the sink before drying them on a tea towel.

"You know. The electric lawn mower. Because you said you didn't want to look out one day and find him keeled over between the roses and the tomatoes," said Sarah, smiling. She stood up and went off to find Ted.

Half an hour later Kathleen was chopping up vegetables to put in a stew when Glynis came inside.

"Give me that roaster. Good Lord, child, you haven't the sense of an ant, out in that sun without a hat. Here, sit down, your face is as red as a ripe tomato. I'll get you some iced tea. Lord, I haven't the brains to rub together myself, seeing you out there it didn't even click; you never do wear a hat unless someone shoves it on your head."

She brought Glynis a glass of iced tea and wet a washcloth and wiped her forehead. "Sweat all over you and you'll have a burn sure as shooting."

"My face was down, I was picking peas. The sun only shone on my back and I've a blouse on." Glynis laughed. "Listen to me, Grandma; I'm sounding like you."

"You've a good ear, going to be an actress like your mother was, I wouldn't be surprised."

"I never thought of that, Grandma."

"Don't let me be putting ideas into your head, now. Better you should be a doctor or a garage mechanic, when you think about it. There. Now sit there, don't move for a while."

"I'll shell the peas, okay?"

"All right, though it doesn't seem fair, since you did the work of picking them."

"Picking them isn't work. Picking them's fun. But shelling them's fun, too. I like the way they sound when you crack them open, and I like the sound of them falling into the pan, too."

Kathleen went back to the counter and banged away with a big knife at carrots and potatoes on the cutting board, as Glynis shelled peas.

"Where's everybody, Grandma?"

"Your mother's lying down, she's got a headache, and Sarah and Teddy are out shopping, and your grandfather, he's sitting out on the front porch like he always does this time of day."

"What are Daddy and Sarah shopping for?"

"Oh, I think I forget; that is, I think she told me, but I forget."

The big knife banged against the cutting board, peas fell with hollow pinging sounds into the big pot Kathleen had given to Glynis.

"It must have been sort of interesting for Daddy, with no other kids around. How come you only wanted one kid, Grandma?"

"Oh, the Lord knows I would have liked a whole stack of kids" (thwack), "a whole big batch of kids" (thwack), "a whole huge herd of kids," said Kathleen. She turned to smile at Glynis. "That's what I would have liked. But it wasn't to be, no, one was my limit, the Good Lord decided. But at least I got a couple of grandchildren out of the one I had." She scooped up vegetables and dropped them into a pot.

"Are you going to put some of my peas in there?"

"Not yet, they don't need the cooking that carrots and potatoes do. But later, yes. You ask your father, someday, what it was like to be the only child. I've a feeling he'll tell you it wasn't all that interesting."

"But he could have you to himself whenever he liked."

"Yes, and sometimes there was a bit too much of us, all concentrated on Teddy. Sometimes he must have felt kind of smothered, I think."

"Grandma, how come you're making a stew on such a hot day?"

"The weather has to get a lot hotter than this before I'll not turn my stove on."

"How hot?"

"One hundred degrees hot."

"Celsius?"

"Celsius! I don't speak in Celsius." She sat at the table. "I'll help you."

Glynis shoved the roaster and the big pot into the middle of the table. The peas fell steadily and the sound they made was shallower now as they fell on top of each other instead of plunking against the bottom of the pot, making echoes.

"I know what they went to buy," said Glynis.

Kathleen kept on working, snapping open the pods, scooping out the peas, dropping them into the pot.

"They went out to buy Grandpa's birthday present," said

Glynis. Kathleen didn't say anything. "We were supposed to do it all together, the four of us." Snap, scoop, and more peas rained into the pot. "I know what they're buying, too. We decided it together. And we were supposed to buy it together." Glynis dropped an empty pod into the big paper bag on the floor and put her hands flat on the table. "He's always leaving me out. He forgets about me when I'm not standing right in front of him. And even then I don't think he sees me very well."

Kathleen reached across the table and took her hand. "Come around here. Come on." Glynis got up and went around the table. Kathleen took her on her lap. "Look at you, ten years old and so big you can't cuddle properly any more. Squeeze yourself down a bit, there, put your head on my shoulder." She rocked Glynis back and forth. "Your dad," she said after a while, "he doesn't appreciate you yet, lovey, like the rest of us do. But he will. One day he'll look at you and his mouth will just fall open, and he'll see you shining there in front of him and he'll say, how could I have not seen that before today, Glynis just a-gleaming away there. And you must frown at him, then, and shake your finger, and you say, I don't know how you could not have seen me, Daddy, when I've been right here all the time."

"How long do you think it'll take before he sees me like that?"

"It might be tomorrow, it might be Christmas morning, and then again you might have to wait until you're all grown up with children of your own. Your dad's a quick learner at some things, but other things . . ."

"Why should I be one of those other things?"

"Maybe he thought since he was the only child in this house, there was going to be only one in his own, too. And maybe when you came he was so surprised that he hasn't got used to the idea yet. Maybe every time he looks at you he thinks, well, that lovely child, it can't be mine, because I was only supposed to have one of them."

"Maybe he thinks he doesn't need me, because he's got Sarah."

"Don't be daft, child," said Kathleen. "We all of us need you. Including him. Now jump up and let's finish off these peas."

*     *     *

The next afternoon Glynis sat on the edge of her grandparents' back lawn and wrote in the dried earth of the flower bed with a twig. Sarah watched her impatiently, sitting on the edge of the porch and swinging her legs.

"Well, don't sulk about it," said Sarah. "For heaven's sake, it's a fact of life. I'm older than you, there's no point in saying I want to play with you when I don't. I'm too old to play any more anyway. You should play with kids your own age. Go call on that kid down the street."

Glynis continued to write in the dust, head between her freckled knees, brown hair falling over her face. "He likes you better than me," she said finally, her words muffled because her chin was pressed against one of her knees.

Sarah's legs stopped swinging and a ruthless light went on in a dusty windowless closed-off room in her heart. "Who does?"

"Daddy does."

"Don't be ridiculous, Glynis, what has that got to do with anything?" Her tongue had tripped, fallen into a hollow in her mouth. "You're imagining things, as usual, your imagination will be the death of you, Glynis, believe me."

Glynis kept scrabbling slowly in the dust with the twig. "I've been thinking about it," she said. "If they had to get rid of one of us, like people drop off dogs and cats by the side of the road in the country because they don't want to look after them, if they had to get rid of one of us like that, then Mommy would want to drop you off and Dad would want to drop me off. They'd have an awful fight about it." She turned her head to look up at Sarah, sunlight in her eyes, hiding their color. "So it doesn't really matter. It's all fair. Mom likes me better. That's only fair." She jumped up and rubbed out the writing in the dust with jerky industrious movements of her sneakered feet.

"Glynis, you're crazy, do you know that? You're totally, absolutely crazy. They can't like one of us more than the other. That's not the way parents are."

Glynis hauled up from the grass an old bike which had been Ted's, and which was dragged out of the garage every time she and Sarah came to visit. She got on it and pedaled down the driveway.

"Glynis! Glynis, you're stupid, do you know that? Stupid!!"

# Chapter 16

ON A DAY THAT SAME SUMMER, AFTER THEY HAD COME home from Kelowna, Ted slumped in a lawn chair on the patio, a straw hat over his eyes. His legs were sprawled out in front of him, his feet in grubby white sneakers. His jeans were dirty and his long-sleeved shirt felt sticky.

Margaret came outside. He winced when the screen door banged, but didn't sit up.

"Why don't you go put on some shorts and a T-shirt or something?" she said, the words separate little hisses of exasperation.

He squinted out from under his hat. "Don't want to," he said. He liked the way she looked in summer clothes, her legs and arms and feet bare and brown. But he shrank from the thought of having the sun touch him that intimately. Sometimes he thought he was happiest in the rain.

"I don't understand how you can mow the lawn on a day like this, all covered up like that."

"I've finished the lawn," he said, settling the hat more firmly over his eyes. He could feel her standing there, getting more exasperated still. He opened his eyes. The straw let in needles of golden light. He slitted his eyes and the light got fuzzy, his sight was shot through with golden streaks going every which way.

Suddenly the hat was wrenched from his face. "What the hell do you think you're doing?" he said, outraged, feeling as though all the clothes had been ripped from him. He sat up and smoothed his hair, sullen.

"You ought to lose some weight," said Margaret from behind her sunglasses.

Ted looked down at himself, flustered.

"Are you going to tell Sarah about the trip? Mom and Dad want to know whether she's going or not."

"I'll tell her." Of course he would tell her. He had to, in order to give her the present.

He refused to let himself pull in his stomach. He slumped down in the chair, resting his head against its metal frame. He found himself looking up into the branches of the dogwood tree at the side of the house. Ted didn't like dogwood trees. He thought the flowers looked artificial, and imagined the provincial government hiring platoons of the seasonally unemployed every spring and fall to creep about in the dark of night and paste wax flowers on the branches of the dogwood trees.

"I'm going to the beach with Moira," said Margaret. She tossed his hat into his lap. "Glynis is coming with me."

"Go ahead," said Ted. "We'll find something to keep us busy."

Glynis came barreling out the back door to throw her arms around Ted and kiss him on the cheek.

"Have a good time," he said to her, smiling. She was a chunky, spunky little person who scraped her knees on her days instead of floating through them, serene and confident, like her sister.

"But wear a hat!" he called after her.

A minute later he heard the car drive away.

He settled back in the chair and covered his face again with the hat. He listened, in the shade, to the summer. A breeze occasionally rustled the leaves of the maple tree behind him; it sounded like someone quietly turning the pages of a book. He wondered where Sarah had gotten to. A bee hummed to itself. In the yard next door a sprinkler spat into life. Jesus, thought Ted, what a stupid time of day to water the goddamn garden. He congratulated himself again for having cut the lawn while the day was still reasonably cool.

He was beginning to feel uncomfortable, sprawled in the chair. Restlessness, a familiar sensation, was gathering inside him. He counted it as an affliction. It was a physical sense of dissatisfaction with the present moment; a faint lurching, a mild churning; and it could be dispelled only by redirecting his energies. He had gotten into the habit of compiling lists in his head of purposeful things to do, so that when the restlessness stirred and his limbs wouldn't stay still he would have something with which to fight it.

Now that they had a bit more money, he had discovered that buying gifts was a particularly satisfying way of dealing with his affliction. In addition to Christmas and birthdays there was a plethora of occasions which demanded presents. This gave him pleasure. He was a generous man who delighted in other people's happiness, especially when he was the cause of it. He could snap into furious action at the thought of buying gifts, and spend half a day shopping for one present.

He lifted his hat and looked around, then sat up and called Sarah a couple of times but nobody appeared. He slumped back down in his chair.

Now and then he deliberately refused to jump up and find himself something to do when the unpleasant sensations clutched at him. He had never managed to last more than ten or fifteen minutes. The churning in his stomach would spread to his limbs and it was impossible for him to sit or lie still. There was no pain, but his arms and legs seemed to see pins and needles coming at them out of nowhere and would want to jerk to get out of the way.

He had always had this problem, but it had gotten worse in the last couple of years. Sometimes he would consider getting into tennis or racquetball; Margaret was right, he could stand to lose some weight, and vigorous exercise should accomplish this and drain off his excess energy as well. But he had never played any games, except soccer in high school, and he couldn't see himself learning one now.

So he usually kept "to do" lists ready in his head, and when the restlessness began creeping up on him one of the lists would come immediately into focus. He would run his eye up to the top of it and whatever was written there, in his own spidery handwriting, would appear as though in neon lights, and he would jump up and take care of it.

And here he was on this Saturday morning in July, caught flatfooted, the sounds of summer dull in his ears, the rebellious churning beginning somewhere in the middle of him. He swept his hat from his head with a sigh—and found himself looking into Sarah's face.

"Where'd you come from?" he said, astonished.

She was squatting in front of him, her hands around her bare knees, her long, thick, honey-colored hair tied back in a ponytail. "The back gate," she said, and at least her smile was still unchanged. "What are you going to do today?" she said, hugging her knees.

She very much resembled her mother, except for her blue eyes. And yet sometimes when Ted looked at her it was as though he were looking into a pond at his own reflection. Her life, he thought, will be a structure of crystal, spun from her clear bright mind.

"I don't know," he said. "First, I have to talk to you about something."

Sarah sat in a chair opposite him. "What?"

"Your grandparents are going to Arizona and New Mexico next month. For the whole month. They want you to go with them. Your Kennedy grandparents," he added, unnecessarily.

Sarah had never been there. But it meant rolling grasslands with horses running free, tossing their manes and whinnying into the wind; and it meant mountains rearing up in the distance, and blue skies without a cloud in them.

"Just me?"

Ted nodded. "They said next time they go someplace they'll take Glynis."

"Daddy," said Sarah, shaking her head, "this is terrible. I want to go so badly."

"Then you should go, chicken."

"But I can't, I can't go. I don't want to go." There were tears in her eyes. "I guess I'm a coward, eh?"

"That's the dumbest thing I ever heard," he said, smiling. "Remember when you had your tooth pulled?"

Sarah shuddered.

"Remember when you were a little kid, and that other little kid beat you up?"

"She was no little kid, Dad. She probably dropped out of school to become a lady wrestler." She looked at him intently. "Lots of kids *do* go away for the summer, you know."

"I know."

"Grandpa said when we were there last week that I can go up to Kelowna by myself next summer and stay with them and work in the store. I'd love to work in the store, Dad. I think it'd be terrific to write out sales slips and work the cash register. I love the way it smells in there, the paper, and the dust, and the way the floor squeaks, and I love to see all the stationery and stuff lined up on the shelves. If Grandpa's store was in Vancouver I'd be terribly happy. I didn't tell him this, but I could never go up there to Kelowna to do it. I couldn't stand to be away from home."

"That's all right, chicken."

"It's a pretty hard thing to understand, though, really. Nobody else I know seems to mind going away from home for a while."

"I do. Every time I have to go away, I can hardly wait to get back. I'm glad I don't have to do it very often."

"But you *do* it, Daddy, see what I mean? You *do* it, even though you don't like it." She leaned back in the chair and folded her arms in front of her. "I'm not going to do it. I'm not going with them."

"And nobody wants to make you. Eventually you'll want to go away from home—everybody does."

"I can't imagine that," said Sarah, shaking her head. "I know it's probably true, but I can't imagine it."

"I know you can't. But it'll happen. I hope it doesn't happen for years and years, though. I like having you around."

"It'll be years and years, all right," said Sarah grimly. "I'll probably still be here when you're ninety-two."

"Meanwhile," said Ted, "I find myself in a quandary."

"What quandary?" said Sarah gloomily, staring at the broken sandal on her right foot.

"Well, I didn't know whether you'd decide to go or not, and just on the off chance that you would, I thought you ought to have something to take with you, to remind you of us."

"You bought me a going-away present," said Sarah in dismay.

"You could call it that, I guess."

"Oh, Daddy, you thought I should go!" She started to cry.

Ted got up and went over to kneel beside her chair. He put an arm around her, hugged her head to his shoulder. "I don't know what I thought you should do, Sarah. I just know that I hoped you wouldn't go. That's why I bought it, I think. If that makes any sense."

He stood up and pulled her to her feet. "I don't see any point in saving it for Christmas, or your birthday, so come on inside and I'll give it to you now."

"But I haven't earned it," she protested, following him into the house. "I'm not going anywhere."

"You don't earn presents, Sarah," he said in the hall, turning to her at the bottom of the stairs. "Go on into the living room. Go on," he said, and smiled at her.

She waited by the front window and when he came down he thrust a small dark blue box into her hands.

"What is it?" she said, taking off the lid. She lifted the layer of cotton and underneath, lying on more cotton, was a locket. Inside was a picture of her mother holding Glynis as a baby on one side, and a picture of her father on the other. Set into the front of the locket was a red stone.

"Oh, Daddy, it's beautiful!" She pointed to the stone. "What's this?"

"It's a garnet," he said.

"Oh, Daddy, it's so beautiful." She held it up and away from her, and the red stone burned in the sunlight, and Sarah put on the locket and told herself that she would never take it off.

# PART III

# Chapter 17

SARAH WAS CERTAIN OF ONLY A COUPLE OF THINGS: HER father was dead, and because he was who he was, his curiosity about the new situation in which he found himself must be intense and would keep him fully occupied for years and years.

Yet—she *felt* something. It had forced itself into her consciousness the day he was buried and had been growing stronger ever since. She had many conversations with herself, usually at bedtime, trying to figure it out. At the end of each conversation she came to the same conclusion: she felt some completely unsupportable responsibility for his death, and this was making her unwilling, in the deepest part of her, to accept the fact that his death had occurred. Sarah thought that having figured this out so rationally ought to have solved her problem. No psychiatrist could have done a better job on her, she thought, than the job she had done on herself. She had been very proud. But it hadn't worked. She still sensed something; a presence—unseeable, untouchable, but there.

She knew it had something to do with her father, partly because she couldn't imagine what else it could have anything to do with, but mostly because it *felt* like her father. The awful thing was that she couldn't tell whether it was sorrowful or angry or loving or what. It was just there, hanging invisibly in the air, maybe standing on invisible feet, how should she know, but she knew it was there.

She didn't know why, though. And that was frightening.

Sarah also realized that it wasn't there at all, of course. She knew it was the creation of her guilt. This was extremely unsettling, since she had always understood that if you identified your demons, and faced them, they would disappear. She was not in any way responsible for her father's death, but she understood why she *felt* responsible, and she accepted that. Why, then, when she was willing to recognize her guilt and let it into her life, did it torment her in this way? She could be very rational about the whole business, most of the time, and it was unfair that even so, she could not make the presence disappear.

She thought it might be easier to accomplish this if she made a change in her life. Only small changes were possible, now that the most unimaginably large one of all had occurred, so one rainy Saturday in April she knocked softly on Glynis' door.

"Who is it?"

"It's me. Can I come in?" She opened the door. "I was wondering if you'd like to trade rooms."

Glynis was lying on her back on the bed, arms crossed behind her head. She was wearing very tight, dirty jeans and a purple T-shirt. "What's so hot about my room that you want it all of a sudden?"

Sarah sat in the chair at Glynis' desk, which was piled high with library books and notes to herself and ballpoint pens with parts of them missing.

"I'm really tired," Sarah said, and pushed things out of the way so she could lean an elbow on the desk and prop her head on her fist. "There's nothing so hot about your room, believe me," she said dryly, looking around at dirty clothes in heaps on the floor and a bedraggled plant hanging in front of the window; the walls were plastered with ABBA posters and pictures. "I just thought you might like to have mine."

Glynis eyed her suspiciously. "You moving out or something?"

Sarah was startled. "I don't think so. No. Why would I move out? Where would I go?"

Glynis shrugged and sat up. "I couldn't think of any other reason you'd be offering me your room."

"I like to think of you sitting in that window seat keeping an eye on the neighborhood, that's all," said Sarah, and as she said it, it became true.

"You've got an awful lot of stuff," said Glynis. She bent over to scratch at a dirty spot on one knee of her jeans. "It wouldn't fit in here."

"You'll never get that off that way. Those things should be in the laundry."

Glynis pushed herself back on the bed until she was leaning against the headboard. "What would you do with all your stuff?"

"There's not much that's really important to me. Maybe I could leave my bookcase in there."

Glynis reached over to pull the curtain back from her window. "Maybe I'd miss my room." She let the curtain drop and turned back to her sister. "Sarah? How long is all this going to last, do you think?"

Glynis had on the floor beside her bed a small rug made of scraps of cloth. Sarah thought she could identify in it clothes she had worn when she still outgrew things. Surely that wink of blue and white was the polka-dot dress she had worn to the beach so often; and the splotches of pink must be the taffeta dress with the ruffles; and there was yellow in there, too, probably from the blouse that had been her favorite when she was twelve because her father had said she looked like a daffodil in it.

It would be good to be able to sink into the normalcy of grief.

"It won't last forever," she told Glynis. "It will change, and just kind of become part of everything else."

But there was more to it than grief, for Sarah, and she could not imagine that it would ever become part of everything else. It was alien, even though she knew she had created it herself, without meaning to.

She was cold, and rubbed her arms.

"I miss him a lot, Sarah. I used to think mean things, awful things about him sometimes. I used to get so mad at him sometimes. And now I miss him a lot. It really hurts me, Sarah, and he won't ever come back, so does that mean it won't ever stop hurting? I don't think it will, and that scares me." Glynis was sitting stiff and straight on the edge of her bed.

Sarah sat beside her and put an arm around her. The feel of Glynis' body next to hers, embraced by her arm, was strange and pleasant. She was strong and stocky, threatening to become voluptuous.

"It'll have to stop hurting, Glynnie. People couldn't stand it forever. I read somewhere that it takes a while, but gradually you start not to hurt, and you remember the person who's died and you smile about him. But right now it's too early, that's all."

She knew that what she had said was true, for Glynis, and probably for her mother. But it wasn't quite true for Sarah, and she wondered how things were going to turn out.

Glynis was crying. Sarah wiped her face with the bottom of a blouse she picked up off the floor, and moved back on the bed to lean against the wall, pulling Glynis with her. They leaned side by side against the wall, Sarah's arm around her sister and Glynis' head resting heavily against Sarah's shoulder.

There was a rap on the door. Sarah climbed off the bed, her knees and hands suddenly trembling. My God, she thought, I didn't think it would knock on doors.

"Who is it?" said Glynis.

"It's me," said Margaret. "Who did you think it was?"

As Margaret came in, Sarah dropped into Glynis' desk chair. She couldn't make her hands stop trembling. For God's sake, she scolded herself, whatever it is, it is not a goddamned door-knocking *ghost*.

"You better go in the bathroom and wash your face and brush your hair," Margaret said to Glynis. "We're going out for dinner."

"Where to?"

"Maybe we'll have fish and chips. Nothing fancy."

"Can I wear my jeans?"

"Yes, you can wear your jeans. Go, now; go. Wash your face."

Margaret sat on the edge of the bed, facing Sarah.

"I told Glynnie she can have my room," said Sarah. "We can switch tomorrow, okay?"

"That's generous of you. Do you think you can fit in here, you and all your belongings?"

"I like the idea of having a smaller room. And Glynis likes the window seat."

"So do you."

"Yeah, but I've had it for a long time now. I don't need it any more."

Margaret smoothed Sarah's hair away from her forehead. "Things will get easier, Sarah, after a while."

"Will they?"

"They will, yes."

"But this has never happened to you before, Mother, so how do you know, for sure?"

Margaret was wearing a yellow dress and a pair of loafers. Her hair was pinned up in a knot, she even had some lipstick on. She looked much as she had before. She was thinner, though; the dress was a bit baggy. And when Sarah looked at her face, her eyes, she did seem different, but Sarah couldn't tell how. She wondered if she looked different, too. Maybe if this thing that was hanging around got stronger, people would be able to see it. Maybe she'd even be able to see it herself. Maybe she'd catch a glimpse of it in a mirror someday when she was about forty, and die of a heart attack, from the shock.

"They have to get better," said Margaret. "So they will."

Sarah missed her mother's voices. The absence of those shifting shimmering cadences had made her decide that part of her mother must have died with her father.

And part of me died, too, and part of Glynis, and part of Grandma and Grandpa. All those little bits of people died when he died, and they must be all together somewhere, wherever he is.

Sarah wished she could remember the last words Margaret had spoken in her voices.

She couldn't remember the last words she'd heard from her father, either.

Glynis came in, her face clean.

"Let's go," said Margaret, but Sarah said she had to wash her hands first.

She didn't really have to wash her hands. She wanted to look at herself in a mirror, and the one in the bathroom had the best light. She looked, but it was like looking at any other object. Certainly there was nothing hovering in the air behind her.

She stared at her face in the mirror, trying to figure out how it was that mirrors never showed you what you looked like to other people, but only what you looked like to yourself. If books were like that, she thought, there'd be no point in reading; all the words would be what you wanted to hear, instead of what somebody wanted to tell you.

Sarah felt completely incapable of doing anything as complicated as living a life.

The mirror reflected only an impassive, blue-eyed stare. The red stone in her locket flickered in the light. The locket's chain was chafing her neck; she lifted it and rubbed the skin under it.

She washed her hands, because she had said she was going to, and then sat on the edge of the bathtub, hands hanging at her sides and dripping onto the floor. The tap in the sink was still running. Finally she dried her hands and turned off the tap and looked into the mirror one last time. She thought she looked a bit worried, but that was all. She didn't mind going around looking worried.

She tapped her head with her fingers as she walked along the hall. All this is just because of guilt, she thought dispassionately. I can wait it out. As long as it doesn't get any worse.

She went downstairs to join Margaret and Glynis. As she went down the stairs she saw them standing at the front door; they turned and looked up at her expectantly, as though she were going to make a speech. She continued down the stairs, looking back at them, and she thought, one of the things I feel is aloneness, which is quite different from loneliness, and she thought that maybe she should talk to her mother about the presence after all.

That night Sarah lay on her bed, not yet undressed, her body thickly, achingly weary. She was determined that she must give herself completely to sleep and let the dreams come if they would. The dreams were disturbing not while she slept, but when she awakened. They were, she thought angrily, the things she should have been experiencing during the day, when she could recognize them for what they were, memories, and allow them to painfully knit past and present together and take their proper place in the future, filtering through the rest of the days of her life, imbuing all the years she had yet to live with nostalgia.

But in sleep they were not memories but reality, and when she woke from them it was like being told all over again that he was dead.

So she had become suspicious of sleep, of dreams that lied, and now even when she had temporarily cowed the presence that frightened her during the day, she was reluctant to abandon herself in sleep.

She knew she was becoming exhausted. Weariness had settled into her bones like a perpetual chill. She began to think that lying awake night after night might make her ill, which was a horrifying prospect. This dreadful time of dying and death was not yet over, and she must remain strong and healthy to cope with the rest of it.

Although her eyes were hot and dry, they would not stay closed. When she forced them closed her eyelids trembled as though in apprehension and snapped open as soon as she relaxed her concentration the slightest bit. She thought it might help if she were to get herself a glass of milk.

What she really wanted was a sleeping pill. She was sure that even if dreams did occur in a drug-induced sleep she wouldn't be able to remember them, and that was all that mattered.

She sat up, wondering if her mother would give her one, suddenly craving an effortless, helpless drifting into sleep—and craving, too, to talk to Margaret, if she could just do it right, and not scare her.

The constriction in her chest was already loosening as she got up and went to Margaret's room.

Her mother lay in bed propped up by pillows, holding a book. She started at the knock on her door, and tried to smile at Sarah, who looked grim and pale.

It occurred to Sarah that her mother might very well say no.

"May I have one of your sleeping pills?"

"Are you having trouble sleeping?" said Margaret.

"No, I just thought it might be a kick to take a pill," said Sarah. She thrust her hands into her jeans pockets. She was all at once convinced that Margaret was capable of deliberately standing between her daughter and a good night's sleep.

"You aren't even undressed yet," said Margaret. "Don't you think you should at least try to go to sleep, before you ask for a pill?"

"I haven't been able to sleep for the last four nights," said Sarah. Her heart was beating faster than normal and her hands were trembling in her pockets. She pressed them flat against her body, her fingers pointing at her groin.

"Have you tried warm milk?"

"Oh, for God's sake." Sarah felt the incongruity of her father's absence strongly. There was something shockingly inappropriate, a month after his death, about her mother trying to occupy the big bed and make decisions without him. She's using both pillows, how comfy. "No, I haven't tried warm milk. Warm milk will not work."

"How can you say it won't work," said Margaret, "when you haven't tried it?"

Sarah felt sick. She could just hear it: how can you think there's something there, when there isn't? how can you blame yourself, when a sickness did it? how can you think he hates you . . . when he's dead?

She turned and walked to the other side of the bedroom, shadowed because the other night-light wasn't on. She went to the window, which overlooked the back yard. There was a zinging in her chest which pulled her upright; she could feel that her back was very straight. She pulled back the curtains and pressed her face against the glass, cupping her hands on either side of her eyes.

"Are you going to sell this place?" she said. Margaret was very much aware of her hostility.

"What's the matter, Sarah?"

"Are you going to sell the house?" said Sarah more slowly, turning from the window.

"I haven't decided yet." Margaret put her book down and smoothed the bedspread across her knees. "I want to talk to you and Glynis about it first."

Sarah went to what had been her father's chest of drawers. Everything looked just the same. All his things were still there. His watch, his wallet, his hairbrush. She leaned heavily against the chest and closed her eyes, remembering her dreams. It was very hard to know what was going on when dreams were so much like reality and reality was so askew.

"What are you going to do with all his stuff?"

"What do you think I should do with it?" said Margaret quietly.

"I don't give a damn what you do with it," said Sarah, turning to her quickly. Margaret could see her blue eyes flash as she came around the end of the bed. "Throw it out. Bury it. Give it away. But if I ever walk down Granville Street and see my father's watch on somebody else's wrist, I'll—"

"Sit down, Sarah," said Margaret, sitting up straight in the bed. "Right now." She patted the bedspread. Sarah shook her head, her face flushed with anger. Margaret let her head rest on the pillows and closed her eyes. "Oh, Sarah. Of course I'll let you have a sleeping pill." She lifted her head and looked at Sarah. "But sit down and talk for a few minutes."

There was a sharp ache at the back of Sarah's throat. She concentrated on keeping her body so stiff it almost quivered, so that she would not cry. She shook her head again.

"I've got some things I want to talk to you about. I have to make some decisions. Will you help me?" said Margaret.

She looked very small in the big bed. She was covered up to her chin in a light, rust-colored robe, but her face was naked in the light from the lamp. Sarah saw the gray that was mixed in with Margaret's fair hair, and the lines in her face that were incipient wrinkles. What happens, she thought, if I screw up with her, too, and then *she* dies?

Sarah lowered herself cautiously onto the chair by her mother's dressing table, the ache in her throat easing.

"If you're talking about the house," she said reluctantly, "I don't know what I think."

"There's no hurry," said Margaret. "There's no hurry about his things, either," she said, looking into the shadows in the other side of the room. "But I think I may pack them away in boxes pretty soon. Sometimes it seems morbid, to let them sit around." Sarah stirred uneasily. "But that's not what I wanted to talk to you about," said Margaret. "I might go back to work. I want to know what you think."

Sarah remembered that during her childhood her mother

used to talk about getting on with her life. There was something ominous about this, as though Margaret might suddenly begin taking giant steps, dragging the whole family along with her so quickly they'd end up being scraped along the ground because they wouldn't be able to keep up.

Now she looked at Margaret and saw a smoldering in her eyes.

Sarah stood up, disoriented. Her hands fumbled at her sides. She hooked her thumbs into the belt loops of her jeans. "What work?" she said.

"I think I might try to go back into the theater."

Yes, there had been another woman in there all the time, jabbering sullenly away, and now that he was dead she'd come out again, this time maybe to stay. Sarah looked at Margaret, lying there so comfortably against both pillows, a novel on the bed beside her, and wanted to hit her.

"How much did you love him?" she said.

Margaret tried to catch her breath, and to remain calm. "Very much," she said quietly.

"I loved him more," said Sarah, the ache in her throat so large and sharp she had difficulty talking around it. "I did."

"We're not talking about the same thing, Sarah," said Margaret. She stretched out her hand toward Sarah. She has cut herself off, thought Margaret, and for an instant felt Sarah's anguish.

"You keep your goddamn pills," said Sarah, and whirled around and ran out of the room.

# Chapter 18

SARAH AT FIFTEEN THOUGHT SHE UNDERSTOOD EVERY-thing pretty clearly, and she knew now what she was going to do with almost all the time she had left to live. Of course that time was endless—she couldn't see all the way to the end of it, and therefore it didn't have an end—but she knew what she would do when she finished school. It wasn't entirely because of her father that she had decided to become an English teacher. She was enraptured by language. Sometimes she even thought she might become a poet, as well. Anyway, it was a relief to have gotten most of her future planned.

She worried about boyfriends, though, which most of her friends had (or said they had) and which she didn't have. She went to things where boys and girls went together, and had a good time, but they had begun to pair off in Grade Eight, maybe even earlier, and that hadn't happened to her.

Once near the end of Grade Ten somebody had asked her to go out. But she discovered she didn't like the boy any more out of class than in it. She sat stiffly beside him in the movie theater and repulsed him sharply when he made a move to kiss her good night on the street outside her house.

Nuts, she thought, and she told her father the next morning in a whisper, "Nuts to that going out." He smiled and said, "There's plenty of time for all that." But at least she had finally gone out with a boy.

Each year there were boys in her classes whom she'd never seen before, and in Grade Eleven, just before she became sixteen, she noticed one of these boys and began to dress each morning as though he might be noticing her, too.

One day he asked her for a date and she said yes and while they were on this date, which was a big barbecue on the beach with lots of other kids, she saw him reach over to toss another log on the fire they'd built. Suddenly her body began to croon and whimper to itself. And a voice like one of those startling, peremptory voices in dreams said, I want him to come over here and put his arms around me.

She pondered, wonderingly, upon this voice, upon the crooning and the whimpering. She felt like slapping herself on the hand. She was flustered, as though she were babysitting a small child who was suddenly, unaccountably misbehaving itself. She didn't think any of this was showing, but to feel it was quite shocking enough. And under the wonder and unease lay a deep, deep cloud of something hot and rosy, building itself there layer by layer, deeper and deeper, and she knew that the start of that rosy cloud had been in her all along, sleeping. In almost a single second she knew all sorts of things she had never known before, one of which was that she was about to learn a great deal more.

She shivered in the heat of the fire and placed her feet primly, closely against each other and clutched her arms.

"Cold?"

She looked up with a lurch of her heart. He sat beside her on the log and looked into her eyes and she was glad that it was night and he could not see her blush.

"Sitting right here, in front of that fire, and you're cold?"

He smiled. My God, she thought, he has a dimple, an actual dimple, his eyelashes are longer than mine, it's not fair, and where did a boy get eyes so purely green . . .

"It's silly, isn't it, it's so hot here I can't be cold, but I guess I am."

"I can fix that," he said. As though he had been doing it every day for all his life, but as carefully as though it were the first time, he put his arm around her and shook her gently into his shoulder, like fluffing up a pillow or adjusting the weight of a puppy in one's arms. She let herself lie there, angled into his shoulder, and his hand on her arm was warm and warmer. "Relax," he said into her hair. She felt his breath, and the cloud in her stomach ruffled in that breeze. "Put your head down on my shoulder." His voice was much deeper than hers. She had never really listened to a boy's voice before. There was something in it, a lilting dangerous rumble, that shivered her.

I had no idea we were so different from each other, she thought, cautiously putting her head on his shoulder, hoping it was the right thing to do but too limp and confused to do anything else anyway. He put his cheek against the top of her head and rubbed it gently there.

"You've got very soft hair," he said.

My God, she thought, is he thinking the same kind of things about me that I'm thinking about him? She tried to imagine what he could be thinking. His cheek rubbed softly against her hair. The cloud in her stomach flickered with determined joy . . .

He was sixteen, and had a car of his own. He took all his other passengers home first. When he stopped the car in front of her house, where the porch light shone and the lights were on, too, in the upstairs window of her parents' bedroom, there were in the car only the two of them. He turned to her and took her face in his two hands and brought it close to his own and placed his lips softly, neatly, against hers.

The thing about kissing, she thought, doing it for the first time, is that you get so close to a person.

He kept his lips against hers for quite a while. They were warm and soft and seemed very large; his mouth covered hers completely. He pulled away and looked at her for a long time, his lips open a little, his teeth gleaming, his eyes extremely soft. He brushed the hair away from her face gently, like a cobweb touching her. He walked with her to the front door and told her that he would call her the next day.

She wondered if they would go out again. She hoped they would, but it didn't seem terribly important. She had had a peek into what she now realized was a rather large part of the world which had remained closed to her, and the knowledge that it lay out there along with work and friendship and the seasons was an enormous revelation. It coated her life with texture and sensation; it splashed a strange foreign color into the sunset; it opened a part of herself which had been locked away until just the right moment.

The next morning at breakfast, which was late and a family thing because it was Saturday, her mother said, "How was the barbecue?"

Sarah's head lifted from her plate of waffles and bacon and turned itself toward her mother blind-eyed, blond hair curving itself along the sides of her head, blue eyes distant and burning.

My God, thought Margaret. I am not ready for this. She watched Sarah's eyes focus, watched her face flush and turn itself toward the plate.

"It was okay, fine," she said casually. She took a bite and chewed with great absorption.

Margaret sat still, fork in hand, looking at her daughter's bent head. Her mind filled with confusion and prickled with warnings.

"How was what's his name, that guy, Michael?" said Glynis, shoveling bacon into her mouth.

"Don't talk with your mouth full," said Margaret.

"He was okay, fine," said Sarah. She pushed her chair back. "I've gotta make my bed, get dressed."

"You haven't finished your breakfast," said Ted. "My waffles, your favorite, you've only had one. What's the matter with them? Have I lost my touch?"

"No, Daddy, they're great. I'm just not very hungry, got to get going. I'll come down in a minute and do the dishes, Mom." Sarah scurried from the room, tossing her hair back from her burning face as soon as her back was turned.

"What's wrong with her?" said Ted, hurt.

Margaret looked at him, and at first she couldn't identify what it was she felt for him, it was so inappropriate. It was compassion.

"She's fine, Ted."

He went back to his breakfast.

"It's that new guy, I bet," said Glynis, pouring syrup exultantly over her waffles. "I bet it's that new guy she went out with."

"What are you talking about?" said Ted.

"I bet she's got a crush on him. I *know* she's got a crush on him. She was all excited about that barbecue, yuck."

"Don't be ridiculous," said Ted coldly. "She's much too young for that sort of thing."

Glynis looked at him in astonishment.

"Be quiet, Glynis," said Margaret sharply.

"A person can't say anything in this house," said Glynis.

"Be quiet and eat your breakfast," said Margaret.

# Chapter 19

SARA WAS AMAZED AT HOW QUICKLY THINGS PROGRESSED.
It took merely weeks.

The first kisses were interesting. The next batch were comfortable and pleasant. The series after that was a whole new thing. Those kisses touched conduits leading directly to her breasts and her groin. She gasped and pulled away, burning, her nipples burning, her crotch burning. Those kisses touched nerves which led directly to the places of her which lived closest to the air.

Michael pulled her face back close to his and this time his tongue touched her lips, his tongue went inside her mouth, poked at her teeth until they opened, touched her tongue, the sides of her mouth. Is there something wrong with this? she wondered, her tongue quickly, shyly reaching out for his.

"French kissing," said Michael, releasing her to grin at her. "Do you like it?"

The question upset her. She said nothing.

She was very hot and her heart pounded and part of her was very tense; but the rest of her was languid as a summer stream lying still beneath the sun, reluctant to move on over cold pebbles, holding itself beneath the summer sun.

The kissing got better and better. She wilted when she thought about it, caught her breath, her lips opened but he wasn't there; and knowing that soon, or tomorrow, he would be there, she buried her face in her pillow or screwed her eyes tightly to the pages of a textbook, and waited.

The kisses were better and better and one night his hand moved from her back to her waist under her sweater onto her bare back. My God, she thought, there are nerves there, too, attached to my breasts, to my groin. Quickly the hand pushed under the strap of her bra, pushed up, moved to the front. She protested. He kept his mouth on hers, pulled up her bra at the front and cupped within his hand her left breast, which settled there, flesh on flesh, warm on warm, not complaining. He continued kissing her, his tongue pushing urgently into her mouth while his other hand released her shoulder and curled itself around her right breast. She had no excuse now; she pulled her mouth away from his and pushed at his hands until they dropped.

"Don't," she said. "Don't do that."

"Ah, Sarah," he said, "ah, Sarah." He turned her around in the back seat of the car until her head rested in his lap. Her feet were up on the seat, knees in the air, skirt falling down her thighs to her waist. Why did I wear a skirt? she thought as he leaned down to kiss her. She put her hands around his neck and pulled him to her, mouth smothered upon mouth, teeth grating. His hand found her knee, slid down her thigh, followed her skirt to the edges of her pantihose. His fingers came under the waistband, down through the hair there to her crotch, wet and hot. She shuddered; she hadn't known he would do that, and couldn't decide whether to let him. His hand pulled away and she cried out; then, mortified, she froze as his mouth left hers. He pulled her toward him, up from the seat, pushed up her sweater, not gently, and his mouth circled the nipple on her breast. She clutched him to her, pressing her breast against him. His hand found her crotch, pulled down the pantihose. His fingers were in the soft wet hot part of her, she felt circles circling inside her somewhere connected both to her breast and to her crotch, not seeming though to exist exactly in either of those places; they were large, lazy circles circling, gaining strength and urgency, becoming smaller tighter whirling faster her hips jabbed at the air, at his hand,

her crotch enveloped his hand the circles whirled fast tight
blurred hips jabbing straining the circles found their center
and exploded, her crotch opened fully embracing his fingers
she could smell the smell of her in the air.

"Oh, Sarah, Sarah . . ."

We sound like we've been running, thought Sarah. The
circles were wider, lazy again, warm, disappearing. Is this
wrong? she wondered. My God, of course it is, but you can't
get pregnant from it anyway.

"Sarah, touch me, please touch me."

She brought up one hand, hesitantly. He grabbed it and
pressed it against him. How swollen it is, she thought; she
knew what was in there, it was terribly big. He pressed her
hand against him there and squirmed and thrust and thrust
again, again, again, screamed a silent whispered scream,
sank back against the seat of the car.

She was in love and selfish and it was to be her sixteenth
birthday soon and there was a New Year's Eve party, too. It
would be her first. Now she had a boyfriend and she knew
about sex and she loved her body and life was pure sensation.

She went to her mother in the kitchen.

"Good," said Margaret. "You've come to help."

Sarah laughed. "No, but I will. I've come to talk to you."

"Make the salad and talk."

"What kind, a green one or an orange one?"

"Coleslaw, if that's what you mean, and don't forget the
raisins."

Sarah squatted down in front of the open fridge and got
out the cabbage, the carrots, and the mayonnaise. Her
muscles were so strong she thought she could squat up and
down about a thousand times and they wouldn't get tired;
she would stop, finally, only because she was bored. She
lifted her body upright with the muscles in her thighs and
they performed well, holding back their strength politely,
not shooting her headfirst toward the ceiling. She took the
vegetables to a cutting board and began whacking at them
energetically.

"For heaven's sake, Sarah, you're getting it all over the
floor."

"Sorry. Mom, it's about to be my birthday."

"There's Christmas in there somewhere, first, isn't there?"

"Yeah, I mean after Christmas."

"I don't believe there will ever be an after Christmas." Margaret looked in at the roast, closed the oven door, and sat down at the table. "My, I do feel heavy."

Sarah looked at her complacently. "You look fine."

"Thanks a lot," said Margaret sharply. "I'm not talking about the way I look. I'm tired. There's too much to do before Christmas."

"Mom, could I ask for a particular present this year?" Sarah stood before her mother, pleading.

"Only if you put the knife down first."

Sarah looked at the large chopping knife flecked with bits of cabbage. Margaret laughed. Sarah blushed and put the knife carefully on the counter.

"I mean, could I tell you what I want?"

"Sure you can tell me what you want."

"And do you think you could make sure that I get it?"

"You're awfully materialistic, all of a sudden."

Sarah sat opposite her mother. "This is incredibly important to me."

"It must be. What do you want?"

"A dress."

"A dress?"

"A special one. To wear New Year's Eve."

"A special dress. Special how?"

Sarah blushed again. The lights in the kitchen were very bright, and her mother was gazing at her with a discomfiting mixture of curiosity, amusement, and wariness. Sarah could feel her face and neck flushing. She had thought she'd outgrown that, and felt suddenly gangly and awkward. She knew that if she were to think about Michael confidence would pour into her limbs and she would throb in the secret shocking parts of her, but she didn't want to think about him now, not even to get back her grace and smoothness, because thinking about him in this particular situation would only make her get redder.

"Special how?" said her mother again, her voice like summer rain.

"Not too stuffy," said Sarah helplessly.

Margaret took her hand. "I think I've got the idea."

"Do you think I'm being silly?" said Sarah winningly.

Margaret frowned. "Don't try the little-girl act with me, Sarah. It won't work. Besides, it's ridiculously inappropriate under the circumstances, don't you think?" She withdrew her hand.

Sarah went back to the salad.

"I'll see what I can do," said Margaret, after a minute in which the roast bubbled in the oven and Sarah's knife slammed at regular intervals against the cutting board.

Sarah turned, joy in her face.

"But don't count on anything," said Margaret. "I don't know what your father will think about it."

Sarah raised her eyebrows. "Why do you think I came to you?" she said, and Margaret almost heard contempt in her voice.

After dinner Ted and Margaret sat in the living room watching the fire and eating Japanese oranges and listening to music. The flames consumed themselves in the fireplace and their muted reflection glowed in the leather of Ted's brown chair.

"It's nice, isn't it," said Margaret, her voice like smoky Oriental tea.

"Yeah. Where are the kids?"

"Sarah's in her room studying, she gets exams this week. Glynis went to an early movie."

He frowned into the fire. "What about homework?"

"She did it after school."

He finished peeling his second orange and leaned over to add the last piece of rind to the neat pile on the coffee table. They smelled sharp and oily, a Christmas smell. His mouth watered as he pulled off a segment of the orange and put it into his mouth sweet and swollen with juice and sunshine.

"I like this house," he said with satisfaction, looking around the room, chewing on the piece of orange. "Buying this house was the best thing we ever did." He saw her smile. "Want to go to a movie?"

"No. I'm happy here. What about you?"

"Me too." They watched the fire. "Now all we need is a dog."

"No dog," she said sharply, glancing at him. "Don't you dare bring a dog in here."

He laughed. "It would be good to have a dog. The kids should have a dog," he added.

"Oh, Ted, for heaven's sake."

"Okay, okay, it was just a thought."

"You get a dog for the kids, who's going to be stuck with it?"

"What's that supposed to mean?"

"It means that Sarah's got only one more year in high school and Glynis has only four and then they'll be gone."

"What the hell do you mean, gone?"

"Just what I said. If they go on to university—"

"Of course they'll go on to university, but the gates to the university are only six blocks away."

"Ted, they might not want to go to U.B.C. They might want to go somewhere else, just to get away from home. That's natural, you can't expect—"

"I expect them to go to university right here, damnit!"

"You can't expect them to stay here because we don't want them to go away."

She hadn't meant to blunder into this so thoughtlessly. She felt as though a highway had disappeared beneath the wheels of her car and changed to mud, thwacking at the tires with hungry sucking sounds, spewing the car from rut to rut.

Irritation prickled Ted's skin. His muscles were knotted. The fire was too hot. He was excruciatingly uncomfortable.

"It's a stupid thing to be talking about," he said.

There was silence. The fire crackled and the stereo played, but silence quivered in the air between them.

"You're right, Ted," said Margaret tiredly.

"It's not a prison, you know," he said. "I've never had the impression that either of them regarded it as some kind of prison. They've always seemed perfectly happy to me, living here."

The silence solidified, strengthened, jeered at him.

"Is there anything on television?" said Margaret.

"I have no idea," he said.

"Sarah was talking about her birthday today," said Margaret.

"And?"

"She told me what she wants for her birthday."

. . . one year he had given her a doll, the biggest in the world; once a bike, the shiniest in the world; another year, a baseball bat and ball. She took the ball and bat to the basement to practice and whanged a lamp stored in the corner—she tried to be conciliatory, tried to be regretful, but she was laughing in her eyes, you couldn't help but laugh with her; Margaret didn't, though. Margaret was furious . . .

He smiled.

". . . she wants a dress."

"But I'd thought—"

"What?"

"Nothing. I'd just thought of something for her, that's all. Not a dress."

"Well, what?"

He knew it was just the thing. The idea was to give people something they didn't know they'd wanted until they opened the package and saw it. He had thought of it weeks ago, just the right present.

"Nothing. It's not important."

"Shall I tell her she can have the dress, then?"

"Oh, for Christ's sake! You don't ask for things you want and then get told you're getting them, that's no kind of birthday, that's no way to get presents, for Christ's sake! The kid's getting far too uppity, too cheeky. No. Don't tell her she can have a dress."

He was flooded with anger. His body twitched, sitting there in the leather chair. It wanted to jerk around the room, throwing off the sticky spines of irritation that pierced its skin all over.

"How about a drink," said Margaret flatly, picking up the orange peels.

"Yeah, sure." He got up. "I'm going to get a book. Do you want anything upstairs?"

"No, thanks."

She watched him go, lumbering petulantly, painfully, across the room, focused, brooding, on things that hurt him. What's my duty here? she thought as she watched him. What's my duty here?

Two weeks before her birthday Sarah sat at her desk, which faced the wall so she wouldn't be tempted to stare out the window and daydream, and she sweated over her history notes. The lamp pointed itself right at her notes. There was no place else to look. She stared at the words and concentrated on them, and flushes and sweats happened to her every time she thought of the exam.

She wanted to phone somebody and talk about it, but she knew that was trying to escape, and she did want to do well. So she started again, at the top of the page, her left hand supporting her head and clutching at her hair, right hand ready to turn the page.

See? That hand is confident that I will finish this page and be ready to go on to the next one. That hand has confidence in me. I will go on, so as not to disappoint that hand.

There was a tap on her door.

"I'm busy!" she yelled.

Silence. Then another tap; louder.

"For Pete's sake, I'm busy, I'm studying, go away!"

"It's me," said her father.

Her wandering mind whacked itself together eagerly, and hope filled her again, as she got up and opened the door. "Sorry, Daddy. I thought it was Glynis."

He stood in the hall with a finger to his lips. "Shhh." He beckoned, and she followed him to her parents' bedroom. They went in and he closed the door, carefully, quietly.

"What's wrong?" said Sarah.

"Nothing. I don't want your mother to hear, that's all."

He went to the closet door, and stopped. He turned to look at her. "I want to show you your present."

"My present! My birthday present?"

"Shhh!" he hissed sternly.

He bent down, reached the bottom of the closet, and dragged out a large bag which seemed to have a box inside. It's not a dress, she thought sickly. It's too heavy to be a dress. What has he done? She walked toward him, staring at the large brown bag.

He looked at her. "It's not wrapped yet. But I couldn't wait for you to see it. Just don't tell your mother." He winked at her.

He struggled with the box inside the bag. She looked down at the top of his head. Graying brown hair was combed from a side part; she could see that some of it was falling over his forehead, as usual. He was wearing old pants and a loose, long-sleeved, dark blue sweatshirt that made his eyes look even bluer than usual. He had seemed to her lately a different man, yet as she looked down on him now he did not

appear much different from how she had always seen him.
But there was a rift between them. It had materialized before
she had had a chance to see it coming, and now she thought
frequently about trying to mend it, but had not decided how
that might be done. It was the only coldness, the only pain in
her life.

"Come on, get down here," he said, looking up at her,
shielding the box from her eyes with his body. "I don't think
I'd better take it away from the closet, in case she comes."
He was whispering.

Sarah crouched and looked. He had pulled the box from
the bag and opened the top of it. Inside was a portable
electric typewriter, keys and metal case gleaming; a gray and
green typewriter. She stretched out her fingers, slowly, and
touched it.

"It's beautiful, Dad. It's a terrific present."

It *is* a terrific present, she thought. Why am I not excited?
Why is my chest not big enough for my lungs? Why do I
want to run oh God why do I have to pretend?

She looked at him quickly. He was watching her carefully,
something hidden in his eyes. He turned away.

"Now don't tell your mother," he said, pushing the box
closed and shoving it back inside the bag. He tucked the bag
away behind several pairs of shoes at the back of the closet.
"She'd be upset if she knew I'd shown it to you." He closed
the closet door.

As he turned, she put her arms around him. It was the first
time she could remember doing that so deliberately, actually
deciding to hug him, putting her arms around him only
because it seemed called for. She put her cheek against his.
"It's a marvelous present, Dad, it's just great, thank you so
much." She felt his middle-aged body against hers and
thought of Michael. My father has turned into someone else,
now, yes, he has, she thought; he's half done it himself and
somehow I've half done it for him. She released him. His
eyes were dull and his lips curved downward; distancing his
face from her, he patted her shoulder.

"You're welcome," he said politely.

When her birthday came there was the typewriter,
wrapped in dull red glowing metallic-looking paper, with a
large white bow on top and a card which read, "To Sarah,
With Love, Dad."

And there was a dress box. She didn't even see its wrapping paper. She ripped it open with a little scream of glee which cut her heart a second later—just one second too late to call it back—and she didn't look at her father while she opened it. She calmed herself as she looked at the dress, and calmly she thanked her mother, but her smile was full of brilliance stolen from her father's eyes.

# Chapter 20

THE APRIL RAIN FELL ENDLESSLY, ENDLESSLY, AND EVEN
the scent of blooming lilacs, the sight of pink and white
blossoms up and down the block, the green-gold leafing
which filled winter-bare branches with a singing, aching
poignance; not any or all of these signs of spring could ease
Margaret this day as she looked into her mirror and saw that
she was aging.

Again, again, a thing had descended upon her implacably
and irrevocably which she had known would eventually
descend upon her but whose arrival was no less of a shock
for that. She had known as a girl that she would become a
woman, known as a wife that one day she would become a
mother, known at thirty that someday her hair would turn
gray and wrinkles would appear in her skin. But it does not
help to know these things, she thought, looking at herself in
her mirror, just as it doesn't help to know I'll die, because
really I don't believe that I will ever die, and really, I never
believed that I would ever age. Now it's here looking at me
and I have to believe it, and one day I'll know I'm dying and
then I guess I'll believe that, too.

I don't feel different, she thought; and yet I see that I am.

Gray had sneaked into her hair while she wasn't looking.

She used to look for it, worried, before it was time, and then she forgot for a few years and now she saw that it was here. She wasn't fat, but her stomach was doughy and there were stretch marks there, and on her breasts, which slumped a little. Sometimes her legs ached when she walked a lot. And she never ran any more, just to get from one place to another in a hurry; she took her time getting places, although she had less time left to spend.

She bent over from the waist and began brushing her hair with long, firm strokes.

And now Sarah had a boyfriend and oh Jesus, thought Margaret, why does that have to be so complicated? . . .

She was sometimes bewildered by the strident presence of her two daughters in her life. At twelve and sixteen, innocently arrogant, they accepted their maturing and their mother's aging with equal aplomb. Margaret sometimes resented—not *being* a mother, but *feeling* like one, as though in the moments when she was a mother she wasn't permitted to be anything else. She remembered seeing a phrase used by real estate agents to describe no-care town houses and condominiums—"empty nesters," they called them. Places for the used-up birds to huddle and wait for death while the chicks flew wild and free. It defined people in terms of their children, as though parenthood was all they had.

Margaret stood up quickly, and flicked her hair over her shoulder like a whip. I am not, she told herself defiantly, a thing made up of softening tissue and facial lines and graying hair; whatever I am, that is not it. And I am more than a goddamned mother, too.

She wanted to go to a big shopping center and buy things—maybe clothes, or books, or hanging baskets full of flowers to hang above the patio.

Instead, she went downstairs and mixed herself a martini and took it back to the bedroom, where she sat in a chair by the window and stared out at the gray and drizzly afternoon.

Perhaps, she thought, the tangled confusion of her feelings toward her daughters was nothing more than a natural preparation for their leaving her. Her mind must have switched into a self-protective gear without having alerted her beforehand. Because although she didn't think she loved her children less, the quality of her love was changing, becoming shot through with unpleasant things like resentment, and frequent exasperation, and—God help her—even envy; and their absence from her life on a daily basis would eventually come as a relief.

She sipped at her drink, thinking.

She had carried in her head for a long time a skittery apprehension about Sarah's adolescence. But she had confidently expected that things would work themselves out, because she couldn't imagine an alternative. She didn't know at this moment whether things would work out or not; yet she still couldn't imagine an alternative. Worry hung heavy on her, and she resented it, and she resented Sarah, too—and Ted.

Screw them all, she thought, downing the rest of her drink. It's time I thought about myself again.

She stood up and faced the mirror, hands on her hips, swinging slightly from side to side as she studied herself calculatingly. I was an actress, she reminded herself firmly. Perhaps it's time I dragged that me out of her grave and tried to breathe some life into her.

She dropped her hands and stood still, looking herself in the face.

Or, she thought, do something, anyway.

# Chapter 21

ON THE WAY HOME FROM SCHOOL, ON A DAY IN EARLY JUNE which had tumbled unexpected heat across the city, Sarah passed a man she thought of as old.

She spotted him a block away, a stranger, heading in the same direction she was headed. He walked jauntily enough. But she imagined she heard knees creaking that full block away.

She saw him ahead of her, and she gathered herself up and she ran.

She loved the ease with which she ran. She jogged down the street, and then broke into a gallop. The man's back loomed up in front of her and she swished around him with an ease, a power, that filled her with strange aggression. She didn't even bother to throw him a smile over her shoulder as she passed. She just flashed by him in a whoosh and, once past, put on even more speed. She wanted him to see that she needn't ever slow down if she didn't want to.

She fled down the sidewalk, blurring the trees and the houses, zoomed around a corner, up a slight rise, and turned into her front yard. Her heart was beating fast but it felt good. Her body was stirred up and ready for anything. She trotted around to the back of the house, to check on the flowers growing there, and the small vegetable garden her mother had planted.

Ted was kneeling beside a bed of flowers that bordered the western edge of the lawn, pulling out little weeds that had sprouted beside some small orange flowers with a strong firelike scent, and wondering what the flowers were called and whether he really wanted to remember, when Sarah burst into the yard from the other side of the house.

Her fair skin was beginning to gather into itself the golden glow which was its gift from summer. Her hair looked windblown and tangled. She wore a blue sleeveless summer dress, the neckline scooped to reveal the locket nestled in the hollow of her throat. She was out of breath and beaming; she looked triumphant, and his heart moved faster. He could see her love for him on her face, and could not remember why he had ever thought it absent, and suddenly felt as close to her as he ever had.

Sarah came toward him silently over the soft spongy grass, filled with the triumph of a life recognized but barely begun. She reached down to hug him where he knelt beside a pile of tiny weeds, and she kissed his forehead.

"Guess what, Daddy," she said softly next to his ear, handing him her secrets. "I'm in love."

She stood straight and whirled around, face lifted to the sun. Dazzled, he laughed. He could see it—sun love, summer love. She ran along the edge of the garden and as she touched the flowers their names came back to him; marigold, sweet pea, peony, and rosebuds, too.

"I'm so happy, Daddy!" She plopped down, tailor fashion, on the grass beside him, blue skirt billowing up then down around her, blue and gold like the day.

"I'm glad, honey," he said. "It's the best time of year, isn't it?" He looked around the yard. "Time to think of where to go for holidays." They still couldn't quite afford the cross-Canada trip they wanted to take, but he'd been thinking about the Oregon coast, or maybe even San Francisco, the girls would love San Francisco, he was sure . . .

"Oh, Daddy, how can you talk about going away! Going away isn't a holiday—staying *home* is a holiday, with no *school*, and a summer job if I can get one, and going to movies. . . ." She laughed and hugged herself. "It's going to be a beautiful summer," she said. She stretched out her thin golden legs, propped up her body on her hands.

Ted wondered if he was coming down with something. His stomach was suddenly disquieted, and he couldn't think of anything to eat or drink that might soothe it. He looked down at his legs, splayed out on the grass; the skin of his feet, in worn bedroom slippers, was pale in the sunshine. His mind was not clear.

Sarah drew up her legs and turned to face him. "You'll like him, Daddy, I know you will. I know you don't know him yet, you've only met him a few times, but you'll really like him. He's going to U.B.C. after Grade Twelve, of course—who knows, maybe he'll even be in one of your classes!"

He felt like a slumbrous animal who had laid alertness aside in the heat of noon, and awakened to find the jungle holding its breath.

"What the hell are you talking about?" he said, and felt his face shape itself into something strange. He watched, appalled, as she reddened.

"Michael, Daddy. You know, you've met him. Michael."

He did not want to see her did not want to be near her did not want her hands to touch him.

"Oh, for Christ's sake," he said, and pushed himself up from the grass. He felt fat, hot, white, old. His heart was beating fast. He was so angry his flesh shook; and sharp and cold he felt hate, as he glared down at her; an impersonal thing, he was sure. "You don't know what you're talking about, you don't know a single goddamn thing."

He saw her move to get up, and he hurried toward the house. His fear was gone, replaced by anger. The house looked dangerous to him. But it was the only place he knew to go.

Sarah sat down on the grass. What a stupid thing to do, she thought dully. Of course he's exasperated with me. What a stupid thing to do . . .

"Yes, it wasn't too bright," said Margaret later, sitting on a chair in Sarah's room. "He probably imagined you running off to elope. It probably didn't even occur to him that by the time you're eighteen you'll have forgotten all about Michael."

Sarah turned away to fumble with something on her desk. "Well, that's pretty silly," she said, and tried to laugh.

Her mother got up. "Don't worry too much about your father. You just sprang it on him rather suddenly. It's your first boyfriend, after all. Give him a chance to get used to the idea."

"But, Mom, I've been going out with him for months now. He knows I've got a boyfriend, he *knew* it.

"He knew, but he didn't know. Now he knows, all right." Margaret went to the door.

"Mom? Do you like Michael?"

"I hardly know him, Sarah. He seems nice enough." Margaret almost asked Sarah what she thought she loved about this boy, but restrained herself. She had had enough of all this. She certainly didn't want to hear a pouring out of all Michael's dubious virtues, particularly since she knew exactly what it was about him that Sarah so enjoyed. . . . Margaret felt a moment's panic. The world would certainly collapse if Sarah became pregnant. In a five-second period, she ticked off all the possibilities for dealing with that kind of crisis and was left with nothing but a mental image of her husband's incredulous, rage-filled face if anybody ever had to tell him that.

She shivered, hesitated at the door. What can I say? Be careful, you're too young, don't get pregnant . . . Then she'll figure that anything goes, as long as it doesn't result in a baby. Should I help her get the pill? That would put my stamp of approval on it . . .

"What's the matter, Mom?"

Margaret turned to look at Sarah, thin, long-haired, sixteen. Oh God, I do love her, she thought. That's the thing, that's what traps you, all right; that's what makes you forever a parent, like it or not.

"Nothing, Sarah," she said. "Nothing's the matter. Good night."

The door closed behind her. Sarah wondered if now was the time to try again with her father. No—better let her mother talk to him first.

Sarah was amazed by the sudden change in the familiar patterns of her life. It had always been her father to whom she went, asking him to explain something to her mother. Now she looked at her mother with alarm, because Margaret held such unexpected power. Could she, *would* she truly explain things from Sarah's point of view? Or would it come out all mixed up with whatever she, Margaret, thought should happen? Sarah felt helpless, but she didn't resent her mother. She had seen something in Margaret's face when she began stuttering away to her, months ago, about Michael. It was what Sarah had expected to see in her father's face, but hadn't; there had been only horror there, which bewildered Sarah and robbed her of joy and conviction, and he had always stalked away without letting her finish. She wished she had remembered that in time, this afternoon. . . .

But in Margaret's face when Sarah talked haltingly about Michael she had seen a wry smile, a warm but ironic salute, a strange kind of welcome; a flicker of uneasiness, too, but that was only to be expected. It was that other thing Sarah dug out of her mind now to look upon and be comforted by: recognition. And with the recognition, something soothing, a split-second message of reassurance: yes, this is part of it, too; new for you but old; unique to you but universal. Sarah liked having seen that in her mother's face.

Because her mother, too, possessed this knowledge, Sarah knew it wasn't something people forgot about when they grew older. She didn't mind so much feeling awkward and inexperienced, because she knew that other people had felt it, too, and grown through it, with it, to something else; something not as exciting, she was sure—and she felt regretful for her mother. But at least Margaret had these things to remember, these things Sarah was now living. That meant that Sarah wouldn't forget them, either. Nor would she remain awkward and inexperienced. She'd polish her sexual skills, she would, and eventually she would no longer blush when her insides became weak and hot and throbbing, somehow she would learn to carry her thoughts along knowing that they could not be seen.

And if her mother had this knowledge, this experience, then her father must have it, too. So eventually she would see the old love and approval in his eyes, and then everything would be all right.

But everything was not all right.

Sarah's mother proved to be of very little help. She would not discuss with Sarah her conversations with Ted. She told

Sarah again and again to be patient. But her father would not even meet Michael any more. She could not invite Michael to dinner except when her father was away, which was seldom. When her father knew that Sarah was going out with him he would disappear into his study and not come out even to say hello. She could not talk to him. He would not listen to her.

"Don't push him, Sarah," said Margaret.

"Push him! He won't listen to me, he won't talk to me! He hides from me, Mother!"

"What do you expect from him? Do you want him to sit there and listen with a smile on his face while you tell him about how you've discovered sex?"

"Mother!"

"Do you think you're the first person to discover sex? Or that you'll be the last? Do you think he hasn't discovered it yet? Is that what you think?"

"Mother!"

"Just what do you expect from him!"

"He doesn't want me to grow up," said Sarah desperately.

"Maybe not," said her mother coldly. "From the look of you, I don't think he's got much to worry about."

"Mother!"

"Oh, stop yelling 'Mother.' Becoming interested in the body of a member of the opposite sex doesn't mean you're grown up." Sarah shivered, humiliated. "Being grown up," said Margaret more quietly, "also means having some respect for the feelings of the people around you. Especially the people you live with."

"He doesn't have much respect for mine!"

"You aren't giving him a chance! You're pushing that boy at him every chance you get. 'Daddy, Michael's coming to pick me up, please say hello to him.' 'Oh, Daddy, I know you'd like Michael if you'd only talk to him.' He doesn't *want* to like Michael, Sarah! Please leave him alone." Margaret stood up. "If you leave him alone," she said evenly, "he'll probably come around, in his own good time. If you don't—then things won't get any better, for you or for him, and they'll probably get worse."

The summer passed. They went for ten days to Victoria, where Glynis inexplicably wanted to have tea in the Em-

# THE FAVORITE

press Hotel every afternoon, and Sarah missed Michael constantly. But she discovered that she could talk to her father about school, about the university, about teaching, about all the things they had talked about in the past. He began to relax. Things were better, even after they got home.

Although Michael didn't think so.

"Why doesn't he like me, anyway?"

"Oh, Michael, I keep telling you, it isn't that he doesn't like you. How could he not like you? He doesn't even know you."

"Why doesn't he want to know me, then? What is it that puts him off?"

"I don't know," said Sarah wearily. "Don't worry about it. My mother likes you. Glynis thinks you're okay. Don't worry about my father."

They were walking from his car to a movie theater.

"He's jealous, that's what it is," said Michael finally, and laughed.

"What do you mean, jealous?" said Sarah indignantly.

"He doesn't like the idea of some punk kid making love to his daughter, that's what I mean."

Sarah stopped on the sidewalk, crowded with coatless strollers enjoying the warm summer evening.

She clasped her hands in front of her and looked at him as though she had never seen him before.

"Oh shit, Sarah. He probably wants to go to bed with you himself, subconsciously—"

She slapped the side of his head with all her strength and turned and ran. He caught up with her and pulled her over to the window of a store. They ignored people walking by, some of whom hesitated at the sight of Michael grabbing Sarah by the shoulders.

"Don't you ever do that again, do you hear me?" said Michael, his eyes alive with anger. He shook her until she looked at him. He pulled her close and hugged her tightly. "Oh God, Sarah, I'm sorry, I'm sorry, I didn't mean it, it's me who's jealous, not him, that's all." He kissed her gently, butterflies on her face, and she thought, he's all I've got, thank God for him, he's all I've got.

*　*　*<br>181

"Maybe you'd like to go away to school next year," said her father one Saturday late in August. Margaret and Glynis had gone shopping and Sarah had made him a sandwich and coffee for lunch.

"Why would I do that?" she said, forcing her voice to remain level.

"Oh, I don't know. Sometimes it's a good idea to get away from home." Industriously he chewed on his sandwich, his eyes bright as he looked at her.

"There's no point in that, Dad," she said. "There aren't many schools better than U.B.C."

"You can find one just as good," he said, brushing crumbs from his fingers.

"But why? I don't want to go away from home yet. Why do you want me to?"

He poured himself more coffee, and opened his mouth to speak. She remembered the moment later as one in which she might have done or said something different. She remembered it many, many times.

"Daddy. You don't want me to go to U.B.C. because that's where Michael's going. Isn't that right?"

"Don't be ridiculous. I just want you to become exposed to new situations, meet new people—"

"There are thousands of people on this campus, Daddy. Thousands of them. You just don't want me to go where Michael is, that's it, isn't it? Isn't it!"

"Goddamnit, so what if that's it!" he roared, and she flinched. "You're sixteen years old, for Christ's sake! That's too young!"

"Too young for what, Daddy!" she shouted at him, and she was actually glad for those few seconds that it had come. People are purged by real arguments, she said to herself as she watched his face mottle; it clears the air. It occurred to her too late that she had never been in a real argument.

His eyes narrowed and seemed to lose their blueness and become all gray, icy granite. "You just want to have your hands on each other, your goddamn hands all over each other!"

She became conscious of silence, then of the sound of his breathing. She heard his chair squeak as he pushed himself up from it.

"Well, let me tell you something, young lady," he said

harshly, his breathing heavy in the air above her. "Let me tell you something. If you plan to go to university on my money you'll damn well live the kind of life I tell you to live, is that clear?" He walked out of the kitchen.

Her father was gone. There was another person inside him, and she and this other person did not like one another.

Sarah thought this, sitting at the kitchen table, looking out the window at the late-summer day.

Sarah seldom looked directly at her father that fall. She didn't have much to do with anyone in her family. She met Michael places, and wouldn't let him come to pick her up. He didn't like it, and occasionally threatened to come unexpectedly to her door and demand to speak to her father. But he sensed that she was right when she said that would only make things much, much worse, and gradually they came not to speak of him at all.

She tried not to think about anything but the day she was living.

Glynis became thirteen that October. Sarah gave her an ABBA record and noticed vaguely that Glynis was actually developing a bust and had a waist now. She wondered if Glynis would have an easier time with her father than she had had. She was almost sure of it. She had paved the way. Her father was too stubborn to change his attitude toward Sarah, but he would know better than to demonstrate the same attitude toward Glynis. And Glynis wasn't dumb; she'd been watching things, she'd know better than to come charging in with joy and announce that she was in love. Sarah shivered. She couldn't understand how she could have been so stupid.

Her mother was quiet, wearing a tired face. She used only her dullest voices. She was gentle with Sarah, and with Glynis, and with her husband, too. Sarah wondered if her mother was still waiting for things to get better, or what.

Her father, even though she didn't look him in the eyes three times that autumn, nonetheless vibrated somewhere within her field of vision, and she noticed that his hair was becoming extremely gray. But his eyes were as deep blue as ever, like the sea, and his mouth was firm, and though the skin of his face was more deeply lined than she remembered from a year ago he still didn't look exactly old. His watch, which he hardly ever took off, and his wedding ring, which he never took off, glinted dully as she glanced sideways toward him at the dinner table. Dinner was a torturous ritual, except when Glynis had had a good day at school. Her father looked thinner, to Sarah, that autumn; and he moved more slowly. She tried to figure out just how old he was. About forty-eight, she thought. He needs exercise, she told herself, and wondered irritably why her mother didn't make him get some.

One Saturday afternoon in late October, Sarah found herself in the house alone with him. She knocked softly on the bedroom door. "Daddy? Daddy? I need to talk to you." There was no answer and she knocked again. "Daddy. Please." She shoved the door open. He was lying on the bed, arms crossed behind his head, looking up at the ceiling. His eyes fluttered as the door opened but he didn't let them look at her. She stood beside him and wished she had more anger to spend. "Daddy, please talk to me. Don't shut me out."

"It's you doing the shutting out," he said.

"I'm not, I'm not! I want to talk to you. Please."

"I know what you want to talk about, and I don't want to listen."

She put her hand on his arm and felt it twitch.

"You're carrying right on with it," he said. "You know what I think about it. Why should it matter what I have to say, all of a sudden?"

"Because you're my father. Because I've always loved you more than anything." She realized, humiliated, that she was crying. "Why does it have to be this way?"

"Don't shout at me."

"Look at me, Daddy, why don't you look at me!"

"I don't like what I see when I look at you." He got up and walked past her to the bedroom door.

"Where are you going?" she said. "You're running away again!"

She followed him out of the room and down the hall. She held on to the banister at the top of the stairs.

He turned at the front door. "I don't have to tell you where I'm going. It's been too long since you felt graciously obliged to tell me where you were going."

He went out of the house. Sarah sat on the top step and

went on crying as she heard him start his car and drive away.

After a while she heard the station wagon in the driveway. The motor stopped. A door opened and closed. Footsteps approached the house, the front door opened, and Margaret came in, shaking rain from her hair.

"Sarah!" Margaret looked at her for a moment, then slowly took off her raincoat and hung it in the closet. She wore a green dress, lacy-looking, and makeup, and her blond hair was done up at the back of her head in a bun, as usual. "Why don't you bring in the groceries for me?"

He's falling apart, just like I am, thought Sarah. We're falling apart, and she just sails through everything looking tired.

"Why does he still wear that same old watch?" she said loudly to her mother. "Why don't you buy him a new watch? That one looks awful. It's old."

Margaret stood at the bottom of the stairs and looked up at her. She held out a hand. "Come and have a cup of tea."

Sarah drew herself wearily to her feet and went down the stairs, and took her mother's hand. They went into the kitchen, where the rain thrummed, muted, on the window-panes.

"Why don't you sit down," said Margaret.

Her mother's voice sounded like wind over a desert, and Sarah was afraid. She sat down.

"What's the matter with you?" said Margaret. "You look dreadful."

"I had a talk with my father, that's what's the matter with me."

"What did you say to him?"

Her mother stood in the middle of the kitchen. Sarah wondered how she had known just where the exact center of the room was, so that she could stand in it.

"Don't hover over me," said Sarah, "I can't think, I feel like I've been arrested."

Her mother didn't move.

"I didn't say anything," said Sarah reluctantly. "I tried to talk to him. He wouldn't let me."

"You're being impulsive, Sarah. That's not like you."

It was amazing, the number of voices this woman possessed. It was disconcerting. It could throw a person right off, not knowing one voice from another, not knowing which

185

one was going to come out next, sometimes not even recognizing the person who spoke.

"You're remarkable, Mother, you really are," said Sarah. She looked at her mother's face. A sweet face, with hazel eyes and a few freckles sprinkled with careful delicacy across the tops of her cheeks and the bridge of her nose. Her lips were full, and looked as though they'd been kissed a lot. Sarah chuckled, shaking her head, and suddenly she was crying again.

Margaret went to her and put her arms around her. Sarah felt like a colt who had these long legs and didn't know how to use them. She huddled into herself and felt her body pressed firmly against her mother's. Her head settled between her mother's breasts. Her own breasts were flattened against her mother's midriff, which felt soft and spongy. Her mother smelled like Ivory soap and Desert Flower bath powder, she decided. She flapped her arms helplessly around her mother's waist and closed her eyes. Margaret rocked, gently, holding Sarah tightly. She did that for quite a while. Then she let go of Sarah and pushed her back a little, to look at her face. She reached into her handbag, which sat on the table, squat and wrapped in its own thoughts, and pulled out a small brush. She began to brush Sarah's hair, which hung yellow and limp to her shoulders. The rain fell outside, breathing softly, dreaming gray dreams. After a while Margaret stopped brushing and sat down at the table.

"You haven't learned much yet, have you?"

"I've learned it, all right. I just don't like it."

"So you pretend that things aren't the way they are. And so you make them worse."

"That's about it."

Margaret got up and poured a glass of milk and handed it to Sarah. She didn't want it, but she drank some of it anyway. Now she was white all the way down her throat and into her stomach. She liked the idea. She drank some more.

"You like Michael, Mom, don't you?" she said earnestly, leaning across the table.

"Oh, Sarah, for heaven's sake," said Margaret. "I'm not going through all that again." She stood up. "I've got to bring the groceries in." She stopped, halfway to the door. "I'm not going to tell you not to see him. Neither will your father." Her voice filled with thistles. "So see him. But do it quietly. Don't rub it in." She smiled at Sarah, a smile which seemed to accentuate her weariness and which instead of soothing Sarah, strangely alarmed her. And when she spoke again it made Sarah think of the time her mother had gotten a cracked rib when she had fallen down the basement stairs. "You will not believe this," said Margaret, "but it is not important, Sarah. It is not at all important." She went out to bring in the bags of groceries, and after a minute, Sarah went out to help her.

"Ted, come to bed," said Margaret that evening. He was sitting in his pajamas, looking out the window. He left his chair and got into bed. She didn't touch him, but he knew she would.

"Let's talk," she said, and smiled at him.

He looked into her languorous eyes and wondered at the stupidity of the human body. It willed itself to age, to tire, to sicken, but at the same time continued stubbornly to house the ageless white-hot center which was its excuse for existing.

"What shall we talk about?" he said. "Shall I tell you about the classes I'm teaching? Will you tell me about Myrtle across the street and her decaying elm? Shall we discuss the phenomenon of Glynis and her excellent marks? Or is it, by some remote chance, that you want to talk about the state of my health?"

"Actually," said Margaret calmly, "I think we should leave the state of your health alone, until you've been back to the doctor. What I want to talk about," she went on smoothly, ignoring his attempt to interrupt, "is Sarah."

Her name seemed to fall upon the bedspread between them. He brushed at it with his hand, as if it had been crumbs.

"She's not looking too well, I think," said Margaret.

"Well, shit, she's probably got VD." Who said that? he wondered, shocked.

"Ted! My God, Ted!"

He shrugged, and refused to let himself get out of bed. He wanted something; a cup of tea, maybe.

What is Sarah for me to fear? Why does the sight of her confuse me? Why do I want to take handfuls of her yellow hair and pull?

He shivered, rubbed his head. He felt the extra flesh quiver around his waist and his mind flipped through all the things he could do to get rid of it as soon as the goddamn doctors finished with him, and he felt better. Tennis—no, too wet; handball or squash in the university gym; lots of swimming. He'd never jog. What a ridiculous sight those gasping, lead-legged creatures were, dragging themselves around the campus every day. God, what a load of crap. Jogging's bad for you, he thought with satisfaction.

Margaret touched his arm. "Ted, don't let yourself hate her, please."

He pulled away from her. "I don't hate her. Don't be ridiculous. It's a simple enough thing. I don't want my daughter wasting her life!" He shouted it. He had lost his temper after all. "Oh Christ, what's the use. Why the hell should I care what she does." He got out of bed. "I'm going down for a glass of milk or something. A drink, maybe."

It will be easier, thought Margaret deliberately, as soon as he's well again.

Her thighs ached.

She went into the hall. The doors to her daughters' rooms were closed. No light seeped out beneath them.

She started hot water running in the bathtub. She added some lemon-scented bubble bath and got out a big wraparound towel. She went back to the bedroom for a book, in case she felt like reading. But once in the water, all she did was think.

The faucet dripped, slowly, one drop forming tiny and growing and quivering and falling helplessly into the tub; the next forming tiny, growing, quivering, falling. She watched for a while, and reminded herself to ask Ted to try to fix the tap.

The big mirror above the sink gradually steamed over. Margaret heard the slurping of water against her body when she moved her shoulders, or a leg, or an arm. She smelled the bubble bath, the Ivory soap. She imagined the feel of the soft towel around her. She felt too relaxed, too languid to get out. And the hot water was soothing her aching thighs.

She sighed, and the sigh drifted off on the steam, skidded through the air, bumped the mirror—she could almost see it write itself, s-i-g-h, all over the steamy mirror.

Once he was well, she could talk to him again. Maybe he

would be receptive, once he'd stopped worrying about his health. And she knew he was worried, even though he usually refused to talk about it. But maybe nothing would ever change his bitter, unreasonable attitude toward Sarah. Maybe they were all stuck with it, forever.

But Sarah will be gone next year, thought Margaret, cleanly, coldly. And then we can get on with our lives.

She let the water out of the tub and wrapped herself in the towel.

If he doesn't make love to me tonight, she thought, I will make love to him; and her mind nodded and smiled inside her head.

Two weeks later they were told that he was dying.

# Chapter 22

GENTLY, GENTLY, SARAH CLOSED HER BEDROOM DOOR, one hand on the knob and one hand on the middle of the door, almost tenderly, as though it were made of heavy crystal and balanced only precariously on its hinges.

She went to the window. Below was the back yard, and then the fence, and then the lane, and then another fence and another yard and another house, with its back to her.

Winter was somewhere nearby, waiting. Sarah could already feel it hovering around. When it came it would strip the trees of leaves, drain the sky of color, empty the air of mildness, and much rain would fall, and maybe even some snow.

I must be in shock, she thought. This must be a kind of shock.

She huddled in the window seat, hugging her legs, and leaned her cheek against the oily coolness of the window. Her mind skipped and skimmed and refused to alight on anything. It pounced on one thing and then another with furious but skittering intensity.

How long since she had washed the long white swagged curtains at her window? What had she gotten in the math quiz? What would she wear on her date with Michael tonight? She had to wash her hair . . .

But I can't go out tonight, she thought.

You don't go running off with your boyfriend when you've just been told your father is dying.

She pulled herself out of the window seat. Blood had retreated from the surface of her skin. She thought her fingernails would drop off if she held her hands down by her sides for very long. She walked around her room, holding her wrists tightly, satisfied by the aches her fingernails caused, grating flesh against bone.

She wanted to be able to cry.

She went downstairs to the living room. Margaret and Glynis were still there. It felt like hours since Sarah had heard her mother say it. I've come through that moment, she thought, looking at them. But she didn't feel capable of getting through any more moments like that one, and saw the days and weeks and months stretch ahead of her as an endless series of impossible moments, her whole damn life looked like a minefield.

"Is he still asleep?" said Sarah. "What do I say to him?"

"Yes, he's asleep. You don't say anything to him."

Hearing her mother speak, seeing Glynis curled up beside her, head in Margaret's lap, Sarah felt suddenly like a visitor. Perhaps a visiting nurse. Or someone pretending to be a visiting nurse. He had been sick for quite a while, she realized, shocked.

"Did you ever think that's what it was? Cancer?" She was surprised that she could say that word out loud.

"I don't know. I can't tell." Her mother stroked Glynis' back. Glynis lay quietly, sniffling sometimes, watching the fireplace where there was no fire.

Sarah saw that her mother was crying, too. She felt a deep and quiet envy. "Do you want a drink, Mom? Maybe some scotch, or something?" She nodded and Sarah got her one, feeling efficient. She thought about having one herself and decided that her mother wouldn't let her.

"I want you to tell me, Mom. I mean, what happens? How is he, what does he do now . . ."

Margaret drank some of the scotch. "They let him stay home as long as they can. Then they let him stay home in the daytime but he has to sleep in the hospital. And then he stays in the hospital all the time." She drank some more. "The doctor says about six months." Glynis began to cry again. Margaret put an arm around her, leaned close to her. "Maybe I shouldn't have told you. I shouldn't have told you. I'm not doing this right."

Sarah crept upstairs and stopped in front of her parents' bedroom door. She listened, but heard no sounds. She opened the door, slowly. There were blinds on the windows, lowered against the cold gray afternoon. The room was filled with a gray light soft as velvet, soothing against the eyes.

Her father lay so still upon the wide bed that for a moment Sarah thought that they were too late, he had already died; and in that second she knew that he had not died, that it would be better for him, maybe, if he had, and that she was fiercely glad that he had not.

She tiptoed close to the bed. His eyelashes lay untrembling against his cheeks. His hair, mostly gray now, lay gently against his scalp. His hands rested on the covers, quiet, untroubled. She watched him breathe, slowly, easily, and wished that she could wish him dead.

Downstairs in the living-room archway she watched as Glynis got up from the sofa.

"I wish I had a dog," said Glynis. "I've gotta go and wash my face."

She passed Sarah without looking at her, walking as though she had fallen moments before from a tall tree. Sarah wondered what things would have been like if Glynis had been the older one.

"Will he have a lot of pain, or what?"

Margaret stirred on the sofa. "Probably. They dance around that question quite a lot. So probably he will."

"When did you find out?"

"They told us this afternoon. They gave him pills then so he could sleep."

"When he wakes up he'll have forgotten."

Margaret looked at her.

"When he remembers, it will be like being told all over again," said Sarah.

The telephone rang and Margaret went to answer it. Sarah waited, tense, ready to calm herself and walk slowly to the phone, but it wasn't for her.

Margaret came back into the room. "I don't know if I

should tell anyone," she said. "I don't know how you do these things. We'll have to tell Kathleen and William, oh God." There were tears on her face. "It would have been easier if he'd just died. Then you can do something." She sat down. "You just call people or send them notes or put something in the paper that says he's dead, and then everyone knows. But I don't know how to handle this."

Margaret finished her drink. She scrounged about for memories, but there weren't any. There was just the present. There'll be lots of time for memories, she thought, and hoped they would be there for her when everything was all over and she reached for them.

But she couldn't believe that it was going to be all over; not yet. She couldn't believe that he would die. She didn't think he would believe it, either. Not for a long time.

"This is not a church," said Ted dryly the next day when Sarah tiptoed into the living room after school.

He sat in his leather chair by the fireplace, holding the newspaper. His complexion didn't look too good, and his eyes were strange, but other than that he looked just the same.

He held up his hand as she sat down. "Don't say a word, not a single goddamn word, if it's about what I know it's about. I have no desire to discuss it, none at all. Talk to me about other things if you like but do not speak to me about sickness."

"You know, Daddy," said Sarah softly, "I keep looking for you, but I can't seem to find you. Do you have the same problem with me?" She tried to laugh.

He thought of lovely things which conceal danger, decay. He thought of the locket, which she now wore underneath blouses and sweaters, so that it would not show. He was not tense, however.

"I've had that problem with you for a while now, yes," he said.

"You're still the person I need when I need help," she said. "Not that I need help," she added hastily, "not really. It's just that—I depend on you. You always said just the right things to me at just the right times."

"You didn't listen to me. I'm not about to stand here dispensing wisdom to the four winds while you gallop off and do whatever you please. I'm not about to talk unless I'm listened to. It's a waste of energy. I can't afford to waste any energy."

She seemed a long way from him, sitting on the sofa, healthy. Too young to have accepted the fact of her own death—but not too young, never too young to accept the fact of somebody else's. Anybody else's.

He leaned his head on the soft leather of his chair and thought that whenever he died, he wanted it to be right here. But if they were right, and it was going to happen soon, would they let him do it here? They had promised all sorts of things, but promising was easy. He could still work, later he could stay at home, eventually he'd have to go to the hospital and get treatments and things—he couldn't figure that one out. If he was going to die of this goddamn thing, why would he go to the hospital for treatments? Maybe they weren't sure it was going to kill him after all. He closed his eyes and chuckled. Jesus, I'd like that, he thought; to prove them all wrong, the bastards.

He opened his eyes and looked at Sarah and saw that she inhabited another world.

"Don't talk," he said gently. "I'm tired and I don't want to get upset, and listening to you will make me upset."

"*I'll* listen, Daddy. Really I will." He saw the skin white on her knuckles as she grasped at her hands.

"Maybe another day, but not today. Not now."

"That's what you always do! You run away, or refuse to talk to me. Daddy, we don't have much more time, please talk to me!"

"You've got all the time in the world. It's me who doesn't have much time. Or so they say. And I don't choose to spend the time I have left going around in circles with you."

He looked at Sarah and thought, she doesn't seem very important to me right now. He couldn't believe he truly felt that way, but it seemed he did. It was Glynis who had crept into the living room an hour earlier and asked, her face white and haunted, if she could read the newspaper out loud to him; it was Glynis to whom his arms had opened, who had fallen into his lap and sobbed and clutched the lapels of his dressing gown and kissed his face.

And then there was Margaret. Of all the pains that came at him, not counting the physical ones, that was the biggest. He

wanted to put his head in her lap and cry: he wanted to hold
her while she cried. He wanted her to die with him: he
wanted her to live a long time and go through two, maybe
three more husbands after him. He looked at Margaret and
he thought he might kill somebody. And he was terribly
afraid that if things proceeded according to the doctors'
schedule there would come a moment when he would hate
his wife because she was not ill.

"Go and make us some tea," he said to Sarah, who got up,
docile, and went to the kitchen.


As the weeks passed, Ted continued to handle his classes
all right. He sometimes thought he might even be able to
finish the year. There were distinct advantages to having
taught the same subject for twelve years, or whatever the
hell it was. He could sluff off now and nobody even noticed.
But he no longer enjoyed looking at the faces of his students.
He wished he could put the information, the perceptions he
had for them into a lot of small plastic bags and just hand
them around.

"The thing that really bothers me," he said to Margaret,
"is that goddamn sabbatical. It was all set. We could have
had such a wonderful year." And he held her while she wept,
finding some satisfaction in still being able to comfort her
physically.

One night soon after Sarah's seventeenth birthday—which
had occurred almost unnoticed by all of them—Ted woke in
bed from a dream, in pain, sweat on his forehead, pajamas
sticking to him. Margaret woke, too, and got him his medi-
cine. As he lay waiting for it to work he felt his detachment
dissolve. He didn't know whether it was the pain or the
unremembered dream that did it, but, like acid, something
began to drip upon his detachment and dissolve it.

And his mind was suddenly full of Sarah. Her childhood
repeated itself for him with a clarity, a vividness that he
would have thought impossible after so many years, so many
happenings. And he knew again his place in the world, and
his mind weaved past and present and hopes of the future
into a panorama of light-skinned, light-haired, light-scatter-
ing Sarahs who, when he looked, made him cry.

He was shocked at breakfast the next morning to see that

her face was pallid and her eyes had lost some of their blueness.

Margaret said Sarah was all right, just not sleeping very well.

"None of us is sleeping very well," he said, and for a moment wished viciously that he could die right then and get it over with.

That evening after dinner he called Sarah into the living room.

"Just what do you plan to do with your life?" he demanded urgently, feeling affronted.

"You know, Daddy," she said cautiously. "I'm going to be an English teacher."

"You'd better make up your mind in a hell of a hurry," he said, as though he hadn't heard her. "Especially if you want to be a teacher. No B.Ed. degree, you remember that. You get yourself an Arts degree first, not all that education crap. Time doesn't last forever, you know. Be pretty terrible if one day you said to yourself, Eureka! I was right all along! I want to be a teacher! And like an axe, whap!" he chopped the air, "down comes something to take it right away from you, the whole damn thing . . ."

He felt that he was wandering from the subject, but he knew that what he had to say was terribly important, so he went on, ". . . your whole life, and all of a sudden you can't do a damn thing with it except watch it trickle away. That'd be a hell of a note, wouldn't it?"

"Oh, Daddy . . . !"

"I'm not talking about me," he said angrily. "Margaret, you tell her." Margaret had been standing in the doorway from the dining room. She came in and sat down. "You've done a few things with your life," he said to her, anxiety pressing him on. "If it started to trickle away you'd scrabble frantically for it, trying to capture all of it in your hand, or at least as much of it as you could—years, months, weeks, days, hours, even minutes . . ."

Like a broken thermometer, he thought; like trying to capture the mercury before it oozed under the tile in the kitchen or down the drain in the laundry room or into a rug somewhere . . .

"At least," he said, "you could sit back on your haunches and sigh and as you fell to the floor dead you could think to yourself, well, at least I've done a few things with my life, at least the part that hasn't escaped me was worthwhile."

He turned to Sarah. "She's been an actress, you know. That's where I saw her first—on a stage. And of course a wife and a mother and all that. And underneath it all, she lived her own life—you know?" He looked at Margaret quizzically. "Underneath it all there was that single mind, working away, never getting tired, never ever getting bored, trying to figure things out, you know? Never daunted. Always working, figuring, trying to make sense of things."

Ted stretched out his hand to Margaret, who took it and knelt beside his chair. He saw that she was crying again, and beneath his enormous anger and pain he was amazed that she had so many tears to shed, just for him.

"Poor Margaret," he said. "Life, death, a dollop of craziness, all mixed up together. Hell of a job trying to figure all that out at one time, isn't it?" He let go of her hand and dropped his head back on the leather of his chair and closed his eyes. "I don't want you to come with me, Margaret. You just remember that, whatever happens. I do not want you to die."

"I think I will, I think I am," said Margaret, resting her forehead against the arm of his chair.

"No, Margaret," he said. "I need you to stay on and keep an eye on things. In case I don't get to do it for myself." He sat up for a moment and kissed her hair. "I think I'll have a sleep. Right here in my chair. Okay?"

Margaret nodded and got up and left the room.

People come and go around here without seeing each other, thought Sarah. We're all locked up in separate little cocoons. No wonder we can't talk properly to each other.

She got up to leave. She wanted to go to her room and lie down on her bed and not think about anything. Maybe after a while she'd find Glynis and play cards or watch TV or go out for a walk, have a Coke somewhere.

"Hey. Sarah."

She turned. His head lay against the leather of his chair, his face was a soft white shadow there, his eyes gleamed blue as the sea on a sunlit day.

"Yes, Daddy?"

"You might not have been able to figure that out. But you get with it. Don't allow yourself distractions."

She thought he looked very ill, and wondered why his sickness had not cured him of other, less important things. This is what they mean, she thought, when they say there is no justice.

Spring had almost come. It was a color in the air, an almost imperceptible plumpness in tree branches dipping dispiritedly in the gusts of the March winds, branches whose awkward sticklike despair was just beginning to think about softening, branches which would not be hurried by the impatient wind but sullenly, stubbornly, dolefully clung to the memory of winter.

Ted's room was filled with a diffused greenness, as though it were floating beneath the sea. Light came through venetian blinds, like long blind fingers poking through the slats. He was in a hospital robe in a hospital bed and the color of his skin seemed the same color as the robe and the walls and the Charon's cocktail they gave him to drink—the color that filled the room seemed like that.

Although it can't be, thought Sarah. Not really green, that sour green of unripe apples.

His face was the white-green of skim milk, all the cream was gone, and he was suffering despite the Charon's cocktails and whatever else they gave him. He was a man subjected to torture, the kind that doesn't leave discernible marks but wraps its victims in an aura of pain that shimmers around them and blinds the eyes of the innocent.

She didn't know whether he could have hidden from her the fact that he was dying, but she knew that dying was something people do try to keep hidden from other people, and from themselves. But dying was a palpable presence in that room. She wanted to get up from her chair and chase it out, and throw open the blinds to let in the realness of the gray outdoors.

He didn't talk much any more. It seemed to exhaust him. Or else something distracted him from talking, something happening in his body or his brain. He would stop speaking and close his eyes. Any day now Sarah would be able to see his eyes through his closed eyelids, they were so translucent, so shimmery thin, stretched protectively across his eyes when he closed them. He was concentrating on something; maybe the pain—getting to know it, or still trying to

198

rout it. She couldn't tell, couldn't ask him. He was truly a stranger now, alone in a strange world.

"It won't be long now," he said in his scratchy, barely-there voice. "It won't be long now."

Sarah thought he meant his death and glanced fearfully at the door, expecting to see there a person from a funeral establishment.

By God, not now, she thought, not without Mom, and she stumbled to her feet to go phone Margaret.

"Everybody, it'll get everybody, everything," he said through his closed eyelids. "Ice age, volcano—do you know the earth is heating up hotter every year, do you know there are more unexplained earthquakes every year?" He stopped talking and breathed; his lips were still slightly pink. "People think of this planet, it's going to last forever, but it won't," he said, with a raspy chuckle.

Sarah felt that the world had already gone. There was just this single room floating through the universe, bathed in its green-gray light; just her and this man, in a room filled with green-gray light.

"Oh no. Could be anything," he said. "Ice age, can't you see them trying to stop that? Bastards'd probably drop a bomb. Could be earthquakes or volcanoes, though, or the earth one day so hot nobody could stand on it."

He breathed some more. Sarah wondered if she should say anything.

"Could be in your lifetime," he said. "Remember what I tell you. Maybe not cancer. Ice age, or an earth that burns your feet, air burning your lungs."

His breathing, slow and scratchy, filled the room. Sarah's dress was damp and her palms were slippery.

"It's very hot in here right now," she said.

He opened his eyes, like a curtain rising, and there was still blueness in them. It was when she looked right at his eyes that she wanted to cry and destroy things.

"Hot?" said Ted. "It's not hot in here. It's cool. Cold, even. But it'll change. Great upheavals, there'll be. Cataclysmic."

"Will you be able to watch it, do you think?" said Sarah, with sudden hope.

He sighed. "Now there, that's the question. I've been reading. Who knows. Who the hell knows."

"I think you will, Dad."

She could *see* him watching; healthy again, young, laughing as he watched, and smiling sometimes, and sometimes sorrowfully shaking his head. She was sure he'd never get angry, not under those circumstances. If death got rid of anything, she thought, it must surely get rid of anger. And impatience, she added, thinking about it.

"Yeah, but you're not the one going, are you? Not yet." He laughed—at least, Sarah thought it was a laugh.

What a stupid thing, she thought, rubbing her face. What a stupid thing to think about. But she desperately wished he believed it. That's all it would take, and then she would believe it, too.

"Where's your mother?"

"She's coming in a few minutes."

"Poor Margaret." His thin white fingers moved weakly, restlessly, on top of the sheet which covered him.

Sarah saw that the nails were getting transparent, too, just like his eyelids. Soon I'll be able to see right through him, she thought in horror.

"But it might not get her," he said. "Something else might get her. Don't know. How to die if you have a choice. Better not have a choice, I think. This way's pretty bad, can't imagine a worse way, but maybe they're all the same. What do you think?" He closed his eyes, breathing.

"You shouldn't talk so much, Dad."

"I should save my strength. Yeah."

She put her two hands over one of his, white, blood flowing through it to no purpose.

Her mother came in. Sarah got up quickly. She kissed Margaret's cheek, kissed her father's forehead, and went out into the hall. She found the elevator, walked across the lobby out into the coolness of the day, and sat on the bench at the bus stop, shivering, while sweat ran from her forehead and down under her arms and wet her dress some more.

That night she told Margaret, "I'm not going to see him alone any more, only if you're there, or Glynis, I won't go alone, I'm too scared, I can't help him—I just won't go there all by myself ever again, ever," and her mother held her as she shook.

\* \* \*

"He doesn't want to see me," she told Michael.

They were in his car, parked by Spanish Banks. Rain mixed sea and sky into an indistinguishable blur at the nonexistent horizon. Sea gulls whirled and cawed, swooping suddenly to earth or ocean. Figures muffled in raincoats or heavy jackets, heads huddled into their shoulders, walked in solitude along the sand.

"He doesn't want to see Glynis, or Harry, or anybody. He doesn't even want to see Mom, or at least not all the time, but she can't stay out of that damn hospital."

She sat close to him, her head on his shoulder. His arm was around her and his cheek was against her hair.

"Mom doesn't go to the hairdresser any more. She's lost pounds and pounds. She doesn't put on any makeup . . ."

"Shhh, shhh," said Michael, holding her tightly.

"She says he changes his mind, that sometimes he really does want her there, so she has to be there all the time, just in case." Sarah sat up straight and looked at Michael intently. "He can't last much longer, you see."

"I wish there was something I could do, Sarah," he said miserably, "I really do."

"The trouble is," she said, looking out at the beach, the gray and restless sea into which the rain fell unnoticed, "I don't know if he ever really believed that he would die, I don't know if any of us did, but now sometimes I wake up in the morning and I hope that this will be the day." She stared at him aggressively.

"That seems pretty natural to me. He must be suffering a lot."

"But it's not his suffering I'm thinking of. It's ours. Mine." She shivered. "Mom says he doesn't want to see us because he's not himself, whatever that means. He's himself all right, he's just dying, that's all. She says he's bitter and angry and stuff, and I think he *should* be. I mean, *I'm* bitter and angry, and it's not even me who's dying."

She pulled away and sat up straight. "I've got to go home now, Michael. I don't want to leave Glynis alone for very long."

"When will I see you again?" He started the car and backed out of the parking space. "Tomorrow? Can you get away tomorrow, for a while?"

Sarah was cut into so many pieces she was often unsure

which were the ones most likely to survive, and therefore most deserving of her attention. Something had to live through this, and she wanted to make sure she didn't invest time on a part of her already condemned to a certain death.

Michael turned on the windshield wipers. They swept back and forth across the glass, smoothing out the ripples and bumps formed by the falling rain.

She concentrated on his black hair, his profile, the strong neck, the shirt open at the throat. She took from her mind her knowledge of each of the parts of his body; and the hot cloud stirred in her belly.

"Tomorrow," she said blindly. "Yes, tomorrow is fine."

He turned and smiled and calmly he winked at her.

Whatever happens, she thought, this does not die; whatever happens, we have this; and it's warm and rolling and will keep us alive.

"Oh, such a lovely dimple," she smirked, and he frowned, embarrassed, and took a hand from the wheel to muss her hair.

It was four nights later that her mother and Glynis came to waken her, her mother's face burning white in the pervasive glow of the streetlamp.

# PART IV

# Chapter 23

SARAH STOOD BY THE GRAVE, SHIVERING. IT WAS MAY, BUT it might as well still have been March. The clouds were thick and low; the light rain that fell seemed like an extension of the clouds themselves, and it was cold on Sarah's face and hands.

They had laid pre-grown grass, in squares, over the place where the dug-up dirt had been. But the fragile wooden cross was still there, and the sight of it made Sarah think for a moment that this whole business might be temporary, that people might still come rushing at her, beaming, to tell her that it had all been a mistake.

She knew it was permanent, though, and that an engraved stone would be thrust into the earth there, to last forever. It would probably have something written on it besides the dates of his birth and death. Sarah had tried to think of something she would like to see written there, but she couldn't think of a single thing.

She found it a relief to come to the cemetery. There was absolutely nothing there but dead bodies and gravestones. She came every Sunday, with her mother and Glynis, and sometimes she came alone, on other days. Today she had come with her grandfather Griffin, who had driven down from Kelowna for the long weekend. She had walked on ahead, while he parked the car, to place her flowers on the grave.

She wished she had thought to get some lilac blossoms from somewhere. She had bought carnations, which her father had not particularly liked, and the heavy spicy scent of them was ridiculously incongruous in the clean air of the graveyard.

Her grandfather joined her and they stood looking down at the grave, not saying anything. Sarah was glad Kathleen had stayed home. Kathleen didn't like cemeteries. She said there wasn't any point in going to his grave because only the dead part of him was there.

It seemed to Sarah that while her father was alive there had been only one of him, but that now that he was dead, there were three of him. There was the dead one, buried here; there was the one she dreamed about, which was pretty well the one she'd known; and there was a third one, which she herself had created to plague and punish her. The dead and buried one was the easiest to deal with, and that's why she liked coming to the cemetery.

She glanced at her grandfather, wondering how he would react if she told him all this. His bald head was wet with rain. She moved close to him and took his arm, and squeezed it. He turned to smile at her.

"I'm going to come and stay with you this summer, Grandpa," she said, "if you'll let me."

"I'd like that. You can work in the store," he said.

Sarah loved Kelowna, and especially the lake. Sometimes things had worked out so that Sarah and her father and her grandfather went to the beach together. William and Ted had sat under a tree and talked while Sarah ran in and out of the water. After a while, though, her father would look at his watch.

"You're twitching, Ted," William would say with a grin. "Did you ever notice that, Sarah? He can't sit still longer than five minutes before he starts to twitch."

"I've noticed that, Grandpa," Sarah would say, seriously.

"Why do you think he does that?" said William.

"Hey, what is this?" said Ted uncomfortably.

"Maybe he concentrates too hard," said William. "Ted, maybe you should let things seep into you, instead of pulling at them so hard."

# THE FAVORITE

"You should learn to relax, Daddy," said Sarah.

"I'm relaxed!" Ted had said, exasperated, and Sarah and William had laughed.

Sarah, shivering in the rain-wet graveyard, said to William, "He's not twitching now, Grandpa, is he? Or is he, do you think? For a person who had trouble keeping still sometimes, this is an awful situation to be in, don't you think?"

William put his arm around her. "I do, Sarah. I do."

"I mean, maybe he *is* twitching down there, maybe there *is* only one of him and he *is* twitching, can you imagine what that would feel like? I saw that coffin and there's not enough room in there for a person to stretch or turn over or anything and of course it isn't possible to get out of it, you could claw and claw at it . . ."

William turned her around until her face was in his shoulder. "Why are you making it so hard for yourself? You know that whatever's down there is just what they say—remains. The *remains* of your father. Not Ted himself."

Sarah pulled back and looked at him. "Then where is he, Grandpa? He can't be in more than one place; he can't be. Either he's down there, all buried under the earth and helpless to get out, with no room to twitch, or else he isn't there, and then where is he? He could be anywhere, and the world is so big I would never find him."

William led her away from the grave, toward his car, which was parked outside the gates of the cemetery, what seemed ten miles away.

"Sarah," he said firmly, "you're doing something to yourself that I don't like, and I know that your father wouldn't like it either." He took her by the shoulders. "I don't know anything about all that where-is-he nonsense. All I know is that he's dead, my son and your father, Ted; and that what we have left of him are the parts of ourselves that were also part of him. That's what you've got to think about, Sarah. That, and all the good memories." He took a firm grip on her arm and led her to the car.

# Chapter 24

SARAH STOOD IN THE KITCHEN, LEANING HEAVILY ON HER hands, which were palms down on the windowsill, and she did not see the lushness of the garden or the weeds invading it because her eyes were flickering from side to side; and she did not feel the coolness of the rainy spring day because her shirt clung hot to the hot sweat of her back; and she did not hear the soft rustling of the rain through the screen door leading to the patio because her heart's frantic beating drove out other sounds.

I will avoid streets where there's traffic, I'll never drive, I'll stay out of airplanes, and when I walk I'll be careful it's in places where there are no people to throw rocks at me; I'll live only in warm sunny places where blizzards won't hunker me down and lightning won't throw bolts at me and I'll live to be a hundred years old, I will, I will, so stay away from me . . . I'll read and have affairs and dye my hair when I get old and have face-lifts and do exercises to keep my stomach flat and I'll travel yes I will I'll go away all right and I'm going to live forever so stay away from me . . .

She let go of the windowsill and whirled around, and beat around her mother's kitchen like her grandmother Kenne-

dy's canary. Oh I should not have let go of my calm I should
never have let go of my calm oh God my feathers are going
to drop off, there's a great big cat in here . . .

She jerked around, but saw nothing. She pressed her back
against a wall.

Should have gone out shopping with my mom, yes I
should . . .

She lowered herself into a chair and wished for a cup of
coffee, but a cup of coffee did not appear. She placed her
arms carefully on the top of the kitchen table and rested her
head upon them. Her cheek felt the soft flesh of her upper
arm against the side of her mouth.

"From where do you peer at me, Daddy? I know you are
somewhere, oh yes I do."

She stopped breathing to listen, but there was nothing
there, the illusion of normalcy continued humming mind-
lessly around her, unbroken, not a rent in it, not the tiniest
tear was ripped in it by speaking aloud to something which
was not there.

She drew herself up, head first, then arms, and shoulders,
and was sitting straight in her chair. She continued to pull
upward from her head and was standing erect, shoulders
back, tummy tucked in, and she walked elegantly through
the dining room and into the living room, just browsing, as in
a department store, intent on casual shoplifting, trying to
note the placement of mirrors and closed-circuit television
and store detectives.

The presence accompanied her. Maybe it was grafted to
her. If she had known precisely where, she could have
quickly lopped off that part of her and perhaps gotten rid of it
once and for all; could have buried the lopped-off part of her
in a grave and listened for sounds of panic from the presence
as dirt fell upon it, shoveled.

She glided to the window and looked out upon the street.
The green of the leaves on the trees was so fiercely alive in
the rain that its glow hurt her eyes. She turned back into the
room, her feet planted wide apart, her arms crossed. She
narrowed her eyes.

She stared into all the corners, in case it had smeared
itself against them and left tiny visible parts of itself behind.
The rug lay upon the floor in graceless abandonment, the
chairs and sofas sat there alertly, waiting blind and deaf for

something to happen. From the roses in a crystal vase came the close cloying fragrance of things removed from their natural place and left to sulk soddenly in greenish water. Dead things, stuck upright in a vase for people to watch them decay. We should have stuck him in a vase, she thought, like a plucked rose; then we could have all watched and seen him die. If I could actually have seen him die, maybe I would have believed it.

Sarah walked stiffly to the dining-room table, which gleamed on its pedestal. She sat at one of the chairs, which had curved legs like a caricature of a ballet dancer's. She felt the sweat on her back, warm like a large hand; it pushed her gently down until her face was upon the gleaming surface of the table. She wanted just to give up, succumb, dissolve into the furniture polish on the top of the table. There seemed nobody in the world of much importance except her and the presence, which felt farther away, now, somewhere near the fireplace, she thought. She wondered what could save her and thought concentratedly of her mother, her sister, of Michael—but they were all far away; she saw them as fuzzy images, out in the surf, perhaps, or halfway up a mountain, or perhaps on horseback thundering away across a prairie somewhere. Anyway, they were not here.

The earth's out there, in all its rainy springtime splendor. It breathes, and throws off scents, and glows, and sprawls beneath the clouds . . .

She stood up. There is, she thought, a wide-mouthed tube in me, it extends from my stomach through my chest up through my throat into my mouth. She thought that if by accident she let herself get too close to the presence again, she might inhale it and then it would live forever inside her.

I must get my calm back, she thought, and ran suddenly and quickly upstairs, into her bedroom, which used to be Glynis'.

She closed the door and flung herself on the bed. It was gone. In a little while she would be calm and could go downstairs again.

But it was getting stronger, day by day, and her calmness splintered more easily now. She wondered if she would be able to outlast it.

The rain spread itself sinuously in sheets that followed one another down across her window. She could hear it murmur-

ing through the glass. Sarah closed her eyes, thinking to
doze off, build up her strength a little more . . .

She became aware of another sound, not the rain; a soft,
huffing sound. Her eyes opened wide. She got up and stood
still in the middle of her room. She went cautiously to the
door and opened it—the sound was a little louder. She
moved silently down the hall and stopped in front of the
closed door to her mother's room. She put her ear to the
door—that's where it's coming from, all right, she thought.
Her heart was going at a tremendous rate. Maybe he's
decided to show himself to me, she thought. She wanted to
run away, but she put her hand on the doorknob.

Sarah saw in her mind her father lying on the bed, dressed,
covered with the bedspread, his hands crossed in front of
him, his head a little to one side, his chest moving up and
down slowly as he breathed. His eyes were closed, some of
his graying hair had fallen over his forehead.

She began to push the door inward, slowly . . .

The bedroom was almost dark. The curtains were closed.
The bed lay smooth and unoccupied. In the corner of the
room, between her father's chest of drawers and the window, Glynis squatted on the floor: Sarah had not known she
was in the house. Glynis' eyes were closed but the faint light
from the window gleamed upon tears on her face. She was
making little sobbing sounds, rocking back and forth on her
haunches, her face buried in the old brown robe that had
been Ted's.

Sarah watched long enough to make sure she was seeing
something that was really there. She looked sharply at the
light, the rust-colored carpet that covered the floor, the
smoothly made bed, the lamps on the two night tables, the
hairbrush and comb that still rested on the top of her father's
chest of drawers. The faint scent of her mother's perfume
hung in the air.

Sarah looked with extreme care at Glynis. Her sister's
hands were clenched into the soft brown fabric of the robe.
Her knees were up, the calves of her legs, bare, in shorts,
were expanded and muscly. Glynis sniffed and gulped and
shivered, clutching the robe to her face, rubbing her cheek
against it.

This is the real thing, all right, thought Sarah.

She closed the door, silently, and stood in the hall outside

211

with her hands in fists. Her body felt very strong. She was sure it was completely free of disease of any kind. With each breath she took her anger grew more powerful. She knew that she had begun to cry, but that was only from rage.

She went down the stairs and vaguely registered the sound of her mother's car pulling up in the driveway at the front of the house.

Sarah pushed through the living room and the dining room and the kitchen and went out the side door and onto the porch. The rain fell upon her back and seemed to sizzle there. She went down the steps and got on her knees on the grass and reached blindly under the porch where the lilies of the valley shone unseen. She fumbled around, cursing, and got handfuls of stuff and pulled, hearing the grunts of the astonished earth, the tiny piercing screams of the flowers as they fluttered into death. She ripped and tore, digging her fingers into the soil like a fat-tined rake, and the leaves and flowers were dying in her hands.

Margaret got out of the car and ran over to her, and put her hand on Sarah's shoulder.

"Where have you been?" said Sarah. She didn't seem to realize that she was crying. "Glynis needs you. Where were you? Nobody's ever around when you goddamn need them. People always show up when you don't need them, poking around, scaring the hell out of you, never saying anything, just scaring the hell out of you. But they aren't there when you need them, oh no."

Margaret pulled her to her feet and with an arm around her shoulder took her into the house, as the rain continued to fall. She put Sarah in a chair in the kitchen and rubbed at her hair and face and legs and arms with the dish towel.

"Glynis needs you," said Sarah, grabbing the towel. "Not me. I don't need you. Where were you, anyway? Come on," she said, clutching Margaret's hand. She pulled her upstairs and opened the door to Margaret's bedroom. "She's in there."

Margaret looked in at Glynis. She watched Sarah go into her room. "Oh God, oh Jesus," said Margaret, and rushed in to take Glynis in her arms.

# Chapter 25

"DO YOU KNOW WHAT I'M GOING TO DO WHEN I LEAVE
here? Where the hell is that waiter?" said Margaret three
weeks later.

"No. What are you going to do when you leave here?"

"I'm going to get my hair cut. All cut off."

The waiter appeared, and Margaret ordered a double
martini and a steak sandwich. Moira asked for a glass of
white wine and a fruit salad.

"I think it's great that you're going to get your hair cut,"
said Moira. "Since when did you start having doubles? Are
you turning into a souse?"

Margaret looked at her, considering. "That's not a bad
idea," she said.

The martini was extremely cold. She thought it tasted like
liquid rock.

"I'm going back to work," she said.

"Good," said Moira. "I was hoping you would."

"I don't know what I'm doing, though," said Margaret. "I
might—Jesus—I might take another brush-up course at
some business school and get a job as a secretary."

"Or?"

"Or I might try to act again." She clutched her hands.

"Jesus. That sounds so stupid. Juvenile. It's a stupid idea."
She took another drink.

Moira stared at her across the table. "Do it," she said,
with a passion that surprised Margaret. "Do it."

"I've got this cousin," said Margaret. "She's quite a bit
older than I am. She used to be a nurse, years and years ago.
When her husband—when her husband died, she hadn't
worked for so long I think she'd forgotten what a bedpan
looked like. He had a lot of insurance and she was in her
fifties. Everybody expected her to sell their house and get an
apartment and go on a cruise or something. But she decided
to go back to work. She had to take courses for a whole year
first."

"Sure," said Moira encouragingly.

"This is a bit different," said Margaret.

"I know. But it's what you want to do, isn't it?"

Margaret sighed. "I don't know. Sometimes I think so.
But I've got to be realistic." She banged her fist softly upon
the table.

"I don't know what you're getting all worked up about,"
said Moira. "I presume you don't have it in mind to storm
Broadway, at this late date."

Margaret flapped impatient fingers. "Of course not, don't
be silly."

"You just want to act again, right? In any old play. In any
old theater."

"Right," said Margaret. "I think," she added. She leaned
toward Moira, whispering. "Moira, I don't even know if I
was ever any good."

"And you're not going to find out by continuing to sit at
home on your duff, either."

They sat in a pocket of silence. The chatter of conversation, the clatter of china and silverware, the drone of Muzak
seemed to have abandoned the area around their table, and
waiters scurried past soundlessly.

"I keep trying to look forward," said Margaret, "and
getting jerked back. I miss him so terribly. Everything
around me makes it hurt more. Everywhere I look I see only
his deadness. There's nothing that doesn't remind me of
him—of the fact that he's not here any more."

Moira reached over and took her hand, and held it until
their waiter arrived.

"And then there's Sarah," said Margaret with an effort. She was looking down at her plate. The steak bore the black streaks of the grill.

"What about Sarah?" said Moira.

"I don't like it," said Margaret bitterly. "She's—clutching at him. I feel—I don't know. I don't like it. I hate it. I'm angry with her. I feel—robbed, or something."

"Of what? What are you talking about?"

"Oh, I don't know," said Margaret despairingly. "I can't deal with it, it's so bloody dramatic. She's in the *way*, standing there all pale and solemn . . . oh, how can I be talking like this, for God's sake, she loved him, half her life has been ripped away, I know that . . ." She dragged a Kleenex from her purse. I do this so often, she thought angrily, dabbing beneath her eyes, wiping her nose, that if I ever again get another cold I'll never even know it.

"How's Glynis?" said Moira.

"Glynis—she's going to be all right, now, I think." Margaret tried to laugh. "She's a survivor, Glynis is."

"Sarah's the survivor," said Moira. "Glynis is—a successful struggler, maybe."

Margaret looked at her sharply. "We'd better eat this stuff," she said, and picked up her knife and fork.

"I have something to tell you, too," said Moira. She leaned back in her chair, wineglass in hand, and her eyes swept across Margaret and beyond her, as she looked the room over critically. "I'm leaving."

"Leaving where?" said Margaret blankly.

"Leaving Jason and the boys."

Margaret stared. She knew that Ted would have said he'd seen it coming. For years.

"I don't think I'm even very surprised," said Margaret slowly.

"It came as a hell of a surprise to Jason, I can tell you."

"And the boys?"

"Yeah. It came as a surprise to them, too." She had purplish smudges underneath her eyes; Margaret noticed them now for the first time. There have been other things going on in the world these last three months, she thought.

"How long have you been thinking about it?"

"Oh, for ages, I guess. But it's been harder than I'd expected."

"When are you leaving? Oh God, Moira. You're not going to leave Vancouver."

"Yeah, I think I better, Maggie. At least for a while."

Moira stabbed at her salad. Margaret took a bite of her steak sandwich, then pushed away her plate.

"I had to tell you," said Moira, putting down her fork. "I decided before Ted died. I waited as long as I could. I didn't want to do it when I thought maybe you still needed me . . ."

"I still need you now. I do."

"I know, but you're making some decisions, you—hell, Maggie, you're even going to get your hair cut off." She laughed a little. "I just can't stay any longer. Not now that I've told them."

"He's your husband. You must love him, you must have loved him once, at least. And your kids, my God . . ."

"My kids are not kids. My kids are nineteen and seventeen years old. And Jason. Well. No, I'm not sure whether I ever did love him. I don't want to go into that." She was staring moodily into her salad. She looked up and grinned. "I'm not much good at writing letters, but I'll try. Maybe I'll send you felt pen pictures, like the things kids bring home from kindergarten. 'My new house,' 'my car,' 'my city,' things like that."

"Where are you going? When?" Margaret saw that there was more gray in Moira's black hair, and the lines bracketing her mouth were deeper.

"San Francisco. I think right away. There's nothing to wait around for."

The waiter came to take away their plates. They ordered coffee.

It occurred to Margaret that it must be possible to live without needing anybody at all. Possible, she thought; but bleak—awfully, awfully bleak. She looked at Moira and tried to smile. "You'll have to come for dinner before you leave. Say goodbye to Sarah and Glynis."

Soon we'll both be husbandless, she thought. But you might run into yours on the street someday, and I won't. You might even call yours up on the phone someday, and I can't do that.

What is this? she thought, dazed. No husband, an absent friend; all the blocks knocked out from under me at once?

\* \* \*

At three-thirty she sat in her car outside the high school watching for Sarah, drumming her fingers on the steering wheel. She was very cold, and tense. She heard a bell ring inside. A few minutes later the doors at the top of the steps opened and kids began pouring outside. She watched a lot of them go down the steps and gather in knots on the sidewalk or wander off toward bus stops and the parking lot. Finally it seemed the school must have emptied itself and she began to wonder if Sarah had gone out a back door. Then she saw her, and leaned over to call through the window.

Sarah stopped, turned, looked at her mother, and walked toward the car. When she reached it she stooped down and looked in, her long hair falling forward to frame her face.

"You've had your hair cut," said Sarah. She got in the car and stared at her mother. Margaret's hair curled around her face gently, like petals. She looked younger, Sarah thought, and her eyes looked bigger.

"Do you like it?" said Margaret politely.

"If I didn't know you, I'd like it."

Margaret started the car and drove away from the school.

"You look a lot different."

"I think that's why I did it," said Margaret.

"Why do you want to look different?"

"Because I am different, Sarah."

Sarah turned to look out the window. Suddenly she laughed. "Maybe I should get my hair cut. Maybe that'd be a good idea, Mom. What do you think?" Margaret didn't answer. Sarah looked out the window again. "I don't think it would work," she said.

They drove along in silence. When Margaret had pulled into the driveway, she put her hand on Sarah's arm. "Don't get out."

Sarah sat patiently, holding her books. Her profile was like marble, tinted faintly pink on the cheeks.

She has not yet basked in the sun this year, thought Margaret, detached.

She felt extremely distinct, fastidious. The child is thin, she thought. She is pale, her hair hangs lank, yet she is as strong as marble, and as easily smitten into smithereens.

"I am angry with you," said Margaret. She hadn't planned anything, she had just recklessly let her anger grow, and now it was so strong that it shook words from her.

"You're trying to steal away my grief," she said. Yes, she thought. That's it.

Sarah thrust her books forward, an instinctive barricade. Margaret pushed them back down into Sarah's lap. It was a small gesture, but in it Margaret felt her potential for violence. They were both breathing quickly in the cage that was the car, but Margaret could feel no heat rising in her face; she couldn't even feel her heart beating. Maybe I'm the one made of marble, she thought.

"You listen for him to come to you," she said, and saw in Sarah's face that it was true. "You hear a knock on the door and you imagine yourself running to it, opening it, seeing your father there and throwing your arms around his neck." Sarah was shaking her head. "God damn you, Sarah, I *know* that you do." She leaned closer to her. "But *which* father, Sarah? The one who patched up your cuts and bruises? The one who gave you the locket?"

She reached out to touch the locket, framed by the open collar of Sarah's blouse, but Sarah pulled away.

"Or is it the one who wouldn't meet your boyfriend?" said Margaret. "Do you think that's the one? The one who hated your boyfriend? The one who found that part of him could even hate *you,* Sarah."

Sarah's face was entranced and stricken, but Margaret saw this as only of peripheral importance.

"I will not be generous with him any more," she said. "I am angry, so angry." She clasped her hands together tightly. "There were years with him that I won't have now, years when you would have been gone. We could have learned to be just two people living together, leaning on one another, but each with our feet planted on our own ground. I know we would have learned that. I think we could have."

Margaret realized that there were tears on her face and she wiped them off with her hands, which were shaking.

Sarah opened the car door and fled, stumbling on the brick walk, toward the front door.

"I will not have it!" Margaret shouted from the car. "I will not have it! God damn you, Sarah! God damn you!"

She put her head back against the seat and closed her eyes.

Now I can feel my heart, all right, she thought.

She was still shaking, and she was unutterably weary. Soon shame began to spill from her, flushed out by her tears.

Sarah went straight from the car to her room. She closed the door, and sat on her bed, still holding her books. Her mother was full of surprises, that was for sure. Confrontation had left Sarah's heart bang-banging and her skin sore and her head aching, and she figured her mother must be feeling about the same. She didn't feel angry with her mother. She thought her mother had as much right to get angry as Sarah did. It was upsetting, though, having her mother shriek at her. Her mother didn't go in much for shrieking.

When she was calmer, Sarah got up and put her books on her desk. Then she lay down to think. Some of the things her mother had said there wasn't much point in thinking about— they just were, and there was nothing to be done about them. But other things deserved a lot of thought. Obviously something drastic was called for. Sarah's preoccupation with the presence was harmful not only to herself but to other people as well. For a minute, there in the car, she had thought her mother knew what was going on, and had felt a gigantic surge of hope. She *almost* knew. But almost wasn't anywhere near enough. She, Sarah, had to somehow find a way to get rid of this thing by herself. She couldn't go on like this.

I can't, she thought, suddenly serene.

I simply cannot go on like this.

## Chapter 26

"GOD, SARAH, I DON'T UNDERSTAND YOU," SAID MICHAEL that evening.

"I thought you'd be glad," said Sarah, and she rolled down the car window to let in the sweet breath of June. She needed lots of air on her face.

"I would be," said Michael, "if I knew what the hell was going on."

"I told you what's going on. If you don't want to do it, just say so."

"Oh Jesus, Sarah. Of course I want to. But I don't want to if *you* don't want to. And I'm not sure you really want to."

Sarah put her face in her hands.

He grabbed her, roughly. "Jesus, Sarah, I love you, Jesus, of course I want to go to bed with you."

Her arms went around his neck and she held him tightly. "Then let's do it, Michael, please, let's do it, right now, please. Your parents aren't home, are they? So let's do it right now."

"At my house? In my room?"

They stopped at a drugstore. Michael had imagined the scene dozens of times. Each time he had groaned and rolled over and pushed his face into his pillow, since he always seemed to be in bed when he imagined it. But when he came out of the drugstore, the package in his pocket, he was amazed at how easy it had been.

He found himself almost hoping, for a second, as they rounded the corner and headed up his block, that his parents had changed their minds and stayed home. But their car was gone. It was really going to happen. He was extremely nervous.

"How do we go about this?" said Sarah heavily, looking around his room.

"I think we should start like we always do. Only we'll have to sit on the bed. There isn't anywhere else."

"Should we get undressed?"

"No, let's just sit down. Come on." He took her hand and they sat on the edge of the bed.

Sarah laughed, lightly. "This feels really strange."

"Just pretend we aren't going to do anything more than we usually do," said Michael, his heart pounding.

"No, I mean your room. I've never been in your room before. It's kind of bare." Sarah thought she might have to be sick, and she didn't want to do that in a strange house.

"What did you expect, *Playboy* centerfolds all over the walls?"

"I didn't expect anything. I guess I was just thinking about my room. I don't know. Haven't you got any books?" she said desperately.

"Jesus, Sarah." His hand dropped from her shoulder. She felt a great deal lighter. "You want a tour? I'll give you a tour. Just sit right there and I'll show you. Look, see? Here's my closet. All my clothes hung up on their hangers, see? And underneath, on the floor, all my shoes. Four pairs. Some dirty laundry in there, too." He kicked it into the corner. "Now here you have a chest of drawers, four drawers, should I open them for you? No? There's nothing much in there anyway, just socks and jockey shorts, stuff like that.

"I've got a desk, too, you might have noticed, right here under the window so I can look out and watch old man Beckett mowing his lawn. There's stuff in these drawers, too, paper, stuff like that—and no books? No books, you say? Just have a look over here, my dear; missed this, didn't you; a little old bookshelf right over here against the wall, and what's it got in it? Books! And some magazines. No

THE FAVORITE

*Playboy,* though, you'll be glad to see—a couple of *Road and Track,* some things like that, you wouldn't be interested. There. How's that?"

He stood in front of her, fists on his hips, his face red and his eyes looking angry.

I will not spend my life with him, Sarah thought. So what.

She reached for his waist and pulled him down beside her. "Don't be angry. It's a fine room, a first-rate room, I love it, really I do."

Michael kissed her, and after a while he sat up to pull off his T-shirt. He threw it on the floor and began unbuttoning Sarah's blouse.

"I couldn't be angry with you, Sarah, oh I see you didn't wear a bra. I'm really glad you didn't wear a bra. And I notice that you have dispensed with panties today, too," he said, undoing her jeans. "I'm really glad of that, too."

Sarah's body was jumping and lurching about, as it always did when Michael put his hands on it. She hadn't been certain that it would respond to him at all, this time, and was both relieved and ashamed.

Michael got up to take off his jeans. After a second's hesitation he left his underwear on and Sarah stared, fascinated, at the bulges there.

"Touch it," he said.

She lifted a hand and touched what she knew were testicles and a penis and as she said the words to herself, testicles and penis, she thought it no wonder that people gave them other words, ones that sounded at once harsher and more real. They rested warmly in her hand, so warm they were almost damp, and as she held them the cock moved, shuddered, thrust itself out.

"You better take those shorts off," she heard herself say. "It's going to strangle in there, poor thing."

She thought the whole thing was very eerie, and wondered if there was anything she could have done to make sure it would all go smoothly. There flashed into her mind an image of the two of them coupling furiously on the rug in her living room, and a piercing giggle whipped through her mind; but she knew even as she imagined it that such a thing would not have been permitted to occur.

They decided they would both take the rest of their clothes off at the same time, so neither of them would be

222

embarrassed. They stood up and Michael carefully folded the bedcovers back.

"It's only meant for one," he said, "but I think we can both squeeze in there, don't you?"

Sarah was relieved to see that they were going to do it under the covers.

She hurried to take off her jeans and slip the unbuttoned blouse from her shoulders, but she wasn't fast enough. When she turned, Michael was already in the bed, covers up to his waist, hands behind his head, watching her. She was somewhat shaken by the look on his face, which was one she had had glimpses of before.

It wouldn't matter to him, she thought, even if he did know why I'm doing this; it wouldn't matter one bit.

She scampered under the sheets and pulled the covers up over her head, and put her lips on Michael's navel. He lurched back, almost falling off the bed, and wriggled down until they were both in almost darkness.

"Jesus," said Michael, "Jesus, no clothes, I can't believe it."

Sarah reached for his crotch and in the second before he pulled away, almost in a spasm, she touched his testicles and felt the hot wrinkles there and on the inside of her wrist felt the hardness of his penis—his cock, she said carefully to herself; that's his cock and those are his balls.

"How do we know if I'm big enough for you?" she said as his lips moved across her neck and down to encircle first one nipple, then the other.

"We just have to trust to luck," said Michael feverishly. Sarah stiffened. "No, I didn't mean that, there's nothing to worry about, we're made especially to fit together." He kissed her forehead and smoothed back her hair, and pulled the covers away from her head. "Didn't you know that? That we're made especially to fit together?"

He turned her onto her side and laid his body carefully against hers and kissed her mouth. It was something her body seemed already to know about, but to her mind it was a great surprise: somebody else's bare chest was pressing against her breasts. In the hollow between her legs there was the now familiar throbbing, but this time somebody's cock was there waiting to get in. She felt Michael's feet against her feet, and that was the strangest feeling of all. Sarah was overwhelmed by a sensation of déjà vu, of suffocating intimacy, of somebody knocking on the door to her soul; but this was only in her mind—her body was sweating in its anxiety for still more to happen.

She fell onto her back in a kind of anguish and opened her legs, her eyes squeezed shut. "Do it, Michael, do it," she said, and lay with her eyes closed, her crotch pounding; it's disgraceful, she thought, but was glad of it. The clamor being set up by her body was quite loud enough to drown out other things.

She heard Michael fumbling around and felt the heat from his body above her before she felt the touch of it.

"Lift up your hips," he said quietly. "I'm going to put a pillow under them."

She gritted her teeth and lifted her hips. She felt as though she were to be examined for the presence of disease; but she quoted to herself, this is to make entry less difficult, and tried to relax.

Michael pushed a pillow under her. "Take it easy," he said, touching her hands, which were clenched into fists. "Take it easy," he said, running his fingers down her body.

She reached up blindly for him, something in her squirming from the vision of herself spread-eagled upon the bed like a butterfly pinned inside a glass-covered box, but he pushed her arms down upon the bed and leaned over to kiss her lips, then her throat, then, more roughly, her nipples. His hands stroked her sides, the insides of her thighs, her crotch; and then his mouth was there, his tongue rough then smooth upon her budlike thing until it began to quiver open. Her fists clenched again, and she banged them upon the bed.

She felt something big and hard press against her crotch. The bud closed up again in a hurry, and her eyes flew open. She found herself staring at Michael's ceiling. She looked down at her thighs spread open upon the pillow, and at Michael's bent head. He was holding his penis in one hand, stabbing lightly at her crotch, and his penis was wrapped in something almost transparent which had a jaunty rolled edge.

She groaned and closed her eyes. "Go ahead, Michael," she said, "go ahead and do it, just *do* it."

He pressed harder. Sarah couldn't get any sense of the possible.

"There's something in the way," she said.

"I know that, Sarah. It's called the hymen."

"You're supposed to break it," she moaned, and felt more sweat prickle out upon her forehead. But this was panic, not passion. "Are you sure you're doing it in the right place?"

"Doesn't it feel like the right place?" he said incredulously.

"I don't know, I guess so, yes, but . . . oh God, just push it in, please!"

"I'm not going to be able to do this much longer," he said grimly. She opened her eyes again. He looked like he was trembling.

She touched his shoulder. "Michael. We can't expect much out of the first time, that's what all the books say. We have to get this over with. So let's just do it, okay? You can't worry about hurting me. It's *supposed* to hurt. I mean, all the books *say* it hurts. So let's just get it over with, *please!*"

It was painful, but not as painful as Sarah had thought it might be. Right up until the thrust that did it, it was painful, and the thrust that did it hurt more than the others, but it was nothing really dreadful.

When it was all over—Michael had given a little cry which Sarah at first thought was an involuntary expression of sympathy—and Michael had withdrawn himself from her and rushed off to the bathroom, she sat up cautiously and looked at herself, still sprawled inanely over the pillow.

There were three drops of bright red blood there, arranged tidily, almost in a perfect triangle. She wondered if that was significant.

She moved her legs a bit. There was an ache in her crotch.

She leaned back on her hands and looked at Michael's wall, and she seemed to see there a heap of leaves and roots and flowers from lily-of-the-valley plants, and she marveled against at how quickly they had withered and died, once removed from the earth.

This ought to do it, she thought.

If anything can do it, this ought to do it.

The locket felt large and heavy on her throat.

# Chapter 27

THE FOLLOWING FRIDAY, GLYNIS, TEARING LETTUCE INTO a salad bowl, said, "Doesn't this seem kind of weird to you?"

Sarah was sitting at the kitchen table, her chin propped up on one hand, looking out the open window. "It's summer," she said vaguely.

"I don't mean the weather, dummy." Glynis gestured toward the door to the dining room. "I mean all these people here."

Sarah continued to look out at the back yard. Maybe she would get out there this weekend and get rid of some of those weeds.

"It feels like the funeral," said Glynis. "When all those people came and ate." She flung the lettuce into the bowl and sat down at the table. "That's what it feels like."

Sarah sat back and smiled. "The funeral was months and months ago."

"What's the matter with you these days?" said Glynis, irritated. "Are you on something, Sarah?"

Sarah laughed. "No, I'm not 'on' something, Glynis. I'm just feeling good. I have solved a problem." She wiggled her eyebrows at Glynis, who eyed her doubtfully.

Margaret came in from the dining room. She glanced

immediately and automatically at Sarah, whose new calmness seemed to Margaret an artificial thing. It didn't make sense. Sarah should have become more tense, more withdrawn after Margaret said to her those things which shouldn't have been said. Margaret had planned to apologize, and try to make things right between them. But Sarah was suddenly so much more relaxed and affectionate that Margaret, perplexed, hadn't been able to say a thing. She thought she should be relieved. She was merely uneasy.

"Jeez, Mom," said Glynis, "every time I see you I get a shock."

Margaret touched her hair. "So do I. Every time I look in a mirror." She looked around the kitchen. "What still needs to be done?"

Glynis got up reluctantly and heaved a long sigh. "I still have to finish the salad."

"I'll make the dressing," said Sarah.

"The garlic bread's nearly ready to get heated up," said Glynis, slicing tomatoes.

"And the lasagna needs—let's see," said Margaret, looking at the clock, "half an hour more. Good. Let's go into the living room." She started to leave, then turned back. "Come on," she said to them.

"You go ahead, Mom," said Glynis. "We'll be right there."

When Margaret had left, Glynis turned to Sarah. "Do you know who's here?" she said. "She invited Harry. I don't like Harry."

"Why not, for heaven's sake?" Sarah got out the oil and vinegar and spices and started to mix the dressing in a small glass jar.

"I used to, but not any more. He's not married any more," she said ominously. "Again."

"Oh, Glynis," said Sarah. "For heaven's sake."

"She's not old, you know. She's very pretty, with her hair cut."

"My God, Glynis." Sarah put the lid on the jar and shook it vigorously.

"He's always been after her," said Glynis, drooped against the counter.

"I know he has," said Sarah. "But she's never been after him."

"Maybe she will be, now."

"For God's sake," said Sarah. "When she's been married to Daddy? Don't be an idiot." She was suddenly trembling. She put down the jar of salad dressing and walked out into the patio to take big breaths of the warm and fragrant evening. Eventually she went back into the kitchen. "Come on," she said to Glynis, and they went into the living room.

Harry was sprawled in an easy chair. Margaret stood by the fireplace talking to Moira. Kathleen and William occupied the sofa, and Margaret's parents sat in chairs opposite them. The room was flooded with evening sun and warmed by the lilting murmur of several non-competitive conversations.

Sarah stood for a moment at the entrance from the dining room. The absence of her father from this gathering of relatives and friends was as striking as it had been the day of his funeral, but today the acknowledgment of his absence was bittersweet, and she could sense that eventually it would become nostalgia.

Someday she would explain to Michael what going to bed with him had been all about. I'll have to explain it to him pretty soon, actually, she thought; he keeps wanting to do it again, and I can't, that would ruin everything.

Kathleen beckoned to her. "There's a light in your eyes and some flesh on your bones again," said her grandmother as Sarah sat on a hassock next to her, "and I'm glad to see it."

Glynis was stalled in the dining room. Sarah saw that she had been abruptly deserted by her self-assurance. Since Glynis had been giving serious thought lately to becoming an actress, she was particularly infuriated whenever she found herself frozen in awkwardness and self-contempt. Sarah watched, sympathetic, as her sister shuffled into the middle of the living room, her face burning, her hands hanging huge at her sides, her shoulders curled in slightly so as to hide the swell of her chest.

"Come and sit down here beside me," said her grandmother Kennedy, smiling behind her glasses. "I brought something to show you."

Glynis plodded over to her grandmother's chair and dropped herself onto the floor next to it. There Sarah knew she would feel smaller, and could begin to gather up her grace again.

"Your hair's getting long," said her grandmother, "and in the sunlight, it's full of red and gold glints."

Glynis blushed. She had thought she'd seen that herself, but was happy to have it confirmed.

"Now," said her grandmother, picking up a scrapbook from the floor on the other side of her chair. "Look at this. I only brought one. You can see the others tomorrow, if you like, when you come for the weekend."

"What is it?" said Sarah, coming over to join Glynis on the floor.

"It's old pictures," said Glynis.

The girls spread it open between them, and Ivy pointed at a photograph. "Look at that," she said. "I've always loved that one."

Sarah looked over at Kathleen. "Do you have photo albums, too, Grandma?"

"Oh yes, child, we do indeed."

"Can I see them, when I come to Kelowna?"

"We've got pictures of Teddy and that dog, haven't we, Mother?" said William.

"Oh yes, that dog," said Kathleen, laughing.

"What dog?" said Glynis.

"William brought it home for him," said Kathleen. "The dog turned out to be an awful digger, it was all I could do to keep a garden in."

"He was accident prone," said William, snorting, his eyes crinkling.

"The dog?" said Glynis, her hand keeping the album open.

"I have never seen," said Kathleen, "before or since, another dog that actually used to fall down."

"Did Dad tell you about this dog, Mom?" said Glynis, and Margaret nodded, and had to smile.

"He got hit by cars, too," said William. "Twice."

"And he used to get into fights," said Kathleen. "We never had him fixed, that was the trouble."

"He was a small dog," said William, "but he never knew it. He'd come out of those fights staggering and bleeding, with his tongue hanging out the edge of his mouth, but with a silly grin plastered all over his face. He always thought he'd won."

"What happened to him?" said Sarah.

"Why, somehow he managed to die of old age," said Kathleen. "I didn't much like the idea of keeping that dog, but when he died I swear I missed him, I surely did." She smoothed her dress where it had wrinkled over her thighs, her hand moving nervously. William put his hand over hers, and it lay quiet again.

"Turn the page, Glynis," said Mrs. Kennedy, breaking the silence, and Sarah and Glynis bent to the photo album.

Across the room Harry got up from his chair and stretched. He ambled to the front window, glass in hand. After a minute Margaret joined him there.

He looked at her appraisingly. "You should have had your hair cut years ago."

"I want to ask your opinion about something."

"I'm full of opinions, you know that. Most of them I give out for free. Some of them I give out without anybody even asking for them. Like the one about your hair."

"I want to know if you think I should try to act again."

Harry looked around the room, then back at Margaret. "Holy cow." He looked at his watch. "When do we eat?"

"Not until you've answered me," she said, trying to keep it light.

"Maybe I should get myself another drink first."

"Stop stalling, Harry." She pulled in her stomach muscles and stood up straighter.

He shook his head, watching Moira walk over to talk to Ted's parents. "I'm in what you call a real dilemma here, sweetie."

"For God's sake, Harry. You're my friend. Who else can I ask?"

"Yeah, but I don't see how I can help you."

"Just talk. Tell me what you think. Don't stall, don't weasel."

"Weasel. I never weasel." He finished off his drink and swirled the remainder of the ice around in the bottom of the glass. "But I'm confused, Maggie."

He looked at her speculatively, and Margaret thought his eyes were cold, but maybe it was just the way the sunlight slanted across his face.

"Why? About what?" she said.

"Why should it matter what I think? If you want to act, act. I'm sure your local Little Theater group would be happy to have you."

Margaret's face grew hot. "That's—not exactly what I had in mind," she said.

Harry studied her for a few seconds. "You're talking about act as in professionally?"

At least, thought Margaret, he's keeping his voice down. At least no one else is hearing this.

Harry felt profound irritation. The familial love at this little gathering irritated him. The still-there grief irritated him. His now empty glass irritated him. Margaret irritated him.

"Oh, hell, do it. Why not," he said. He shrugged and looked out the window. "It's been done before. People do start new careers in their middle age."

"But it wouldn't be a new career," said Margaret. "It would be picking something up where I'd left off."

Harry looked with interest at her hand on his sleeve. "Ah, now she's offering me her body." Margaret pulled her hand away. "You're wrong, Maggie," he said. "If you were an actor you never would have 'left off.' You were in a few plays, that's all."

He seemed to be standing so close to her that she could hear him breathing. Margaret stepped back, and her body felt clumsy. She was hot and her clothes felt rumpled. She was suddenly humiliated that she had had her hair cut.

Harry was looking uncomfortable, and Margaret became aware that she was staring at him.

"How are you feeling these days, Harry?" she said.

"Not too bad, Maggie, not too bad. And yourself?"

"You're not looking particularly well," said Margaret. "That's why I asked. You should take better care of yourself, Harry."

He looked confused, then shocked.

"Let me get you another drink, Harry," said Margaret. She took his glass and smiled at him. "It's scotch on the rocks, right?" she said, and walked away.

Good for me, she thought. That son of a bitch. He liked telling me that. He actually enjoyed it.

"Hey, Mom," said Sarah. "Do you remember this one?"

Margaret stopped and bent over to look at the photograph.

For what seemed a long time, she saw nothing that she recognized. Finally, "I sure do," she said heartily, and looked over at her father. "It's you and me, Dad. In Stanley Park."

She went on into the dining room to refill Harry's glass. I'll think about it later, she thought. I can't think about it now. I'll think about it later, when I'm all alone.

Sarah peered at the photograph intently. Margaret looked to be about ten years old, and was sitting beside her father on a park bench in front of a lot of trees. Her hair was in shoulder-length ringlets and her whole face was smiling. Her father was leaning forward, his arms resting on his knees, looking at the camera patiently. Two things occurred to Sarah as she looked at the picture. First, her mother seemed filled to bursting with energy and joy; and second, why is it, thought Sarah, that not once since he died have I looked at any pictures of my father?

She sat back, leaving the photo album to Glynis. Pins and needles swept up and down the calves of her legs. She got to her feet and stamped them to make the blood flow. Then she went to the kitchen.

She tried to remember the photographs of her father which she had seen many times before he died.

As she sat quietly at the table she began not to feel the heat in the kitchen, not to hear the muted voices from the living room. But the lasagna, sizzling, sounded very loud indeed.

Margaret came in, startling her. Sarah's heart gave a couple of tremendous leaps, and then settled down.

Margaret turned the oven off and opened the door. The heat struck her face, but she didn't particularly notice.

"Where's Jason?" asked Sarah.

"He couldn't come," said Margaret. She took out the casserole with a pair of potholders and put it on the counter.

"I'm sorry I've been so hard to live with," said Sarah, and her heart began pounding.

Margaret turned swiftly to her and put her arms around Sarah, resting her cheek against Sarah's hair. "No, I'm the one who's sorry," she said. "Sometimes I'm not very smart, Sarah."

Her voice came to Sarah from far away, and had a muffled

232

sound. Sarah hugged her dutifully and pulled gently away. Her mother patted her shoulder and went back to the counter.

Things keep on changing, thought Sarah. Her mother had once been a two-year-old, peeking out from under a sunbonnet; and ten, crammed full of joy; and a long-haired actress; and a wife. Now here she stood in her own kitchen becoming something else and not seeming to mind that, because she kept it in a different part of her than where she kept her grief.

Sarah shook her head, wearily. She would have liked to have gone to bed and straight to sleep, and wakened up somewhere else with this whole entire part of her life behind her.

Margaret called people to dinner and poured wine while they settled themselves around the table. Moira sniffed approvingly at the lasagna, and Mrs. Kennedy complimented Margaret on the place mats, which she thought were new.

"To Margaret," said Harry, lifting his glass, "and whatever awaits her." He nodded at her, smiling a little.

The other people raised their glasses, slightly confused but polite, and drank.

"To Moira," said Margaret firmly.

"Okay," said Harry, and again, they toasted.

"What's the occasion, Moira?" said Mr. Kennedy, who had been fond of her since the days when she and Margaret used to watch him build things in his garage.

"I'm not sure you'll approve," said Moira, fiddling with the knife at the side of her plate. "I'm leaving. I'm going to San Francisco."

There was a pause.

"By yourself?" said Glynis, incredulous.

"By myself."

"But what about Jason?" said Mrs. Kennedy.

"He's kind of what I'm leaving," said Moira.

"Oh, Moira. That is terrible. Does your mother know?" said Mrs. Kennedy.

Moira spread her hands and looked around the table. "Let's not talk about it. Okay? I don't want to spoil anybody's dinner. Which is delicious," she said to Margaret, "but I wish you'd kept your mouth shut."

"It's a sad thing, a sad thing," said Kathleen, shaking her head.

"Grandma," said Sarah, who sat next to her, "do you still talk to things? My grandma," she said to the table at large, "talks to flowers and tomatoes, to God and the devil, don't you, Grandma?"

"I do, yes," said Kathleen.

"I once heard her talk to her gate," said Glynis.

"And dogs, and maple trees," said Sarah.

"That gate, it sticks," said Kathleen, "and when I'm feeling black I do believe it sticks on purpose to spite me."

"Do they ever talk back to you, these things?" said Sarah. She felt like a balloon someone had let go of.

"Of course not," said Kathleen shortly.

"Oh, Grandma," said Sarah, "I used to think you knew all kinds of secrets." Her face was hot.

Kathleen looked at her closely. There was other conversation around the table now.

"I'll be all right, Grandma," said Sarah.

She picked up her fork and began eating. She could hear everyone's voice clearly, but she couldn't distinguish what they were saying. She could also hear herself, humming something. She ate dutifully until Kathleen stopped glancing at her every couple of seconds, and then she only pretended to eat, because she wasn't hungry at all.

She was suspended somewhere in a circle of serenity, while voices and fragrances and colors and movement swirled around her, at a distance. Her eye caught the flash of silverware, glimpses of rose petals, the red-brown throb of polished wood; but it was all in bits and pieces, nothing fit together with anything else.

She felt herself put her fork carefully on her plate, felt her body move slightly away from the table to rest against the back of her chair, felt her head lift and realized she was looking into a corner of the dining room.

She wondered if she could be getting sick.

She thought she felt someone pass behind her, and glanced over her shoulder, but there was nobody there; everyone was still sitting at the table, talking, eating—they were not making any jokes, nobody was laughing, but there was some smiling going on. They seemed far away from her,

234

although she could see they were actually quite close; especially Kathleen.

Again she thought someone had gotten up and walked behind her into the living room . . .

. . . oh God, she thought, I have been in the eye of a hurricane all these lovely days, these three lovely days since Michael, and now it's going to happen again right here right in front of all these people.

Her heart pounded in her chest. She would have to sit still. She couldn't go dancing about the room. All these people would stare at her and demand an explanation. I could pretend happiness, I could pretend to have swallowed some pepper . . .

She made herself remain utterly still, staring at the wall in front of her, just to the left of the kitchen door, and then her eyes moved slowly to the left and came to rest in the corner, where a small desk sat beneath the window and through the window came the rich molten sunshine of the evening, making the corner golden; and then something began to happen there as her heart pounded even harder and her hands trembled in her lap; she could almost hear them clattering.

It filtered through the sunlight, like light, but distinguishable from the light, not golden or yellow or white; it was like fog, yet it was not cobwebby, not moist-looking, not the oyster-white color of fog; it was like smoke, but it did not drift upward like smoke and did not have the tinge of gray that smoke has . . .

Sarah looked at it, her dry throat trying to swallow, and sought in her mind for comparisons but none of them helped . . .

It was in the sunlight, but not of the sunlight; the light did not illumine it; where the two things met, the light disappeared. It formed itself precisely, replacing sunlight, in the corner, by the desk, under the window; but it was not forming itself into anything, it was just becoming, it was there . . .

. . . it fluttered and swayed, a resplendent translucent mass of something pale, and it was *aware* of her—she felt with all her flesh and bones this exchange of awarenesses, across a room which now existed in another, separate world.

She thought she might crack in the middle of herself and fly apart, dividing herself neatly between the world where people ate and talked and smiled and looked at the sun and that other one, a small two-occupant world which still managed to fill all space, all eternity—but she looked at it, and didn't look away . . .

. . . it fluttered and swayed; colorless, shapeless; it didn't move from the corner, by the desk, under the window, where it had replaced the sunlight and was outshining it; and when it had finished being there, it left.

Sarah watched it go, conscious of the thumping of her heart and the pressure in her head and the incongruous taste of ice cream in her mouth.

"What's the matter with you, child?" said Kathleen.

Sarah turned to look at her. "I don't feel very well," she said.

Her eyes swept around the table. Margaret, watching, caught her breath; Sarah's eyes were so dense with color they seemed to leave soft swatches of blue upon every face they touched.

Basically, thought Sarah, looking at the people around her, I am not a bad person.

"Do you want to go to your room and lie down?" said Margaret.

Glynis watched Sarah apprehensively.

I've had a relapse, Sarah wanted to say.

"I think I'll be all right."

Her mind was extremely clear.

I looked right at it, she thought. And it did not harm me.

# Chapter 28

"COME ON, SARAH," SAID MARGARET, KNOCKING ON THE bedroom door the next evening. "It's time to go." She turned away and had reached the top of the stairs when Sarah's door opened. She glanced up and saw Sarah standing in the hall.

"Come on," said Margaret. "It's going to be late by the time we get there."

"Listen, Mama," said Sarah. "I'm not going."

"What? Why? What do you mean?"

"I'm not going."

Margaret sat on the top step. "Why?" she said again, looking down the stairs at the front door.

"I want to be by myself."

"I thought you were finished wanting to be by yourself all the time," said Margaret.

"No, Mom, this is different," said Sarah, and sat down beside her. "I just have to think, that's all."

"I can't let you stay here by yourself. It's a ridiculous idea. Your grandparents will want to know why you didn't come. We'll all stay home, then." She stood up.

Sarah took her hand and pulled her gently back down onto

the step. "Listen, Mom. I just saw them last night. Their feelings aren't going to be hurt."

"But what do you want to *do?*"

"Nothing, Mom. Just think, that's all. Here. At home."

"Okay. Then we won't go to Haney until tomorrow."

"Mother, I want you and Glynis to go. Good heavens, what on earth are you worried about?"

"I can't leave you here alone all night."

"Mother," said Sarah patiently. "In six months I'm going to be eighteen. Face it, Mom. I'm just about all grown up."

"Oh God." Margaret looked down into the hall. She glimpsed the living room through the archway and saw the hardwood floor by the front door gleaming except where shadows lay in dark sprawling puddles. She was filled with incoherent dread.

Sarah put an arm around her shoulder. "Please, Mom." She seemed perfectly calm.

The car horn tooted impatiently.

"Glynis," said Margaret. She stood up, looked from Sarah to the front door.

The car horn tooted again; twice.

"I'll lock all the doors," said Sarah. "And if I get nervous I'll call Michael's mother and ask if I can stay there, or something." She smiled." I love this house, Mom."

The front door burst open. "For Pete's sake," said Glynis. "What's going on? Let's go." She waved them forward.

Margaret started down the stairs. "Sarah's staying home," she said.

"What's the matter with her?"

"Nothing's the matter with me," said Sarah.

"Is she going to have Michael over?" said Glynis, sly and innocent.

Margaret stopped in the hall and looked doubtfully back at Sarah. "I don't think so," she said.

Sarah shook her head. "I don't want to see Michael."

"Then come with us," said Glynis.

Margaret hustled Glynis out the door. "Sarah," she said, looking up at her.

"Go on, Mom. I promise, I'll be fine."

Sarah sat still until she heard the car start. She went quickly down the stairs and watched through the small window in the door to make sure they left. The car was

238

backing slowly out of the driveway, its headlights cutting through the dusk. It turned onto the street, and Sarah could see Glynis watching the house as the car passed it. Sarah closed her eyes and rested her forehead against the glass in the door.

There was probably something she could have done to prepare herself, she thought. Perhaps somewhere in the public library downtown there was a book with dusty leather covers, the edges of the pages painted with gold, and a title carved delicately into the front cover—a book which contained things she ought to know. She imagined some unknown person laboriously writing it all down, catching his tongue between his teeth. He would have sat at a desk in a dark room, with light from a lamp or a candle throwing itself protectively across the top of the desk. She saw him using an old-fashioned pen, the kind you dip in an inkwell after every three or four words; she saw him leaning forward in his concentration, trying to describe everything just the way it had happened to him, trying to explain precisely what to do should a reader of his words find herself in the same predicament.

Afflicted by a presence.

She lifted her head, seeing fleetingly the empty front porch, the bare brick walk, the unoccupied driveway, the trafficless street. She turned to face the inside of the house. It was very quiet.

The refrigerator hummed into life, lazily, as though it could do it by now in its sleep. From as far away as the front door Sarah heard the kitchen clock, its precise ticking slurred by distance.

She moved away from the front door and a board sighed in weak complaint beneath the shifting weight of her body.

She went upstairs into her room and closed the door. She had to turn on the light; it was almost dark outside now.

She reached up and took off her locket, and sat on the bed to study it. It fit perfectly into the palm of her hand. She opened it, nervously, and looked at the photographs; her mother with long hair pinned up on her head smiling at Glynis as a baby, and on the other side, her father. She had almost expected that photograph to be gone. He smiled out at her, just the way she remembered, his hair falling over his forehead, as it usually did; she could even see the very slight cleft in his chin that her mother used to tease him about sometimes. Now, looking intently at the photograph, she wasn't nervous at all, just enormously relieved. She stroked the photograph with her finger.

Sarah turned off her lamp and lay down on her bed, the locket in her hand. She closed her eyes and didn't think about anything. She was aware of the soft bed beneath her, the position of her arms and legs, the slow and steady movements of her chest as her heart went on with its work, dreamy and dependable.

She lifted her head and held the locket by its chain. She could see it swinging in the little bit of light that came through the window. It swung back and forth and the swinging became slower and slower and then it hung in the air almost completely still, shivering slightly from the slight movement of Sarah's hand, and every so often the faint light from the window caught the stone in the front and a red splinter appeared for an instant.

Sarah sat up and held the locket in her hand, moving it to catch the light. It flickered red and then the redness stayed, glowing; Sarah bent closer to it, looking intently at the red glow. It began to hurt her eyes, so she closed them, but the redness glowed in the center of her mind behind her eyelids; it shivered and altered itself and became an explosive mass of color, every shade she had ever seen and some she hadn't, prismatic, colors shifting as she watched them, gleaming silver as they changed.

It was no longer her locket at all, but something huge, that floated somewhere in limitless blackness, bleeding the blackness away from it on all its rounded, shifting, silver-limned sides, so that it seemed to be suspended in a pale luminescence which was in turn suspended in blackness. It was something colossal yet tranquil; dispassionate. She watched it behind her eyelids, discerning patterns. She watched ivory swing through cream into opal, saw lemon deepen into gold and then apricot; caught a glimpse of ruby and watched it bloom into russet and then mahogany. But as soon as she had identified a pattern it vanished, and what she saw was silver-circled iridescence—she sensed that there was a deep, languid current which created the color shifts; she felt it there, emotionless, inexorable, unhurried, and she thought that this pulsation was the essence of what she saw, and that it showed itself as color because in that way she might, if not understand it, at least not be frightened by it. . . .

She watched, transfixed, and after a long time the colors caused themselves to disappear, fading away, backwards and still further back. They retreated and retreated to a glowing red speck and then that too vanished.

Sarah opened her eyes to see the locket resting, a small black shadow, in her hand. She closed her fingers around it and lay back on her bed, and soon felt wetness trickle from the corners of her eyes down across her temples. On the ceiling were speckles of light and through the window moonlight slanted, now.

She lay there quietly. She liked the idea of having all those colors in her head. Though she wasn't sure that she could call upon them at will.

After a while she sat up and fastened the locket around her neck again.

She looked around cautiously for fear, and it was there, but it was smudgy-edged and did not gnaw at her.

She got up and looked around the room, brushing her eyes across it, tinting it delicately with the white and black and putting husky hints of color in the objects which lay in shadow.

She went into the upstairs hall, closing the bedroom door behind her, to decide where first to look for her father.

# Chapter 29

"YOU CAN PHONE HER WHEN WE GET THERE, MOM," SAID
Glynis.

Her voice startled Margaret, who had been thinking busily, with nothing to distract her but the thrumming of the
motor and the occasional whoosh of another car passing
hers.

"I know, honey. I probably will."

Jangled, she peered into the darkness to spot something
familiar.

"We're about halfway there," said Glynis.

Margaret nodded, and shifted behind the steering wheel,
trying to get comfortable. Maybe I'm worrying about Sarah
deliberately, she thought, so I won't have to worry for a
while about me.

"Why did she want to stay by herself?" said Glynis.

"She wanted to think."

"Ha," said Glynis. "I think all the time. No matter where
I am."

Margaret glanced at her, smiling.

Glynis looked out her window, hoping to glimpse the river
in the moonlight.

"I was sitting in my window seat the other day," she said,

self-conscious of the possessive pronoun. "I was sitting there," she said, "reading this magazine. I don't remember which one. Anyway, I read something funny in it, and I was halfway to the door to go read it to him before I remembered he was dead."

Margaret concentrated on her hands, persuading them to relax their grip on the wheel. "I know, Glynis. It's happened to me, too."

"After more than three months, though," said Glynis, "I wouldn't have expected it to happen."

"A part of you doesn't believe it yet. It depends on how stubborn that part is."

"I'm a pretty stubborn person," Glynis said, despondent.

They were quiet again. Margaret figured they were about ten miles from Haney. A cup of coffee with her parents, and then they could go to bed. But first she would call Sarah.

"Do you think Sarah loved him more than I did?"

The question lay heavy in the air; Glynis wasn't looking for something soothing.

"I think each of us loved him differently," Margaret said.

"Well, I know you loved him differently. You were married to him, for Pete's sake. But how did Sarah love him differently from the way I loved him?"

Margaret could feel her tension. She thought, this is a brave person. "Your father and Sarah were very close," she began.

"Did he wish she'd been a boy?" said Glynis quickly.

"No," said Margaret, wishing she could have said yes. "He only wanted daughters." I lie, just a little, you bastard. . . . "It was probably because she was the first one," she said, her fury with him growing; if I mess this up I swear I'll get you for it. . . . "But he and Sarah were always very close." She looked over at Glynis. "I sometimes felt left out," she said, and laughed a little, for Glynis.

"And then I came along," said Glynis, grimly.

"Yes. And there were four of us, instead of three, and things worked better that way."

"Not for me. Then *I* felt left out."

"Oh, Glynis, I hope not . . ."

"Yeah, I did. I knew I had you, but I didn't have any choice, you know? I always thought that if she'd wanted to, *she* could have had you."

"Oh, Glynis, that's terrible, terrible."

Margaret pulled the car onto the shoulder of the highway. She looked over at Glynis, and was surprised that she was not small and furtive, crouched against the window: she sat straight and tall, looking out through the windshield, and her face in the moonlight was thoughtful. They really look very much alike, thought Margaret, astonished. Her hair is darker, and her eyes are brown, not blue. But in profile, she could be Sarah.

"Look at me," she said, and Glynis turned, and one side of her face was in moonlight, the other side in shadow. "I don't give a good goddamn about any of this. I love you both, very much. I can't possibly tell you how much I love you. And you're two different people, you always have been, and sometimes I love you better than Sarah and sometimes I love Sarah better than you. But if you were both under the wheels of two cars lying on the highway in front of me, I swear to God I'd pick one car up with my left hand and one car up with my right hand and both of them would lift up off of your bodies at exactly the same instant."

Astonishment swept over Glynis' face and settled there, immobile. Then she burst out laughing.

"Oh, Mom," she said, "oh, Mom. Okay. Okay."

They arrived a few minutes later. Margaret's father came out on the porch as her car pulled up in front of the house.

"They've been waiting for us," said Margaret.

"I told you we should've left earlier. They probably thought you smashed us up."

Glynis got out and ran to hug her grandfather, who then walked slowly to the car to greet Margaret.

He kissed her cheek, smiling, and looked into the car. "Where's Sarah?"

"She didn't feel too well, Dad," said Margaret. "She decided to stay home."

"She has to think," Glynis called from the porch, and went inside.

Margaret's mother said later, "She should have come with you. What's wrong with her, anyway?" She had stopped, frowning, halfway to the kitchen.

"She has to think," said Glynis patiently. She was peeking under the cover of the canary's cage, trying to coax it to sing, or at least to chirp. She went over to her grandmother.

# THE FAVORITE

"Can I help you?" Her grandmother hesitated and then led the way into the kitchen, where she soon began responding to Glynis' chatter.

Margaret and her father talked of relatives, and old friends, and gardens, and politics. She wished she could talk to him about herself, and about Sarah. She needed comfort and advice. But they had never been that close; which was one reason, she knew, for her resentment of the closeness between Sarah and Ted.

The door to the kitchen was pushed open. "Maggie," said her mother. "You better go and phone that girl. Make sure she's all right."

Margaret nodded, and stood up.

"Use the upstairs phone, if you like," said her father.

Margaret went up to her parents' bedroom. She sat on the bed and looked at the Princess phone on her father's night table. It was anachronistic, sitting on that walnut table, next to an old brass bed, near a refinished chest of drawers covered with framed photographs, in front of a window hung with new drapes and behind them, glass curtains.

Margaret stared at the telephone as though trying to communicate without picking up the receiver. She reached for it half-heartedly, but had known since she got up from the chair downstairs that she was not going to phone Sarah.

She knows where we are, she'll call me if she needs me, she thought, trying not to consider the hour-and-a-half drive that separated them.

She watched the telephone carefully, but it did not ring.

# Chapter 30

SARAH WALKED SOUNDLESSLY DOWN THE HALL IN HER OLD scuffed sneakers, and fear fluttered in her throat.

She had turned on no lights but there was some light from the moon, which shone obliquely past the window at the end of the hall. She knew it would be brighter in her mother's room.

She crossed directly to that part of the room which had been her father's and sat in a chair by the window, moonlight falling smoothly across her shoulder and disappearing into the carpet. She sat still, her hands in her lap.

Her body was tense, as though she were peering over a high wall, huddled on top of a ladder, ready to jump back down to the ground on the safe side if she sensed so much as a tremor of movement in the black jungly garden into which she was compelled to look. But there was no movement. There was not even the thick stillness which she had learned preceded the movement she feared. She saw and felt nothing in the corners of her mother's room.

Her father's silver-backed brush slept quietly on top of his dresser. She knew that his clothes still filled the drawers, and the closet on this side of the room. But nothing moved, nothing happened, except that Sarah continued to sit in the chair, tense, becoming more and more aware of her lungs and her heart—but it seemed they were unnecessarily expectant.

Eventually she pulled herself up and walked to the door, where she stopped and looked again around the room, and found it empty.

So you're not here, she thought, and fear hiked itself up a notch. What will I do, if I cannot find you?

She went to Glynis' room, which had been Sarah's. She turned the doorknob blindly and fumbled her way across the room to sit once more in the moon's cool light. She wiped trembling hands on her thighs and huddled into the window seat. She rested her head against the glass of the window and thought she could feel the moonlight on her face, stroking it through the glass; and she thought that when she turned away, her face would be forever pale and luminous, and that her eyes would be forever the color of the black sky from which the moon shone.

She could see through the window the shadowed back yard, and the dogwood tree which grew at the side of the house. She could see the cleared space, knee-deep in shadow, by the back fence, which should have been the vegetable garden, and glinting in the moonlight, the latch on the gate.

She saw herself, smaller, thinner, blue-eyed and yellow-haired, sitting here and looking out the window. She thought her younger self looked amazingly calm and self-possessed. There must be some of that in me still, she thought. She saw Sarah looking out evenly upon the day, sniffing the fragrances of summer through her half-open window. That whole child is inside me somewhere.

She imagined herself growing, still; but invisibly now, to accommodate newer Sarahs, creating around herself an intangible aura which became wider and wider as she grew older and older, and she imagined it as a rainbow which would shimmer around her more and more brightly. I must watch for people's rainbows, she thought . . .

The moonlight still sheeted through the glass, but its angle had changed. She huddled still in the window seat, but was beginning to grow stiff.

She put out sensors, tentatively, then raised her head and looked around her old room, now filled with Glynis' things, and there was no one there, nothing, except what was always there—objects, and dim light, and some signs that in sunlight or lamplight the room would be splashed with color.

Sarah stood up awkwardly and walked out of the room. In the hall she closed the door and leaned against it. She thought that the night must be nearly over, and nothing had happened, nothing at all.

And then she realized that there was only one more place to look.

# Chapter 31

MARGARET'S PARENTS HAD ONE EXTRA BEDROOM IN WHICH was a double bed, a closet, and a small table with a lamp on it. They provided sleeping bags for Sarah and Glynis. Margaret wondered if this night Glynis would be expected to sleep in the double bed with her, because there were only two of them. Perhaps Glynis had thought about this, too. She went upstairs first, and when Margaret came into the room one sleeping bag was unrolled against the wall and Glynis was already climbing into it.

Margaret took a long time brushing her teeth and combing her hair and taking off her makeup in the bathroom down the hall, but when she got into bed Glynis was still awake.

"Did you phone her, Mom?"

"Didn't you hear me tell your grandmother she's all right?"

"Yeah. But did you phone her?"

"No."

Margaret lay with her eyes open, staring up at the ceiling.

"It must have been awful for you," said Glynis, resuming a conversation, "feeling left out."

Margaret closed her eyes, but they wouldn't stay closed. "I didn't feel left out all the time. Just sometimes." She hesitated. "Like you, probably."

249

"Yeah."

There was silence for a moment. Margaret could hear the old tree outside the window creakily adjusting its branches.

Glynis said, "There were times, it's true, when I thought he loved me as much as her."

Margaret ached, as though she had spent the evening in violent exercise. She had been aching ever since that talk with Harry. I talk too damn much to too many people, she thought. That's my problem.

Glynis raised herself on one elbow and strained to see her mother in the dark. "When he was sick, before he went into the hospital for good, I felt a lot closer to him then."

"I know, honey," said Margaret. "I'm glad."

The tree sighed, settled into itself.

"Was that only because he wasn't getting along with Sarah?"

"I don't know, Glynis. But it doesn't matter. It would have happened sometime. I'm just glad it happened in time, and I don't care at all why it happened."

She wondered if Ted could have bequeathed her his restlessness. Agitation was clutching at her aching limbs. She threw off the covers and sat up.

Cautiously, Glynis asked, "What do you think she's doing right now?"

"I hope she's in bed asleep."

"Are you worried about her?"

"Why should I worry about her? I'm just restless. Come down to the kitchen with me. We'll have some tea or something."

She was out the door before she finished speaking. Then she stopped and came back and held out a hand for Glynis. She felt Glynis' hand, square and solid, and remembered that there were after all many differences between her daughters: Sarah's hand in hers felt like a broken-winged bird.

My God, thought Margaret. How could I have left her there?

She looked at Glynis, and said, "Let's go home."

# Chapter 32

SARAH KNEW SHE COULD SIT WAITING IN THE KITCHEN, where they had all four had breakfasts together; or in the dining room, where they had eaten dinner; or outside on the patio, where he had liked to sit with his straw hat over his face. She could stomp bravely through the basement, where he had stored things, and frowningly examined furnace and hot-water heater, and once talked about building another room.

She knew she wouldn't find him in any of those places.

She started going down the stairs, and was afraid again, more afraid than ever. She sat down heavily on a stair halfway down and clutched one of the posts of the railing.

Surely he would not kill me, she thought, and licked her lips, and listened to the pounding of her heart. Even if he doesn't love me now, he used to love me. But she didn't know much about dead people. Maybe death has made you murderous, she thought. She looked down the stairs into the darkened hall and her legs wanted to carry her pell-mell-fast-as-hell straight out the front door.

She got up and went down the rest of the stairs, holding on to the banister with both hands.

At least it's a place to sit, she thought.

With her heart making so much noise she couldn't hear anything else, not the muffled ticking of the clock or the humming of the refrigerator or the squeaking of the hardwood floor beneath her feet, she stumbled on rubber legs into the living room and across the room toward the fireplace and there she let herself fall into the cool leather lap of her father's chair.

For a minute she waited, just waited, her body supported by the chair, waited for a roar of rage and triumph, waited for an axe to split her skull or a knife to bury itself in her chest; she waited with such an intensity of doom that she made no sound and felt nothing; hoped only that it would happen so quickly that it would not hurt.

The arms of the chair made themselves felt beneath her hands, and the hollow in the back of the chair reached down a little to cup itself beneath her head, and she became aware that although she could not feel them yet her legs were still attached to her, dangling to the floor where her feet lay slumped. She was so hot she might have been set afire.

She opened her eyes.

That's got to be the worst of it, she thought. And I did it to myself.

She felt the coolness of the chair.

She could not have moved if he had formed himself, of dust or starlight or pink cotton candy, six inches in front of her nose.

Give me a minute, she said inside her head, panting, and somewhere felt him smile.

She closed her eyes again. No frightful images attacked her this time. She willed her heart to slow down, her breathing to deepen, and brushed her face with her arm in a long-sleeved sweatshirt. It's handy I wore that, she thought.

She remembered that when she had been beaten up at school she had felt that only her fragile tearable skin kept her from falling into tiny pieces, bloody and shattered, and that the trauma of weeping, mild as it was, would be enough to burst that skin.

She opened her eyes and saw only real things, some drenched, some skirted by the ubiquitous moonlight.

She rubbed her eyes and sat up in the chair. She put her hands carefully on the padded leather arms and said silently, I'm ready.

# Chapter 33

THE CAR SPED ALONG THE HIGHWAY, ALMOST ALONE THERE, with only the moon for company.

"Granny and Granddad think we're crazy," said Glynis, watching the lights of the city as they approached.

"As long as they don't worry," said Margaret.

"I don't think they're worried. I think they're mad at you."

"Forty-five minutes now," said Margaret. "Half an hour, maybe."

"Mom," said Glynis after a while. "Sarah says you're going to be an actress again."

Margaret laughed. Oh Christ, she thought.

"Well? Are you?"

Margaret shook her head. "Somehow I don't think so, Glynnie."

"I think *I* am. Going to be an actress."

Margaret nodded. She hoped that if it happened, and Glynis turned out to be good, she would be able to be glad.

"One actress in the family," she said, "is probably enough."

"What *are* you going to do, then?"

"I don't know. Something. I don't know what."

Glynis thought for a minute. "You could sell real estate." She looked at Margaret hopefully. "I hear you can get pretty rich doing that, selling real estate."

"Oh, the whole world is open to me, Glynis," said Margaret bitterly. She reached over to pat her daughter's knee. "I'll think of something. It might take a while. But I'll get it all sorted out."

Glynis was silent. Then, "She's probably sound asleep," she said, "with the TV still on. I told you, we should have got a dog. Ages ago."

"If she's asleep," said Margaret sharply, flashing past exits to New Westminster, "why does she need a dog?"

Glynis didn't answer.

# Chapter 34

IT WAS A SAD AND SILLY VISION, SITTING THERE IN HIS chair waiting for him.

Maybe I'm doing this all wrong, thought Sarah as she sat there with nothing happening all around her.

Maybe he's not here.

Maybe he's somewhere else.

Maybe I should walk out of here right now, out into the moonlight, and keep on walking and walking in a straight line no matter what gets in my way, wild animals or rivers or lakes or oceans or mountains or deserts; if I just keep on going, walking, walking, walking, eventually maybe I will find him again, my father, somewhere on a straight line from me right around the globe and back again; somewhere on that path he's sure to be waiting, with the brilliance of his smile and the crackling excitement of his restless curious mind and the love that swept from him over and around me and protected me and built me tall and strong and invincible.

I wish I had not killed those lilies. Next year I will look under the porch and there will be only darkness there, like there is darkness here, and all around me . . .

You had no right to leave me in the dark! she said silently. I can't see anything, I don't know where I am—damn you, she said, who do you think you are, leaving; you didn't even like me any more; couldn't say anything useful, couldn't stay to fix it, oh no . . .

She felt her body dissolving and thought incongruously of the Wicked Witch of the East. Am I on the wrong side, then? Am I one of the bad ones? Oh, Daddy, oh, Daddy, I hate you, I do . . .

. . . on the place inside her head where her closed eyes blindly focused, light showered and scattered and made a picture, and as the tears continued to flow and her lips continued to move, tasting brackish words, she watched . . .

. . . and saw two figures sitting on the steps of a white stucco house. She recognized the house. It was the only other house she had ever lived in. She had moved into it when she was a year old, had learned to walk there, and to talk, and lived there until she was ten. She saw it, and recognized it, and was amazed.

And then she was there, at that house, as though a pane of glass had been removed from in front of it. She was invisible, watching herself.

The child was very young, not going to school yet, sitting on the steps next to her father. They were looking across the lawn that sloped to the sidewalk, across the street to the woods beyond, and the watching Sarah saw that it was summer. The two people sat there, next to each other, a small yellow-headed girl who was just beginning to get that summer's tan, and a man wearing an old pair of pants and a white shirt with the sleeves rolled up.

The child said, "Daddy, where do dead things go?" and the watching Sarah could not remember ever having asked him that. But she saw that the child looked nervous, and disconsolate. Sarah remembered a neighbor who had died. And she remembered a friend's dog which had died, a long time ago. She looked hard at the child, trying to see into her mind.

"I know they get buried," said the child, "but then what happens?"

The picture took on still more substance—Sarah could smell the nasturtiums as she watched, and hear the restless rustling of trees behind her, and feel the warmth of the sun.

"What happens then?" the child said again, gloomily.

The man didn't answer.

The child got up to pick a flower. She chose one that was mostly yellow, like her hair, and abstractedly sucked the sweetness from it; Sarah, watching, tasted it. The child put the flower on the grass and sat down again beside her father, wriggling close to him. She arranged her body like his—feet straight out, crossed at the ankles; hands behind her, leaning on them. She waited for him to say something . . .

. . . and Sarah waited, too, wanting to make something up for him to say, and wondering if this whole place and these two people would dissolve, disappear, if she were to cry out—would she then be caught there, in this nameless place, and find herself alone, forever, in blackness? Or would they turn to her, astonished, and then smile, holding out their hands to her? Oh my God I am not in charge here, I must be very quiet and not breathe a word, she said to herself . . .

The man sighed, and looked across to the woods, where the trees fanned themselves with the wind from the sea. Finally he turned to the child . . .

And then he was looking not at the child, but right into Sarah's face. He was not a younger father, but the one who had died. He reached for her hand and held it, and she looked down to see that her hand was seventeen years old. She could do nothing but look up again and see that his eyes were looking right at her eyes, calmly, blue to blue, and that he didn't seem to be at all surprised.

His hand reached out, slowly, slowly; slowly it cupped itself around the back of her neck and slowly it drew her head close to his. Terror rushed through Sarah. Then she felt his fingers on the clasp at the back of her neck; and then, on her cheek, she felt a kiss. His eyes were blue like cobalt, and as warm as a tropical sea; there was nothing, anywhere, except that blueness, her mind was filled with it; and then, slowly, subtly, it began to embrace new colors, became delineated with silver, faded, growing smaller, and disappeared.

Sarah tried to open her eyes, but they were already open. She looked into blackness, waiting.

Slowly the room formed itself around her. The moonlight had retreated toward the window.

In Sarah's mouth was the sweet taste of a nasturtium.

She thought she could sit where she was forever, watching the moonlight withdraw, waiting for sunrise, then watching the passage of the sun through the day as marked by the infinite variety of light it would carry into the house, through windows, perhaps through cloud, as well.

Tears flowed from her eyes, and she knew the difference between crying and weeping. She got up from the chair and fell onto her knees on the floor, and she felt like a willow tree, surrounding itself protectively with silver filaments of tears.

On the floor lay her locket.

She heard a car pull into the driveway.

The front door opened, quietly, and she thought of her mother and Glynis standing there, listening, their minds full of dreadful possibilities. She pushed her hair back from her forehead and wiped her face with her hands.

"In here," she called out, and her fingers closed around the locket and its chain.

They appeared almost immediately in the archway from the hall.

"I've been watching the moonlight," said Sarah.

## Chapter 35

"Where's your locket?" said Glynis in surprise the next morning.

"I lost it," said Sarah.

Margaret looked up from the kitchen table, which she had been setting for breakfast. Sarah's throat was bare. Margaret could see the pulse beating unprotected there.

"We'll help you find it," said Glynis soothingly.

Margaret went to Sarah and put her arms around her. Sarah's body was slim and supple, leaning against Margaret like a young tree leans against a breeze, and it felt terribly, achingly familiar.

"Yes, we will," said Margaret.

"The thing to do," said Glynis, "is try to remember exactly where you saw it last."

"I saw it last night," said Sarah, turning to her.

Glynis and Margaret helped Sarah search the house. But they didn't find the locket.

Alone in her room, Sarah took out her exercise book. It was almost filled with poems from high school English courses which she had copied there because she admired them. She found the one she wanted between Hardy and

Wordsworth, and typed it out carefully on a sheet of white paper.

Then she got from a drawer the tin box with a hinged lid which her mother had given her, years ago, to keep things in. She folded the poem and slipped it into the tin box with all her other treasures, and closed the lid, and put the box away.

Even with the drawer closed she seemed to hear the locket, faint but clear, like a distant night bird singing to itself in the dark.

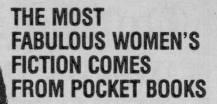

# THE MOST FABULOUS WOMEN'S FICTION COMES FROM POCKET BOOKS

LACE Shirley Conran 46714/$3.95

DECEPTIONS Judith Michael 46968/$3.95

FOREVER Judy Blume 46942/$2.95

WIFEY Judy Blume 46899/$3.50

ANY MINUTE I CAN SPLIT Judith Rossner 42739/$2.95

ATTACHMENTS Judith Rossner 44100/$3.50

EMMELINE Judith Rossner 81681/$3.50

LOOKING FOR MR. GOODBAR Judith Rossner 49622/$3.95

NINE MONTHS IN THE LIFE OF AN OLD MAID Judith Rossner 42740/$2.95

ONCE A LOVER Diana Anthony 42183/$3.50

DOUBLE STANDARDS Aviva Hellman 45048/$3.95

OPTIONS Freda Bright 41270/$2.95

AS TIME GOES BY Elaine Bissell 42043/$3.95

THE FAVORITE L.R. Wright 45186/$3.50

# Outstanding Bestsellers!

## THE WORLD ACCORDING TO GARP
45217/$3.95

and

## THE HOTEL NEW HAMPSHIRE
44027/$3.95

by John Irving

•

## THE WHITE HOTEL
46535/$3.95

by D.M. Thomas

•

## THE DEAN'S DECEMBER
45806/$3.95

by Saul Bellow

•

## RIDDLEY WALKER
45118/$5.95

by Russell Hoban

Pocket Books continues its tradition of providing splendid books of quality in beautiful formats everyone can afford.

These are the ones you are proud to own—the books you read again and again.

## All available from POCKET BOOKS